Mishella heard the front door open, then slam shut.

For a split second, fear paralyzed her.

Footsteps followed, coming toward her. She managed to take a breath, gather her courage and turn in the direction of the living room. *He's found you.*

But no satanic creature stood before her. Only a man— a tall, broad-shouldered man, his angular jaw covered with stubble, his raven-black hair falling well past his shoulders. Clad in faded jeans and a matching jacket that fell open to reveal a white T-shirt stretched over a well-muscled chest, he looked very real. Still, she knew the evil could take on human form if it so chose. Hadn't she been warned?

"Be gone," she whispered, her back pressed against the kitchen door. "There is nothing for you here. *Nothing.*"

"But there *is* something for me here," he said, his voice rich, deep—human. *"You."*

Dear Reader,

This month, you get a chance to welcome a new talent to the Silhouette Shadows lineup. Kimberly Raye is making her debut with *'Til We Meet Again,* a haunting tale about a couple whose past lives have been interwoven, and whose present provides their final chance for happiness. And *you'll* be happy, too, because Kimberly's second book will be out in just a few months.

Next month, search the shadows for *Mystery Child,* Carla Cassidy's latest book for the line. Like all her past books, it won't disappoint.

Until next time, enjoy your journey to the dark side of love.

Yours,
Leslie Wainger
Senior Editor and Editorial Coordinator

Please address questions and book requests to:
Silhouette Reader Service
U.S.: 3010 Walden Ave., P.O. Box 1325, Buffalo, NY 14269
Canadian: P.O. Box 609, Fort Erie, Ont. L2A 5X3

KIMBERLY RAYE

'Til We Meet Again

Published by Silhouette Books
America's Publisher of Contemporary Romance

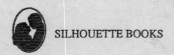 SILHOUETTE BOOKS

ISBN 0-373-27060-7

'TIL WE MEET AGAIN

KIMBERLY RAYE

has always been fascinated by the supernatural, including ghosts, vampires, demons and other creatures of the night. She loves writing a story that frightens, yet thrills. Likewise, she enjoys creating a hero so dark and dangerous that the heroine doesn't know whether to fall in love with him or run for her life.

Kimberly lives in Pasadena, Texas, with her own dark hero and husband of three years, Joe. She writes at least four hours a day and holds down a full-time job. In her spare time, she attends writing workshops and works with an active critique group.

To Nina,
for making me believe in myself
and my characters.

To Gerry, Audrey and Donna,
the best of writing friends,
who bring out the devil in me
and make me strive for every word.

To Donna and Lindy,
for objectivity, encouragement and honesty,
and for listening to me no matter
how much I complained.

And to my very own guardian, Joe,
for showing me the miracle of love firsthand.

PROLOGUE

Spain, 1493

Ever since Maricela de Ruiz had sought him out, Esteban Malvado found himself cursing his own birthright. A birthright that had given him wealth and power, when all he had ever craved was freedom from the demon that haunted his soul. Freedom to join with the beautiful creature who'd sold herself to him for the meager gift of her husband's life—a life not even her own. A notion that had baffled him at first, never being a man to consider anyone worth dying for. Yet, the more she filled his thoughts, the more he came to understand why she'd done what she had. And despite his being brought up in the ways of darkness, reared to fulfill the damnable pact made with the demon Belial by his father and grandfather before him, Esteban came to yearn for the enchanting Maricela to love him with the kind of passion that would sacrifice eternity. The kind of passion that would reach from the heavens to cool the very fires of hell. The kind of passion that would destroy the evil within him and save him from a forever filled with darkness. Sadly, however, he knew nothing could be that powerful. Nothing.

CHAPTER ONE

Fuel the flame that burns within,
Brighter, brighter, overcome the sin.

Darkness awaits, beckoning to me,
Enshrouding an evil only the soul can see.

I must resist, no weakness can dwell,
For within my hands rest heaven and hell.
Three times to touch, to heal, to live,
Of myself, my soul, I freely give.

Mishella Kirkland recited the ancient words revealed to her in her visions, her voice a hushed, frantic whisper as she leaned over the sick girl who tossed restlessly in the throes of a raging fever. Not that Mishella had to bother speaking the words aloud. She needed only to think them to serve her purpose. But speaking each powerful phrase, feeling each syllable on her lips, strengthened her in a small way, and she needed strength if she intended to see Stacey, her stepsister, survive.

She rested her hand on Stacey's forehead. A blazing heat singed her fingers. With every word Mishella murmured, the sensation intensified, until she felt the bubbling of skin at her fingertips and the almost unbearable throbbing.

Please! she screamed silently, the agony rushing up her arm, surging through her body, expanding in her chest until each breath took great effort.

She concentrated on speaking the words, which caught in her throat until she felt herself choking. *Pull away,* a voice commanded, only she knew she couldn't. Not until the sun vanished over the horizon. Then and only then would the second touch be complete.

Determined, she fixed her teary gaze on the window. Staring past the trees and overgrown pasture, she concentrated on the orange blaze that lingered in the distance.

Hurry! As if sensing her haste, the fiery ball inched lower, but not quickly enough.

She heard the slam of the front door first, like a loud clap of thunder breaking open the still quiet of dusk. Then each door throughout the house opened and closed in succession, the loud bangs causing her to flinch as they moved closer, down the hall toward her.

Closer... Closer...

The bedroom door crashed open, and Mishella shut her eyes to the sight. Then she tried to shut her mind to the presence.

Over and over, she recited the words, pain and fear be damned, as she battled for power—the power of life.

If only she wasn't a novice with the special power that had been born to her. The visions showed her when and how to administer the touch, yet she still didn't fully understand the power. All she knew was a terrifying dread felt clear to her bones since the moment she'd dared to use it.

Evil. The power came from an evil she didn't know how to fight. An evil she hadn't wanted to rouse in the first place, but she'd had little choice. And now that evil had finally come to take his power back. Only she couldn't let him have it. Not yet.

A frigid draft of air surrounded Mishella. Icy fingers played up her spine, down her arms and legs, until goose bumps covered her from head to toe, with the exception of her right hand. Had she opened her eyes, she knew she would have seen smoke rising from the point where her palm contacted the sick girl. The smell burned her nostrils and throat. Tears seeped past her clamped eyelids to slide down her face.

Her stepsister's faint, fever-induced cries now mingled with demonic growls—low, throaty animal sounds—which taunted Mishella, eager to break her concentration and force her to lose the touch.

No! You can't. She has only you, Mishella. You are her only hope. Her only chance to live.

Mishella squeezed her eyes tighter and recited the ancient prayer again.

Against the backdrop of her closed eyelids, she saw a spark. A split second later, fiery flames lit the blackness. An agonized scream pierced her ears. *Her own voice?* It couldn't be. She still mouthed the prayer, her lips forming each word with a steady rhythm that remained unbroken.

In the midst of the blaze, a woman's writhing form materialized. Her body was scorched from the fire, her expression anguished. Only her eyes remained distinct, the rest of her consumed by the flames.

"Mishella!" she cried, her blue eyes wide, pleading. "Remember, Mishella. Three times to touch, to heal, to live. You must touch her three different times, each at the exact moment that the sun touches the west. Three moons...three touches." As she spoke, three bloody gashes appeared on her cheek. *Three.* "Remember, Mishella. Remember and beware!"

Then the blue-eyed woman dissolved and another form appeared. A man, also bearing three gashes on his face. The fire licked at his dark features, searing his flesh, but he didn't scream or beg. He seemed to delight in the blaze. The brilliant glow of his eyes, intense like the flames surrounding him, didn't fade. The fire seemed to fuel their potency. The more he burned, the brighter his gaze glowed.

"Mishella," he called, his voice low, beckoning, tormenting. "You will not escape me. You will burn with me, for it is written. Now that you have used your power, I will find you. I *have* found you." He laughed, his face a distortion of flame and melting flesh.

"No!" she whispered urgently, willing the vision away. The flames dissipated. The man vanished, yet the coldness remained, and she knew that whether or not she could see him, *he* remained—the embodiment of evil. The demon set on seeking and destroying her.

She recited the words again. "Darkness awaits, beckoning to me—"

"Traitor!" his voice growled in her ear. A rush of cold air lashed at her.

"I must resist, no weakness can dwell—"

The window shattered, as if hit by a giant fist. Shards of glass flew at her. She lowered her head to protect her face. Grabbing Stacey's hand, she leaned closer to form a shield with her body. Pieces of glass rained down on her, pricking at her flesh through her thick sweater.

"Be gone," she commanded, drawing strength from the knowledge that she had to save the frail girl. That was why she'd broken her vow, used her power and unleashed the darkness. Only to secure an innocent life. "Gone, gone, gone."

Suddenly the cold air warmed. The door creaked shut. Silence ensued, interrupted only by the pounding of Mishella's own heart and her rapid breathing. She slumped forward, resting her cheek against the woolen blanket that covered Stacey. For a brief moment, she wondered if she really had won.

"Shelly?"

Mishella heard the faint murmur of her name and glanced up into the glistening eyes of her fourteen-year-old stepsister.

"It's all right, Shelly," Stacey whispered through cracked lips. She touched a weak hand to Mishella's tear-streaked face.

"How do you feel?" Mishella asked, placing her hand over her stepsister's and entwining their fingers.

"Cooler," the girl whispered, the corners of her mouth hinting at a smile. "You?"

"Don't worry about me," Mishella replied. She glanced at the angry red flesh of her right palm. Careful not to let Stacey see it, Mishella slipped her hand beneath the edge of the blanket.

Stacey had no memory of the first touch, and Mishella was sure she would be spared any recollection of this one, as well. The fever heightened during the touch, rendering Stacey unconscious for the few moments that Mishella used the power.

Mishella took a deep breath, her hand throbbing, her back stinging. She knew that when she lifted her sweater, she would find endless scrapes and cuts from the glass. But the suffering was a small price to pay when Stacey's life hung in the balance.

Gently Mishella smoothed the damp strands of short blond hair back from Stacey's perspiration-damp forehead. The small bedside lamp cast a faint glow on the girl's skin, still a ghastly white—the result of several months of chemotherapy that had drained the vitality from her young body. But her gaze revealed the success of Mishella's efforts. Her eyes seemed clearer, less glazed than usual. In the pale blue depths, Mishella could almost see the vibrant adolescent her stepsister had once been, before that fateful day when the phone call had come.

"Miss Kirkland, your sister has been injured," the head-mistress of one of New York's most elite prep schools had informed her. "It would be advisable for you to come here right away."

Within the hour, Mishella had abandoned the portrait she'd spent the past month working on, commissioned by one of Dallas's wealthy who delighted in seeing himself preserved on canvas, to board a plane for New York City. She hadn't given a second thought to the self-centered Randall Morgan or any of his friends who clamored after her talent. Her only thoughts were of Stacey, the one and only person she had left in the world to love.

Upon arriving at the hospital, she discovered that Stacey had broken her hip playing softball. The doctor had called the injury "unusual," since the activity hadn't been strenuous. She could still hear his matter-of-fact voice when he'd revealed the cause of Stacey's injury.

"Your sister has multiple myeloma."

"What?"

"Multiple myeloma," he repeated, "a form of primary bone cancer, Miss Kirkland. Our tests indicate the disease is a result of chronic myelogenous leukemia."

"Leukemia?" Mishella whispered. Her heart skidded to a stop. *Leukemia.*

"Yes. Your sister is in the advanced stages."

"But how?" Mishella demanded. "She's never had anything worse than a little asthma, a few sinus problems—that sort of thing. How could she have something like that and not know?"

"There are symptoms—a low-grade fever, weakness and pain in the joints, anemia. I've talked with the headmistress at your sister's school. She said Stacey had been complaining of muscle pain. They thought it might be from her numerous extracurricular activities—volleyball, softball, tennis. She was a very active girl.''

Was. The word lodged in Mishella's mind.

''The cancer has progressed rapidly,'' the doctor continued, mindless of the sudden tilt of the floor that forced Mishella to lean one palm against the wall for support. ''An amputation of both lower limbs will be required if chemotherapy fails to put her condition into remission.''

The entire room seemed to vibrate, and Mishella sagged fully against the stark white wall of the emergency room. After the hours spent worrying on the plane, she thought she'd anticipated every possible scenario. But she had never, not in her wildest imaginings, anticipated the doctor's terrifying news.

''We'll begin treatment right away.'' Then he cleared his throat—a harsh, crackling sound that grated on her nerves. ''I'm very sorry, Miss Kirkland.'' Bowing his head, he turned and disappeared down the hall, his heels clicking much the way an empty gun clicks when the trigger is pulled over and over again.

Sorry. Her world had been shattered and her sister had received her death sentence. *Sorry* was little consolation.

And that was the beginning of months of praying and painful chemotherapy treatments that had proved worthless. The cancer hadn't gone into remission.

Three times to touch...

The moment she'd first placed her hand on Stacey, Mishella remembered the dreams that had plagued her through her adolescence, ever since she'd first discovered her cursed power.

''The evil will come for you, Mishella,'' the blue-eyed woman had told her in her dreams. ''Once you use the touch, the demon will see you, know you and destroy you.''

A life for a life...

Had Mishella not felt the power inside her, seen the destruction it could do firsthand, she wouldn't have believed the blue-eyed woman. She would have relished such a healing gift. Only the power had terrible repercussions.

A life for a life...

Her power was too frightening, too fantastic—like a made-up story to tell in front of the fire on a cold night while sipping hot cocoa. A touch that heals, yet destroys at the same time. It was too unbelievable and, at the same time, all too real.

Mishella hadn't even known of her power, not until that day nearly fifteen years ago when she'd touched Millie, her cat. That discovery had altered her life forever.

The dreams had started then, showing her the power, what she could do if she chose. But at a cost. She must pay a price to heal, the blue-eyed woman had said over and over.

A life for a life...

Fearful of the consequences, Mishella had vowed never to use her touch again.

Mishella hadn't revealed her power to anyone, afraid that just talking of it would bring about evil things. Not that anyone would've believed Mishella if she had. She doubted even her own mother would've swallowed such a wild tale. That was part of the reason Mishella hadn't told her. That and the fact that she hadn't wanted to endanger her mother's life. Not again.

Never speak of the touch. Never use it. Mishella had promised herself both. Until recently.

Since learning of Stacey's leukemia, the dreams had become much more frightening and much clearer than ever before. The burned man had urged her to use her touch while the blue-eyed woman had warned her against it. But Mishella had no alternative. She couldn't stand by and let Stacey die.

When she'd touched Stacey the first time, exactly twenty-eight days ago, the dreams had escalated into visions.

The blue-eyed woman cried out to her, still warning her, yet guiding her, as well, for better or worse. *A life for a life...*

At the woman's urging, Mishella had left New York. She'd brought her stepsister to Three Rivers, Texas, the small town her mother had lived in, about one hundred miles from the Mexican border, in hopes of hiding out from an evil spirit strong enough to destroy her and keep her from healing Stacey.

She only needed to complete one more touch, she reminded herself. One more lunar phase. Then, at the exact moment when the sun caressed the earth and gave way to night, she would touch Stacey for the final time.

"Don't cry," Stacey whispered, drawing Mishella from her thoughts, back to the small bedroom, to the mahogany bed with the patchwork quilt and the faint breeze that filtered through the shattered window.

Self-conscious, Mishella wiped away the telltale moisture that streaked her face. "No, don't *you* cry," she said, tracing the faint bluish hollow beneath one of her stepsister's eyes and wiping away the wetness. "There's no reason to cry, baby. Everything is going to be all right."

Stacey glanced toward the window, to the sheer tattered curtains billowing with the night breeze. "What happened?" she asked.

"A big gust of wind, that's all. That's why all these windows have shutters. Mom used to tell me they always had windstorms out here." Mishella smiled, but Stacey didn't look the least bit convinced.

"I'm scared," the girl said, her voice soft, weak, heartbreaking.

"Nonsense. You have nothing to be scared of, sweetheart. I'm here, and you're getting better," Mishella assured her.

"Still, I'm scared."

"Of what?"

"Dying." A tear trickled from one corner of the girl's eye, and Mishella felt a vise tighten about her heart.

"There's no reason to be afraid," she said, her voice fierce, confident as she held her stepsister's gaze and gave her hand a squeeze. The small fingers felt like ice against her palm, as cold as the metal railing on the hospital bed that Mishella had come to detest. But no more. No more cold metal railing, blinding fluorescent lights, unnatural hums of heart monitors and respirators. No more.

"You're not going to die. I won't let you," Mishella vowed. "I won't let you, Stacey. Do you hear me?"

Stacey nodded. "You always were a bossy older sister," she murmured, closing her eyes, her mouth crooked in a half grin.

Mishella didn't have to force a smile this time. "And don't you forget it, little sister."

Several seconds ticked by while Mishella studied her stepsister. The steady rise and fall of her chest indicated that she slept. Her smooth, delicate brow revealed the peace she felt, and in that instant, Mishella had a small taste of victory.

Easing her hand from Stacey's, she smoothed the covers around the girl and stood up.

Pieces of glass covered the floor, the dresser, the overstuffed blue velour chair in the corner. With careful steps, Mishella crunched her way across the room, grateful she'd thought to put on tennis shoes. She hurried through the doorway, eager to get a broom and clear up the reminder of the battle she'd just waged. And won.

A faint stream of light drifted from the partially open bathroom door at the far end of the hallway, but otherwise, the rest of the hall was concealed in the shadows.

Squinting, Mishella walked through the darkness toward the kitchen, thinking that one of the first things she had to do was drive to town and buy, among other things, some light bulbs. She'd been in such a rush when they'd arrived that she hadn't had time to anticipate what the house would be like after a year of neglect.

Only a few steps from the kitchen, she heard the front door open, then slam shut.

For a second, fear paralyzed her.

Footsteps followed, coming toward her. She managed to take a breath, gather her courage and turn in the direction of the living room. *He's found you,* a voice taunted.

From the end of the hallway, the dark shape of a man appeared. He seemed to fill the entire corridor as he neared her, his steps slow and steady. She inched backward, wanting to turn, to run, only she had nowhere to hide. She'd known that when she'd fled New York. Leaving had been a ruse to buy her time. Time that appeared to have run out.

"Be gone," she whispered, her back pressed against the kitchen door. "There's nothing for you here. Nothing."

"But there *is* something for me here. You," he said, his voice rich, deep, *human.*

She blinked to see better as he closed the distance between them. The stream of light from the bathroom silhouetted his massive frame. When he stood just inches from her, so close she could feel his breath caressing her face, she stared up at him. Light seeped from the corners of the kitchen door she pressed against, the faint rays illuminating him.

No satanic creature stood before her. Only a man—a tall, broad-shouldered man, his angular jaw covered with stubble, his dark, raven black hair falling well past his shoulders. Clad in faded jeans and a matching jacket, which fell open to reveal a white T-shirt stretched over a well-muscled chest, he looked real and very earthly. Still, she knew she shouldn't be fooled. The evil could take on a human form if it so chose. Hadn't the blue-eyed woman said so?

Reason told her to beware, yet his words, his strength, his musky scent disarmed her.

"The second touch is finished," he said. "I've come to see that you complete the third touch, as well."

He knew. He had to be the evil manifested, but something in his eyes—a tenderness maybe—proved him merely a man. And a man she could face.

"Who are you?" she demanded with more bravado than she felt.

"Only a man," he replied, as if reading her thoughts, "with powers like yours. With one foot in the darkness and one in the light, Mishella."

Mishella. "How do you know my name?"

"I know a lot more about you than your name," he said. "I've come to help you. A guardian, you could call me. Someone to pull you over to the light and keep the evil from taking your life." He dropped the worn knapsack he carried to the floor and reached for her right hand. Closing his fingers around her burned palm, he stared deep into her eyes. "Not an angel, not a devil, but a guardian."

"Guardian," she whispered, feeling the heat in her hand dissolve beneath his cool, lean fingers. Staring into the compelling midnight of his eyes, she wondered if she dared believe. She shouldn't, except something in those dark depths pleaded for her trust, and she needed to trust someone. The burden felt too heavy to bear alone.

Believe in me, Mishella. Trust in me.

After what seemed like endless minutes, she broke the silent communication and forced herself to look away. Pulling her hand from his, she stared at the once-burned flesh. Not a trace of the blistering remained, as if she'd never touched her hand to Stacey. "You have the touch," she gasped, staring up at him, her eyes wide.

"Yes, like you. Only my power is stronger. Much stronger. I can help you. That's why I'm here."

"But why would you want to? If you're like me, using your power makes you weak, susceptible to the evil. The power *is* evil," she whispered. She searched his face for some clue to his thoughts, but found none. "*If* you're like me," she added, her fears overriding her reason.

His eyes remained dark, unreadable, even beneath her suspicion. "I've been waiting to find you," he said. "When you made the first touch, I felt you, Mishella. I was drawn to you, driven to find you because you're like me. Because I'm like you. I'm threatened by the evil, too. The touch we possess is life-draining. You already know that." He touched his fingers to the shadows beneath her eyes. "But if two people with the same touch combine powers, they become stronger. You can give your touch to Stacey, and I in turn can give you mine, and save your life."

"That would be too great a risk for you," she reminded him, all the while feeling a ripple of hope. "Whoever you love the most will die should you use your touch. You don't even know me. Why would you chance death for someone you don't even know?" The question tumbled from her lips.

"But I do know you, Mishella. All along, I've known you were out there somewhere. We were destined to come together. That's why the demon's been after me—because I figured out that together, with our powers combined, we can escape him." His voice lowered, sending a shiver down Mishella's spine. "I've always known there was another like me. I have dreams, visions—"

"I have them too," she cut in. "They show me the power, warn me—"

"Mine show me *you*. You're in my dreams. The touch bonds us. I'm here to help you because you're a part of me. Your soul cries out to mine, and I can't resist. I felt the evil at my heels for so long, desperate for my life, my soul. He almost had me—until you made that touch."

His fingers drifted across her cheek like a cool, soothing breeze. His voice was low and so very compelling as he added, "You drew his attention from me by making the first touch, but when he finishes with you, he'll come for me again. By helping you, maybe I can save myself. The last thing he wants is for you to make the third touch. He'll do all he can to stop you."

"No," she whispered, wanting to deny the truth. But she knew. Even before she heard his next words, she knew. Like him, she'd always known.

"Yes." His gaze, as deep as midnight, dark and consuming, bore into hers. "Together we can make the touch and destroy him. Alone, the evil will swallow each of us." She heard the anguish in his voice, just below the surface as if he tried to deny the carefully hidden pain in his words. Only she felt his pain, as real as her own.

"Together," he repeated. "You can save me, Mishella, and I can save you. Without me, you won't perform the third touch. Already, the demon knows where you are."

"Yes," she replied. "I've heard his voice, felt his presence." And I see him in my dreams, she added silently, remembering the burned man and knowing that he was the demon that pursued her.

"The evil is strong," he said. "Stronger than you can imagine. If you want to resist him and save your sister, you'll let me help you."

"And if I don't let you help me? What then?"

"You will both die," he replied, enunciating each word with a slowness that sent a shiver through her. "You've completed two touches, but only because he let you. He's toying with you, testing your strength. He'll crush you before you make the third touch." He trailed his fingers down the slope of her jaw, tracing the shape of her face. "You can't see the process through alone, *querida*. Your power isn't strong enough."

Querida. Darling. The word niggled at her memory the way a childhood picture does. She knew she'd heard it before.

"Not nearly strong enough," he added, disrupting her thoughts. "You need my help, and I need yours. *Together.*"

She wanted to refute his words, only she couldn't. Afraid that, should she fail, her stepsister would die, she could only nod. He knew of her, of her powers, of her desperate situation—all proof he spoke the truth. He promised help. A help she couldn't refuse, for Stacey's sake.

"What's your name?" she asked.

"Raphael," he replied, letting his hand fall away from her. Still, his gaze didn't waiver. "Raphael Dalton."

"Raphael," she echoed the familiar name. Any lingering suspicions about his identity slipped away. She knew of Raphael. He was one of the archangels . . . now, a *guardian* angel. *Her* guardian angel.

CHAPTER TWO

A loud rap on the front door startled Mishella. She tore her gaze from Raphael's and stared down the hallway to the living room.

"Someone's at the door," she said. Only there couldn't be. They were miles from town, on an isolated stretch of land at least three miles from the nearest neighbor.

"Are you expecting anyone?"

She watched as he glanced behind him, then back at her. His brows knit together in a frown, his gaze concealed beneath a thick veil of dark lashes.

She shook her head, desperate to deny the truth—that she did expect someone. Hadn't she been waiting for the evil to manifest itself? The burned man kept telling her how close he was. How she wouldn't escape him.

The knock sounded again, louder, more demanding this time as if unwilling to be ignored.

"I guess I'd better answer it," she said, forcing her fear aside long enough to take a step forward.

She moved past him, down the hall and into the living room. Sheets still draped most of the furniture. The stale odor of age filled the room. Only a year empty, the house might well have stood a lifetime that way.

"Do you want me to answer it?" he asked, touching a hand to her arm as if sensing her misgivings.

She did, only she couldn't admit that to him. She had to be strong in her own right. "No," she whispered.

"Are you sure?"

When she nodded, he dropped his hand. Reluctance glimmered in his eyes, showed in the sudden tick of his jaw muscle.

Turning, she unbolted the door. "Give me strength," she said softly to herself and pulled the door open a fraction of an inch.

Through the crack, she spotted an old Mexican woman, head bowed, digging in an oversize purse the size and color of a grocery sack.

Mishella breathed a sigh of relief. The woman was a far cry from the devil she'd expected.

"May I help you?" Mishella asked, opening the door a few inches.

The woman glanced up, her search abandoned. For a second, Mishella could have sworn she saw something flicker in the woman's eyes—fear maybe, yet she sensed relief, as well. Guarded control slipped into place before Mishella could wonder.

"I knew it!" the woman cried. "I just knew you were here already." She slapped a few strands of gray hair back from her face. "You had me worried. I was ready to use my key. What took you so long? Is everything all right?" The questions poured forth as the woman scanned Mishella from head to toe, her brows furrowed, her gaze unblinking.

"I—I'm sorry," Mishella said, feeling as if she stood accused of some crime for which she needed to make immediate restitution. "I didn't mean to keep you. Is there something I can do for you?"

The woman regarded her for a long moment. Finally, a smile wrinkled her ruddy brown face. The gold crown of a tooth glittered in the lamplight from the living room. She grasped one of Mishella's hands between her callused palms. "Ah, Señorita Kirkland, I have waited a long time to meet you," she said. "You are the spitting image of your mama, God rest her soul."

"You knew my mother?" Mishella swallowed at the sudden lump in her throat. Her grip on the doorknob faltered. She let her hand fall to her side while the other remained in the woman's warm grasp. The loss of her parents was still so fresh, the wound unhealed.

"*Sí.*" The woman fingered the cascade of ebony curls falling over one of Mishella's shoulders. "Your mama had hair this exact color." Her smile turned wistful as she touched her palm to Mishella's cheek. "Such smooth, pale skin, too. You, *mija,* are as beautiful as your mama," she declared. "Blue eyes and all."

Mishella fidgeted beneath the woman's scrutiny.

As if sensing Mishella's discomfort, the woman pulled her hand back. Her smile disappeared as she clutched the rosary suspended around her neck. "Such a terrible car accident," she added. "One week after I heard the news, me and my Domingo went to mass for the novena—nine days of prayer—so your mama and stepfather would rest in peace."

"Thank you, um… I'm afraid I don't know your name."

The woman's cheeks stained. "But of course you don't, *mija.* Forgive me," she implored. "I am just a foolish old woman for going on and on when you have no idea who I am. It's just that I feel like I know you. Your mama told me so much about you and the little one."

"My mother told you about me and my stepsister?"

"*Sí, mija.* I am Inez," she stated, obviously expecting her name to strike a familiar chord.

Mishella could only shake her head. "Inez?"

"Inez Santibanez. I used to cook and clean for your mama when she and your stepfather moved here. Now I just keep an eye on this place."

Inez. Mishella searched her memory. "Yes, Inez!" she exclaimed after a moment. "I'm sorry the name didn't ring a bell at first. I've had a lot on my mind lately. My mother did mention you in some of her letters. In fact, I seem to recall that she said you kept her company quite often."

"Your sweet mama never wanted to move out here," Inez said. "So far from everything, but that husband of hers..." She shook her head. "A good man but awfully stubborn."

"My stepfather wanted to retire someplace he could relax. He spent his entire life in a three-piece suit, building up his business." For nothing, Mishella thought.

For you and Stacey, Mishella remembered her mother's words. *He doesn't want either of you to ever have to worry about anything.* But no amount of money could have prepared Mishella and Stacey for what they were facing. No amount of money could save them.

"He used to tell your mama this place was like heaven," Inez was saying.

"For Dad it was. Anyplace without a telephone or a fax machine seemed like heaven, though I know my mother never shared his enthusiasm."

"She didn't like being so far from her girls," Inez said. "I know she'd be happy to know both of you are here now."

She wouldn't be so happy if she knew the circumstances, Mishella thought. She'd be heartbroken. "I'm sure my mother would be happy that you took the time to come and welcome us. You're very kind."

"Your mama was the kind one. I miss her. She was a very good friend to me."

Mishella felt the tears brimming in her eyes. Mention of her mother always had that effect. Except now, she couldn't cry. Crying meant weakness, and she had no room for weakness. Only strength. Strength would see Stacey through.

Inez breathed a heavy sigh, her generous bosom heaving beneath her flower-print dress, and said, "I knew you would come."

"You knew?" Mishella felt the faint stirring of apprehension. How could Inez have known? Unless she was the presence Mishella had been waiting for... She looked into the woman's soft brown eyes.

You're letting your imagination get the best of you. You'll know when the presence comes. You'll know.

"Señor Morris, the attorney, called me a few days ago," Inez quickly explained, as if she could see straight into Mishella's mind and was eager to assuage her fears.

Mishella's heart started to beat normally again. *See? Just your imagination.*

"He told me you were on your way and asked if I could come out here and make sure everything was ready for you. I planned on coming tomorrow, but tonight while I was fixing supper, I had this feeling. As soon as my Domingo came in from work, I told him we had to come out here tonight. Sure enough, when we pulled up at the road, I saw the lights." She motioned toward the large bay window. The lamp cast a distinct shadow against the draperies. "I knew I was right." She tapped a finger to her chest. "Whenever I get the *feeling,* I'm always right. My Domingo can tell you that."

Mishella's gaze went to the man standing a few feet behind Inez. Moonlight silhouetted his short, stocky form, but the shadows of the porch concealed his face. He stepped forward into the small beam of light from the living room.

Mishella noted his wrinkled, leather-brown features, his bushy gray eyebrows set close together above hard, glittery brown eyes. The silver-white hair that framed his face reached the shoulders of his dingy, navy blue workshirt. He looked old, worn, as if he'd been breathing forever. The knowing light in his eyes reinforced the notion.

"Señor Morris said you were not coming until Saturday," Inez said.

"I arrived yesterday," Mishella explained, forcing her gaze back to Inez. "I left New York a few days earlier than I expected." She'd had to leave in order to reach Three Rivers and get Stacey ready for the second touch. "My lawyer didn't know of my change in plans."

"I didn't bring anything to clean with, but I'll be back tomorrow to help get you settled in," Inez offered with a wide smile. "I only wanted to see that you had made it here all right."

"Thank you, but you don't have to bother coming back tomorrow. I can wait until Sat—"

"It's no bother," the old woman said, waving Mishella to silence. "In fact, why don't I come in now and straighten a little for you?" Inez stared past her into the living room. "At least pull the covers off the couch and chairs. That won't take but a minute, not nearly as long as it will take to get this place like it was when your mama was here. She always kept every window in the house open." The old woman sniffed. "Smells like this place could stand some open windows."

Mishella glanced behind her at the now empty room, her gaze riveted on the spot where Raphael had stood only minutes before. *Gone?* Her uneasiness grew. Her heart started to drum. She took a steady breath and turned back to the old couple.

"There's no need to go to any trouble tonight, Inez," she said, casting another glance over her shoulder to confirm that he really had vanished. Yet he had to be close by. She could still feel him. The palm of her hand still tingled from his cool fingers.

"Is something wrong, señorita?" The man spoke this time, his voice thick with an accent that required her full attention.

"No. Nothing. I mean...everything is fine. I thought I heard my sister call." *Liar,* she scolded herself.

"I'd almost forgotten you brought the little one!" Inez cried. "I've seen so many pictures of her I feel like I know her."

"She isn't so little anymore."

"As old as I am, to me she'll always be a little one. Where is she?"

"Asleep," Mishella replied. "She's not really feeling well."

"It's no wonder with this crazy weather. I've never known it to be so cold in September. Crazy weather," she muttered. "Does she have a cold? The flu?" She stared expectantly.

"The flu, I think. I'm not really sure. But she'll be all right." Mishella said the words more for her own benefit than the old woman's. "The sickness is passing. She'll be fine."

"Tomorrow I will bring some soup for her. She will be up and about in no time," Inez declared. "Domingo will bring me bright and early." She gathered the frayed edges of her faded pink shawl. "It's cold," she said. "Time for us to go. Come, Domingo." She turned and crossed the small porch to the front steps.

Domingo paused. "Keep the child warm," he said after several seconds. "You must keep her warm." His words sounded more like a warning than advice.

"I will."

"The cold is too much for her," he pressed, staring past Mishella into the house, his black eyes searching.

In that instant, Mishella felt that something was wrong.

"Domingo," Inez said, her voice sharp. "Leave Señorita Kirkland to rest," she said. "We'll come back tomorrow."

Domingo shot Mishella another glance before turning to follow his wife down the steps.

Mishella sagged against the edge of the door, relieved, yet terrified. Relieved that the couple had left her alone, but terrified that when the demon did reveal himself, she would be powerless to fight. Each day, each night, each moment, sapped her strength. She was dying. Soon, in four weeks, it would all be over.

Raphael. He'd come to renew her strength, only to disappear. She wondered when, or even if, he would return. He had to. She would surely die without him.

A life for a life.

Death waited for her, but she didn't want to die. If Raphael was telling the truth, then with his help, she wouldn't. Together they could defeat the demon.

But what if he was lying? He was a stranger. A mysterious stranger who had appeared out of nowhere and promised salvation. Why? Because his own life really was in danger, and he needed her as much as she needed him?

Yes! a small voice screamed. The same voice that told her to believe. To trust him because she had nothing and no one else to put her trust in. Already she felt weak, her spirit being drained like water dripping slowly, torturously from a faucet.

A life for a life.

Unless . . .

Despite everything, Raphael didn't seem like a stranger. The few moments she'd spent with him might well have been a lifetime. She felt his power as intensely as she felt her own.

Together they could save Stacey, she thought as she stepped back to close the door and slide the bolt into place. *Together.*

* * *

Raphael leaned against the corner of the wood-frame house and let his knapsack fall at his feet. Safely obscured by the shadows, he watched the old couple climb into a battered pickup truck parked at the end of the driveway.

"Tomorrow," he said. "I'll deal with both of you tomorrow."

A movement near the front window of the house drew his attention. He saw Mishella's silhouette moving about the kitchen. The two touches had worn her down, but still she boasted a strength he hadn't anticipated. *A power to rival my own,* he thought, *if she so chooses.* Only she didn't seek to rival his power. She only wanted to complete the third touch, even though it meant angering the demon. Even though it meant death.

"Death it will be," Raphael whispered, knowing that Belial would drain every breath from her, despite her strength. Raphael knew how powerful, how overwhelming, the demon could be. That was why he'd come to her, why he'd been drawn to her light.

He rubbed his hands together as a shiver went through him. Startled, he took a deep breath, willing the cold away and the numbness to return in its place. He hadn't felt the cold in a long, long time. Not since he'd heeded his own nightmares, realized his ties with Belial and discovered his power.

Raphael exhaled, watching the pale white cloud that blew from his nostrils—warm breath meeting the cold air. She the warmth and he the cold. The cold would swallow her.

The silver ring on his left hand felt like a chunk of ice against his palm. A reminder of his past, of *their* past. He clenched his fist and closed his eyes. Yes, the cold would swallow her, just as it had swallowed him....

* * *

"You are Señor Malvado?" The woman shoved the hood back from her forehead and pushed a stray black curl away from her face. She stared at him with brilliant sapphire eyes, as bold as the jeweled ring that adorned Esteban's left hand.

"*Sí*, and you, señora, are . . . ?" Esteban knew even before he heard her reply.

"Maricela de Ruiz," she stated, her soft voice barely audible above the fierce storm that raged outside.

"Ah, Señora Ruiz." He leaned back in his chair and eyed her across the wide expanse of the room. Yes, he had known of her impending arrival. He knew all who dared to venture to his castle. All who dared to seek his powers. "Come closer."

She glanced around, her gaze sweeping the grand interior. The beads of water that nestled against the velvet of her cloak glistened like crystal teardrops in the candlelight. She lifted her heavy brocade skirts and stepped across the room.

"Tell me what brings you to my home on such a hellish night?" The wind beat a satanic rhythm against the stone walls surrounding the Castillo de Malvado.

Flames in the stone hearth behind him cast flickering shadows across her face as she neared, stopping a few feet from his velvet armchair. Esteban took a sip from the brass goblet held loosely in his palm.

"I am here to ask for your assistance, señor," she said, finally meeting his eyes.

"I am flattered, señora, but what would bring you seeking my services when you've a husband to see to your requests?" He studied her over the carved rim.

"He is the reason I have come," she replied, arched ebony brows wrinkled worriedly over her magnificent eyes. "He is very ill."

"So I've heard," he remarked. "But what does his illness have to do with me?"

"I—I fear he is dying and..." Her voice faltered.

"And?" He prompted, placing his drink on the table beside his chair, his gaze never wavering from hers. "Do not tell me you have traveled such a great distance to lose your nerve now, señora. Not when you have my undivided attention."

She looked uncertain for a moment. Licking her full pink lips, she whispered, "There is talk, señor, among the servants and others in the village."

"Talk of what?" He quirked an eyebrow.

"Talk of you. That you have certain, um, how shall I say...*abilities* that might help my husband."

"And what abilities are these, Señora Ruiz?" He gave her a mocking smile.

"He needs a remedy for his sickness," she said, seeming not the least bit bothered by his sarcastic manner.

"I am no doctor." He frowned. "You should have traveled to Barcelona if it's a physician you seek. I am sure they can bleed him or concoct some other form of torturous cure," he said. "I have no such remedy for your dear Miguel."

"No, but you have..." She paused, then said, her voice a whisper, *"Powers."*

"Powers!" he scoffed, his voice echoing above the wind.

"Shh," she said, her gaze nervous as she glanced behind her at the stoic-faced servant stationed at the door.

With a flick of his wrist, Esteban dismissed the uniformed man. "Better?"

"Si," she breathed, yet she cast another worried glance over her shoulder.

"Gossip floats through the village, but whether such talk holds any truth is questionable. Surely you do not believe all that you hear, Señora Ruiz?" Without waiting for a reply, he added, "I never would have thought Miguel would marry a gullible woman, even one as beautiful as you."

"I know only what I have heard," she murmured. "You have quite a reputation."

"Tell me," he urged, leaning forward to rest his forearms on his knees. "These powers of which you speak, are they courtesy of our Heavenly Father or do they come from dear Lucifer himself?" He was baiting her, he knew. But the flare of her nostrils, the blue blaze of her eyes was well worth the effort.

"You tell me, señor," she challenged.

"You could have gone to any church were you seeking powers of the Holy One," he assessed. "I trust then that the powers you require are those of his enemy." He smiled knowingly.

"Please keep your voice down, señor," she admonished, glancing again over her shoulder.

"Of course. Such talk could see you burn, señora, should anyone discover that the wife of one of the Crown's highest-ranking officers seeks any powers other than those granted by the Holy Father." He watched her stiffen before adding, "The Inquisition, of which your husband is a loyal supporter, holds such as evidence to prosecute the vermin heretics, which make the Church weak. Tell me, Señora Ruiz, are you one of these heretics?"

"Maybe your reputation *is* unfounded," she replied, her voice tight, her gaze suddenly icy. "I beg your forgiveness for having disturbed you." She cast him a freezing glare, then turned in a swirl of skirts.

Esteban reached her before she could take a step toward the door. "Wait," he said, touching a hand to her shoulder.

Slowly she faced him. He breathed in the heady scent of jasmine mingled with the wine he'd consumed. A few glasses—a paltry amount compared to what he usually imbibed—to forget and escape the cursed demon Belial who haunted his soul. But he'd been waiting for her arrival. For her, he had exercised restraint.

For her...

"So you have come seeking my powers," he said, sliding his hand from her shoulder, down her arm, feeling her flesh quiver beneath the cape. In her eyes, he read the desperation and fear that had brought her from the carefully guarded walls of the Ruiz castle to the lush countryside that was his domain.

"My husband has very little time." She untied her cape and pulled a small satin purse from the bodice of her dress. "I have gold." She held the bag out to him, her hand quaking ever so slightly.

"And so do I, señora," he said with a sweeping gesture to indicate their lavish surroundings. "More, in fact, than you can fathom, despite your husband's esteemed position. I am afraid your gold will not serve as a means of exchange for my assistance."

"Please," she said, imploringly. "I have no one else to turn to."

Her eyes shimmered with unshed tears, but Esteban was hardly moved. Rather, the rapid swell of her breasts, which spilled over the bodice of her low-cut dress, stirred his interest as no amount of despair could. He forced his gaze upward to the fullness of her trembling lips and said, "The price is very high."

"How much? If you require more gold—"

"The price is far more than gold, *querida*. Far more." He touched a finger to the slope of one creamy breast. She flinched, but she made no attempt to pull away. She knew. The instant their gazes locked, she knew.

"Whatever the price, I will pay," she murmured, her breath catching when his palm brushed the taut peak of one nipple. The first of several tears slid silently down her ivory cheek. "Whatever you wish, Señor Malvado. Just help me."

"Damn," Raphael muttered as another shiver gripped him. He snatched up his knapsack and stalked toward the dilapidated building that had once served as a barn. He needed to refuel his powers, to channel them so that he no longer felt the cold—or the regret. Until the only thing inside him was a driving force that Mishella Kirkland didn't stand a chance against.

That was the way it was meant to be.

The way it had been such a long time ago.

The way it would be again.

CHAPTER THREE

Mishella scooped the last few pieces of glass into the dustpan and dumped them into a wicker trash basket. She straightened and stretched, glancing at her stepsister, who lay in a tangle of blankets and pillows in the center of the bed.

A gust of wind rushed in through the window. Goose bumps rose beneath the thin covering of her long-sleeved blouse. Mishella caught her bottom lip between her teeth to keep them from chattering. It was unusually cold for September.

The evil brings the cold, a voice whispered. *It will get even colder as he comes closer... the burned man... the demon.*

Stepping to the closet, she pulled another quilt from the top shelf. As she tucked the warm cover around her sister, she remembered Domingo's words. *Keep her warm.* Another rush of wind came through the window and Mishella shivered. She had to find something to cover the opening.

In a few quick strides, she reached the doorway. First she would cover the window, then she'd start a fire in the fireplace and—

"Oh!" She stopped short of Raphael's towering frame. He stood just outside the door, partially hidden in the hall shadows.

"I—I'm sorry. I didn't see you," she apologized, making yet another mental note to get some light bulbs the first chance she had. Then her voice turned slightly accusing, and her eyes narrowed. "I thought you were gone."

"Did you?" He cocked one dark brow at her. "And I thought for sure you could feel me close by," he said, his voice soft, mocking even. Only his eyes held no malice. "The same way I feel you."

"Okay, so I felt you," she admitted. "Where did you disappear to?"

"Not far, Mishella. Never far," he replied. He stared past her into the room. "We need to cover the window." He'd brought plastic bags and a roll of tape with him.

Mishella glanced at Stacey. The peace that had followed the second touch had been only temporary. Her forehead now had a thin film of perspiration, despite the chill of the room. She whimpered, tossing about as if fleeing some unseen pursuer. The fever still fought for control of her body.

Another shiver gripped Mishella. "Can you help me move her to another room first? The plastic won't keep the draft out, and I don't want her to develop pneumonia."

Raphael nodded, tossing the plastic and tape onto a nearby chair. He stepped to the bed where Stacey lay, her breath coming in short, shallow gasps.

At her bedside, he hesitated. Mishella stared at the muscles of his back, which went rigid beneath his white T-shirt as if he didn't want to touch Stacey. She sensed the tension in him.

"You don't have to pick her up," she said with every intention of telling him she could look after Stacey herself. But before she could finish, he bent down.

The moment he lifted Stacey, she stilled. He gathered the girl in his arms, blankets dangling almost to the floor, and turned back to Mishella.

"I don't mind helping you out. Where to?" he asked, avoiding Mishella's gaze.

"Follow me," she said, hurrying through the door to the next bedroom. She flicked on the light and motioned to the quilt-covered bed. "You can put her down there."

As soon as Raphael eased Stacey onto the bed, Mishella brushed past him and started arranging the blankets.

"How long has she been sick?" he asked, stepping back so she could move to lean over her stepsister.

"It's been nearly four months now since the doctor diagnosed her."

"Then you didn't touch her right away?" He sounded surprised.

"No, I was hoping the chemotherapy would put the cancer into remission, but the only thing it seemed to do was make her worse." She touched a few strands of dull blond hair. Her stepsister's once glorious mane was now thin and short. She could still remember Stacey's heartbreaking tears after the first few treatments, when the hair had started to fall out.

"And the touch?" he asked, his deep voice pulling her from her memories. "Has it helped?"

"I don't know." She focused her gaze on the starlike display of oranges and browns that patterned the quilt, suddenly self-conscious beneath his scrutiny. "After the first touch, she gained a little strength, but then when the time came for the second, she became sick all over again. Worse than before," Mishella added, catching her bottom lip between her teeth to stop the trembling.

"And what about you, Mishella?"

"What do you mean?" she asked, smoothing the edge of the quilt over the side of the bed, but she knew what he meant even before she heard his next words.

"The touch is wearing you down fast. When was the last time you slept?"

"I slept a few hours last night," she murmured, tucking the last corner of the quilt under Stacey's legs before turning to face him. He stood so close to her. So close she could reach out and touch him, only her arms felt heavy, the same as her heart. Tears—exhausted, worried, tears—burned her eyes, but she held them back. She'd cried too much already.

"You need more than a few hours to keep up your strength."

"Thanks for your concern, but the only thing on my mind right now is my sister, not sleep." She couldn't sleep. The visions wouldn't let her. The burned man wouldn't let her.

"That's the reason you should sleep. Your power is weak without rest. You have to be alert. How do you expect to face the demon and win if you can hardly stand up?"

The demon. She blinked back the tears. "I'll win," she whispered, trying more to convince herself than him. "I have to." She stared at him now, her gaze pleading for strength, for understanding, when the words refused to come. "*We* have to. *Together.*"

He took her hand and laced his fingers through hers, his touch cool, comforting. Pulling her closer, he stared down into her eyes as if looking straight into her soul and seeing every fear and misgiving that plagued her. She felt his strength feeding hers, his power fusing with hers.

"The power you possess is purely an accident of fate, Mishella. It isn't really yours. It's the demon's—a demon more powerful than you can imagine. We both have to be strong if we intend to win this. *You* have to be strong." His intense eyes held her immobile. "You know, no one would blame you if you didn't go through with the third touch. Not many people would be willing to sacrifice so much for someone else. Most wouldn't inconvenience themselves to lend a hand to somebody in need, much less risk death."

"I know," she said. "But Stacey isn't just anyone. She's my sister..." Her words faded. "I have to go through with it. Besides," she added, clinging to the seed of hope Raphael had planted, "you're here. If we combine our powers, then I'll live. I won't be sacrificing my life. We'll defeat the demon." *We have to,* she screamed silently.

"We will, but you must try to rest," he said. "You can't let yourself become weak."

She nodded. "I still don't understand how you found me."

"The touch. I felt you when you touched your sister the first time. I felt your power."

The demon will come for you. Mishella remembered the blue-eyed woman's words. But the man in front of her wasn't a demon. He might be dark, handsome, overpowering, perhaps even bewitching, but he made her feel safe and, for the first time, not quite so alone. He made her feel alive. He could keep her alive. *Together.*

"Why me?" she asked. "I still don't understand why I have this power. Why you have it. What it means." She shook her head. "Were we cursed or something? Are there others besides us?"

"We are the only ones with this power, Mishella. Only you and I, and in a way I guess we were cursed. I'm not really sure how it happened. Or why. Only that it did."

"But there must be some reason," she insisted, her sanity dangling by a thread.

"Maybe we were born on a certain day at a certain moment that makes us what we are. I don't really know." He swung his gaze to Stacey briefly before again leveling it on Mishella. "I only know that the touch is evil. As much as it can heal, it can also kill. You're using it for good, Mishella. That angers the demon. He doesn't intend to let you succeed. To see his evil power give life is an abomination to him. It contradicts all that he stands for.''

''But why me?'' she asked once more, needing to understand. To make some sense out of something too fantastic to believe. Shockingly enough, she did believe. Gazing deep into Raphael's eyes, she saw truth and understanding and something else. Something that pulled at her emotions, begged for trust and warmed her insides, though the hand that held hers felt cool.

She forced her eyes from his and pulled from his grasp, suddenly unnerved by the strange tightening in her stomach. *Stacey.* She had to keep her mind, her energy, channeled on her stepsister. She could search for answers later.

''The window,'' she whispered, eager to distract them both. His face remained expressionless, his dark eyes unblinking as he studied her a moment longer.

''The window,'' he finally echoed. He touched a finger to her cheek and she closed her eyes to the strange but thrilling sensation.

When his hand fell away, she opened her eyes to see him turn and disappear through the door. A few moments later, she heard him moving around in the other bedroom. Next came the sound of plastic tearing, then the ripping of tape.

''Shelly.'' Stacey's faint voice reached her ears.

''What is it, baby?'' She turned and knelt beside her sister.

''Who was that?'' Stacey's eyes fluttered open for a brief moment.

''Just a...a friend of mine,'' Mishella whispered. ''An old friend, that's all.''

''Do I know him?''

''No, baby. He's someone I met at, uh, college,'' Mishella finished. ''He lives nearby and thought he'd stop in and say hello.''

"He sounds real nice," Stacey whispered, her lips curving into a smile. "He smells good, too."

"I'll tell him you said so. Now, enough talk," she said, patting the girl's arm. "We don't want his ears burning. You try to get some rest. Don't think about anything or anyone. Just rest."

"I'm not scared anymore," Stacey whispered, her eyes closing. The worried frown that almost always creased her brow had disappeared.

The statement took Mishella by surprise. Tears spilled from her eyes and she quickly wiped them away. "Me, either," she replied. "Me, either, baby." And she wasn't. At that moment, with Raphael so near and Stacey smiling, she wasn't scared anymore, only bone-tired.

Mishella leaned her head against the blankets and closed her eyes. She should have wondered why the vision of the burned man—the demon—didn't come this time. Instead, she relished the temporary refuge she'd found from the haunting nightmares.

"Sleep," she heard Raphael's deep, hypnotic voice, clear, distinct, as if he murmured directly in her ear. "No more fear," his voice promised. "No more waiting. Sleep, *querida*." And she did.

Hours later, Mishella stared out the kitchen window at the first signs of dawn. Faint smudges of orange streaked the otherwise gray horizon. She watched as a black sports car maneuvered onto the main road, leaving a trail of dust in its wake. She glanced at the piece of notebook paper in her hands.

"I'm staying in town if you need me," it read. "I'll look in on you later." Below his name Raphael had scribbled a phone number.

A fat lot of good a phone number would do her. She hadn't had time to have the phone hooked up. But then, he had no way of knowing that.

She crumpled the piece of paper as she watched the billows of dust settle. If only she'd heard the front door a moment sooner. *Why? So you could have begged him to stay?* She dismissed the disquieting questions. She couldn't expect him to baby-sit her. He had a life somewhere, responsibilities to take care of. She couldn't expect a virtual stranger to give up everything, even temporarily, to stay by her side for the next month. Like Raphael had said, most people wouldn't inconvenience themselves to help someone else. Then again, though Mishella knew very little about him, she would wager he wasn't like most people. Not by a long shot.

She swallowed the last of her orange juice and tossed the paper at an open trash can. When it missed, she rushed over, snatched it up and went to drop it into the trash. But her fingers didn't want to uncurl. She stared at the crumpled paper for several more seconds, then she smoothed out the edges, folded it and stuffed it into her purse. Why, she had no idea. Maybe because the paper was a link to him.

If only she didn't feel so god-awful alone knowing he'd left. Not that she'd seen much of him since his arrival. Last night, after he'd patched the window, he'd disappeared. Still, he hadn't gone far. She'd felt him nearby, every nerve in her body screaming with awareness.

Yes, he'd been close by. The blanket she'd found tucked around her had proved as much. He'd picked her up from Stacey's bedside and settled her in an overstuffed chair from the living room.

Guardian. The concept was almost too much to grasp, too good to hold any truth. But Raphael was real. Or was he?

She shook away the disquieting notion. Of course he was real. She'd seen him, touched him, smelled the real and very masculine scent of him.

Mishella forced a deep breath and tried to calm the sudden quickening of her pulse. She shouldn't feel so attached to him, but she couldn't help herself. The past few hours had been the most peaceful she'd spent in a long time. That was why she hadn't heard the door. Not even the blue-eyed woman had come to her while she'd slept.

And the burned man...the demon, as Raphael had called him. Most of all, she'd been free of the hideous burned man, his eyes as brilliant as the orange glow on the horizon.

She crossed the tiled floor. She had to give Stacey her medicine.

Opening the cabinet, Mishella stared at the numerous prescription vials—an array of medicines purported to lessen Stacey's pain and ward off infection. The medicine would help her, albeit temporarily. Then the third touch would approach and she would deteriorate again. Such was the cycle, the struggle between sickness and health, life and death, light and dark, good and evil.

Taking a deep, determined breath, Mishella grabbed two bottles and popped them open. Two blue ones and one red. She stared into the empty vial. Closing her eyes, she chided herself for being so careless. She should have had everything refilled before leaving New York. If only she hadn't been in such a blasted hurry.

With the two blue ones in her palm, she grabbed a glass of juice and headed down the hall. She would have to drive into town and get the other refilled. Soon. The red ones helped the fever.

"Stacey, honey, here," she whispered, trailing her fingers across her stepsister's forehead. The girl stirred, her eyes drifting open.

"Shelly?" came Stacey's groggy voice.

"Yes, baby. Medicine time." Mishella eased one hand behind Stacey's head and helped her sit up. Placing the pills on the girl's tongue, she tilted the glass to her lips. The fever had returned in full force, giving Stacey an unnerving, glassy-eyed look. Yes, she would have to get the prescription for the red ones refilled *very* soon.

A thin trickle of juice wound its way from the corner of Stacey's mouth as Mishella eased her head back to the pillow. With the gentlest touch, she wiped the moisture away.

"Go back to sleep, honey. Morning will come soon."

"I'm cold, Shelly."

"It's the fever, baby. Just close your eyes. The weatherman promised sunshine today."

"Good." Stacey smiled and closed her eyes without further encouragement. "Draw me a picture, Shelly," she whispered. "Draw the sunshine, the flowers..."

"I'll draw you the best picture ever," Mishella assured her. "Just go back to sleep, sweetie."

Mishella hurried to the bathroom and shoved a cloth into the sink. Ice-cold water poured from the tap. She twisted the hot water knob, but the water seemed to flow even icier.

"Does anything here work?" she murmured. No lights, no phone, a broken washing machine and, it seemed, no hot water. Funny, how barely a year could see the place deteriorate so much.

She warmed the cloth a little between her palms before hurrying back to the bed and placing the folded compress on her stepsister's forehead.

Saying a quick prayer, Mishella sank into the chair beside the bed and settled in to wait for full daylight.

Grabbing her sketch pad from the nightstand, she stared out the window for a full moment. She should draw sunshine, flowers, all the things Stacey wanted. Only she couldn't. Compelled, Mishella put another vision of the burned man to paper. She had a whole notebook full of his image, and the blue-eyed woman's, too. In some vain hope, she'd thought that by capturing the images on paper, she could free herself of them. But nothing seemed able to do that.

Mishella busied herself until his likeness covered the paper in front of her and she felt purged enough to lay her charcoal aside and close her eyes.

"He is near, Mishella," the blue-eyed woman whispered. The flames lit the blackness of Mishella's mind, hiding the woman's face but not stifling her voice. "He fears you, be certain about that. He fears you because of your light. In giving your sister life, you sacrifice your own. Such is the ultimate love, such is the light. He cannot surpass your power. He will lose against you, and he knows it."

"Why doesn't he leave me alone, then?" Mishella heard her own voice. She'd thought herself asleep until that moment when she realized she stood on the edge of the darkness, watching and waiting for the woman to guide her.

Slowly the flames died down until Mishella saw the flawless ivory skin of the woman's face—familiar and hopeful. Her blue eyes were alight with strength.

"See, Mishella? We are getting stronger, you and I." This was the first time Mishella had seen the woman clearly. Always before the fire had distorted her features. But now Mishella saw her—beautiful, unnervingly familiar and not nearly so frightening.

"Why doesn't he leave me alone?" Mishella asked again.

"He cannot. He is drawn to you, but make no mistake. History will repeat itself. He will fail, like before. As long as you believe. *Three,* Mishella. Three touches to neutralize his three touches and free us both.''

''Free us from what?''

''From him. He is the master of darkness, a man filled with the very power of one of Satan's own.''

''The demon,'' Mishella whispered.

''*Sí,* the demon. And because of me you must face him. For that I am sorry. Sorry that I could not redeem him as I redeemed myself, sorry that you must face him now. No matter how powerful he appears, remember that he is weak, as well, as long as you stay focused. Think of the girl. Only the girl. She will keep you strong.'' Without warning, the woman's face faded into utter blackness.

''Stop!'' But the vision vanished and Mishella waited, dread filling her, for *he* always followed the woman.

''*Mija.*'' Mishella heard the voice a second before she felt a pudgy finger poke her shoulder.

Her eyes snapped open and she found herself staring into the concerned face of Inez Santibanez.

''Are you all right? I heard you whispering and—''

''Uh, yes,'' Mishella whispered. ''I must have dozed off.'' She blinked and stared blankly at her surroundings—the antique mahogany armoire in one corner, the matching four-poster where her sister lay. Gathering her wits, she clutched the sketch pad to her, unwilling to let Inez glimpse the drawings of the visions that haunted her. She took a calming breath and asked, ''Did I leave the door unlocked?''

''No. It was locked up real tight. I still have my old key.'' Inez waved a dull piece of metal. ''Your mama gave it to me so I wouldn't wake her and your papa when I used to come on Saturday mornings. That man sure liked his sleep. Speaking of which, I hope you had more sense than to sleep on that lumpy old chair all night.'' Her face puckered in a frown. "I know the little one is sick, but you have to keep up your own strength. Sleeping in an old chair will not help either of you."

Guiltily, Mishella scrambled to her feet. "No, I slept in the other room. I gave Stacey her medicine a few hours ago and sat here to watch the sun rise." She glanced at the window. Sunlight streamed through, brightening the otherwise gloomy bedroom. Several rays fell across Stacey's pale face, and Mishella blinked back a sudden swell of tears.

"The little one, she is better?" Inez asked, her voice hopeful as she followed Mishella's gaze.

Mishella nodded. "She will be. She's still weak, but she'll be all right."

"Good," Inez replied, her plump hand patting Mishella's arm. She waddled over to the bed, her hips swaying beneath a bold flower-print dress similar to the one she'd worn the night before. She frowned again. "It looks like the fever is back."

"Yes, I noticed this mor..." Mishella's words trailed off as she watched Inez, seemingly oblivious to her presence, lean over Stacey and place her hand on the girl's cheek. Mishella searched her brain, trying to remember if she'd mentioned Stacey's fever the night before, but the woman's voice disrupted her thoughts.

"Poor *niña*. This awful fever will break soon," Inez said, her gaze sweeping over Stacey's blanket-wrapped form, from the tips of her toes hidden beneath the blanket to her limp blond hair tangled across the daisy-print pillowcase. "*Sí*, it will break soon."

A sudden chill raced up Mishella's spine and she trembled.

"Cold?" Inez turned, her eyes watchful. Too watchful, it seemed.

"A little."

"The weather will change. My bones have been aching something terrible, and that always means the warm weather is coming. That's what I tell my boy, Thomas. He's always nagging me about being so superstitious, but my bones are always right."

"I hope so." Mishella attempted a smile.

"The warm weather will do this little one a world of good, I think." Inez sighed. "But now time for work. I think I'll start in the living room. The dust is so thick I felt it in my throat when I came in." She moved to the door.

"Inez, I need to go into town for a little while. Could you keep an eye on Stacey? I'm sure she'll sleep the whole time, but if she wakes up—"

"Go," Inez said, pausing to wave a hand at her. "The little one will be fine. You take care of your errands. I've got a whole day's worth of work here and then some. I'll look out for her."

And somehow Mishella knew that Inez would. The unease she'd felt dissipated as she held the Mexican woman's soft brown gaze. Strength, courage, concern—all glistened in the woman's eyes. "Thank you, Inez. I promise not to be gone long."

"Take your time. I have all day. Domingo will not come for me until suppertime."

The mention of the man's name struck a chord of trepidation in Mishella. She made a mental promise to be back long before suppertime.

Mishella watched as Inez disappeared down the hall. Minutes later, she heard the sound of rustling sheets as Inez uncovered the living room furniture and started to bring the old farmhouse back to life.

"I'll be back, Stacey." But the girl didn't hear. She was lost in a world of fever.

A good half hour later, Mishella steered her Mazda down the gravel road leading to town. The morning sunlight blinded her and she flipped the visor down. Maybe the warmth was returning. Somehow she felt more hopeful that all would be right again. The blue-eyed woman had said they were getting stronger. Mishella certainly felt it. She might actually make it through this entire ordeal.

Correction—she *would* make it through. She had Raphael now. Together they could keep the evil away and stay strong long enough to see the third touch. Then all would be right again.

A life for a life.

Mishella dismissed the thought and wiped away the tears that glided down her cheeks. "You won't win," she whispered a second before the road blurred and a dust devil appeared out of nowhere, engulfing the car.

"I will win."

She heard his guttural voice. The car trembled from the ferocious wind, rocking back and forth.

"*You* will not win against me," he assured her. "Never."

"Please stop!" she cried, but the car rocked all the more violently. The leather-wrapped steering wheel heated, scorched her fingers and forced her to let go.

The car lurched as she slammed on the brakes. As quickly as it had appeared, the dust cloud dissolved. She fought for control, the brakes screeching, the tires spinning. The car swiveled and came to a bone-jarring stop nose-first in the ditch bordering the road.

Heart pounding, Mishella leaned her forehead on the now cool steering wheel and marveled that she was still alive. She felt the blood race through her veins, heard the consistent echo of her own breathing and said a silent thank-you to whatever being she owed her good fortune.

"No, *you* won't win," she said more for her own reassurance than some belief that the burned man still listened. She took a deep breath and glanced up into a cluster of drooping cattails.

She knew her next effort would be wasted, but she turned the key, anyway. The engine ground but didn't catch. "Idiot," she chided herself. "Mishella Kirkland, you are a careless idiot." She could have died in a mangled heap of red metal, and then what would happen to Stacey?

"I don't know about idiot, but careless seems a fitting description. Do you always drive so recklessly?"

She jerked around and found herself staring through the half-open window into the familiar eyes of none other than her guardian.

"I—I lost control," she said, but her reply was wasted. He scowled, surveying the car with a cold thoroughness that roused her temper.

"Obviously," he muttered, wrenching open the door. "Are you all right?" Without waiting for a reply, he grasped her by the wrist and pulled her from the seat, intent on seeing for himself.

"Fine," Mishella said, her tone cool and clipped as she plucked her hand from his. She couldn't help but feel a little resentful that he showed up after her mishap rather than in time to prevent it.

"You're lucky you didn't flip this little car. Weren't you watching the road?" He pierced her with his gaze, his eyes dark, unreadable. He sounded worried, yet she sensed an aloofness, as if her answer didn't really matter, so she opted not to give him one.

"Thanks very much for your assessment, but I don't need a lecture. I'm perfectly aware of what could have happened." Her heart still pumped furiously. But Mishella found herself wondering whether it was from his nearness or what had almost happened. "Some guardian you are," she added.

"Had I known you needed to go to town, I would have offered to take you." His voice was soft, deep, rumbling in her ear and soothing her anger. She saw concern flicker in the dark depths of his eyes.

"Thanks, but I didn't know myself until this morning. One of Stacey's prescriptions is out, the refrigerator is nearly empty, and I need light bulbs."

"The food I anticipated," he said, motioning to the sack of groceries just visible through the tinted back window of his car. "But the light bulbs..." His words trailed off and she read the wicked gleam that lit his eyes. "I rather enjoyed our little encounter in the hallway. Light bulbs would have spoiled the effect."

"You sound as if you speak from experience," she countered, her lips curving in a half smile at his attempt to lighten the mood. "Do you make it a habit of creeping into people's houses and cornering them in dark hallways?" She said the words jokingly, yet an underlying seriousness laced her tone.

"Only you, *querida*. Only you." He smiled, yet the softness didn't quite reach his eyes. "But I don't think your car is in any condition to make the rest of the trip. If you're determined to light up the house, then you'll have to come with me. When we get into town, I'll find a towing service for the car." He gripped her elbow and ushered her to the passenger side of his sleek black Jaguar.

"Beautiful car," she commented as he threw open the door. Climbing into the cushioned interior, she inhaled the scent of rich leather and unmistakable maleness. As she sank back against the seat, her senses were overwhelmed.

Seconds later, Raphael climbed in beside her and then they were speeding off down the road, the engine purring softly, mingling with the steady thud of her heart.

"What about the groceries?" she asked, casting a sideways glance at him.

"Nothing that'll spoil. It's mostly preserved stuff. If you want, we can pick up a few more things."

"Stacey's not eating much lately," she heard herself say. Not that he didn't already know. He seemed to know an unsettling amount about her and her stepsister.

A guardian. That had to account for his extra sense when it came to reading her mind. What had he told her last night? That their power bonded them? Maybe that was what made him so attuned to her every thought. If they were the only two people with such a power, then they had a common link.

If...

How could Raphael be so sure they were the only ones with the touch? Did his dreams tell him that?

Maybe. Her own visions revealed a great deal, but not enough. Not nearly enough. She wanted, no, needed to know everything. Was the touch truly an accident of fate, or something else? And Raphael? Surely the same accident of fate couldn't occur to two complete strangers. Or could it?

And he was a stranger, logic reminded her. A stranger she should be wary of until she better understood everything. A stranger who claimed to be her guardian—someone like her, with the same powers. Someone to help her, to save her. Or curse her?

Mishella pushed the troubling thoughts from her mind. She would die without him, and maybe with him. Either way, she faced the same risk, but believing in Raphael gave her a small sliver of hope. Hope she desperately needed.

Raphael promised life, and she couldn't ignore or dismiss such a promise. Any more than she could the fact that he seemed so attuned to her every thought, as if the power they shared really did bond them.

"You need to eat, Mishella," he said, his deep voice breaking into her reverie. "To keep up your strength. Stacey is draining you."

"You're the second person who's told me that today."

"And who was the first?" His gaze pinned her to the seat. For the first time, she felt the faint stirring of fear deep inside her. Then his hand closed over hers, his long fingers cool, comforting and strangely familiar as they laced through hers. The fear and wariness disappeared as quickly as it had come.

"Inez. She said the same thing to me this morning."

"She's at the house?" He looked none too pleased.

"I left her to look after Stacey." He tightened his hand around hers for a brief, almost painful second. Then he relaxed, and Mishella was left to wonder if she'd only imagined his strange reaction.

"We're here," Raphael announced. Turning off the gravel road, he steered the car down the main street of Three Rivers.

The town had changed little since she'd visited her parents more than a year ago. She'd spent only three precious days with them because she'd been right in the middle of finishing portraits of a Texas senator and his wife. That left little time for her to see the town. She and her mother had traveled the dirt road to Three Rivers only once, but the town had left an imprint on her memory. It was a place where time seemed to stand still.

Mishella stared out the window as they passed a few small stores and a couple of gas stations, all rusting dinosaurs compared to the modern offerings of the large cities. The whole place stood untouched by the hands of progress, at least until they turned a corner. Then Mishella saw the one clue that proved they hadn't reached the far edge of the earth.

A familiar grocery store stood out like a beacon, surrounded by a concrete parking lot that contrasted with the shell drives that served most of the other businesses. Raphael drove a block past, then pulled up in front of the town pharmacy.

"I doubt they'll have a computer link here. I hope you have the prescription with you," he said, drawing her attention.

"Yes," she said, fishing in the side pocket of her purse, more than a little conscious of his scrutiny.

"Do you want me to pick up some extra groceries while you're inside?"

"It looks like you bought plenty. I'll just get the medicine and we can head back. I don't want to be gone too long." She had until supper, but she declined to mention that to Raphael. He probably wouldn't understand her doubts where Domingo was concerned. The old man had really done nothing to rouse her suspicion. Still, she couldn't help the unease she felt around him. *He could be the demon,* a voice whispered. Mishella dismissed the thought. If he was, she would know.

Would she? the voice asked. Of course she would. As strong as the demon was, she would know when she came face-to-face with him.

"I'll be back in a minute," she said as Raphael opened the door for her and she climbed out. She tilted back her head and looked up into his eyes, which glittered like dark mysterious pools in the sunlight.

"I'll drive to one of those gas stations we passed," Raphael said. "One of them may have a tow truck. I'll pick you up when I'm done. And I'll get you some light bulbs.'' The wicked light returned to his eyes.

''Thanks,'' she said, feeling her face heat. He held her gaze and Mishella seemed to stop breathing altogether.

Think only of the girl. Mishella remembered the blue-eyed woman's words. She had to get back to Stacey. That thought gave her enough strength to break the trance he held her in, to turn and hurry inside the store without glancing back. She couldn't let the strange pull she felt for Raphael distract her from her mission. She could use his strength, his power, but she couldn't let herself fall victim to anything else. She couldn't be attracted to him. She *wouldn't* be, she vowed.

CHAPTER FOUR

Mishella tried to keep her vow in mind more than an hour later as she sat next to Raphael again. Silence surrounded them as they drove down the road toward the farmhouse. The engine hummed, disrupted only by the faint sound of gravel pounding the underside of the car. Mishella clutched the prescription in her hand and stared out at the passing fields.

"Remind you of home?" His voice cut the silence.

"I—I'm sorry. I didn't hear what you said," she murmured, glancing at him. She allowed herself a few moments to study his profile—high cheekbones, angular jaw covered with dark stubble, a firm and sensuous mouth, a strong chin. She'd never seen another man with such classic features. And the eyes that he turned on her were no exception. Nearly midnight black, they seemed to see straight through her, prompting her to talk yet rendering her speechless at the same time.

"I asked if these fields remind you of home." Thankfully, he turned his attention back to the road and Mishella was able to find her voice.

"Not hardly. Concrete parking lots and freeways loaded with rush-hour traffic remind me of home. This is a far cry."

"And home is?"

"Dallas."

"So you're a native Texan."

"As far as I can remember." Actually she was having a tough time recalling the details of her life before the doctor's diagnosis. Her existence since had become a monotonous ritual of prayer and waiting. Her home the stark white walls of a sterile hospital room.

"I should have known by your drawl."

"I don't drawl," Mishella insisted, rising to the challenging grin he flashed her. "I left my drawl back in my first speech class in college. I can still hear my instructor—'Ms. Kirkland, if you wish to study and use the language to your advantage, you must learn to speak it correctly. That excludes butchering the melodic flow with your detestable Southern twang.'" Mishella enunciated each word, which drew a smile from Raphael—an arresting smile that made her regret her small attempt at humor.

He laughed, the sound rumbling from deep in his throat, warming her ears. "Your instructor would be disappointed to hear you now."

"At least I spared her further misery by switching my major from speech and drama to art."

"An artist," he said. "What kind of art?"

"I do portraits, landscapes, the standard bowl of fruit— whatever I'm commissioned to do. But I love drawing people most of all."

"Are you good?"

"Yes," she replied without hesitation. Too good sometimes, she thought, remembering the drawings of the burned man. She had an uncanny eye for detail and a photographic memory, both of which made for very vivid creation. Her pictures of the burned man were grotesquely accurate and very, very frightening.

"You've still got a bit of twang left." His smile broadened and it was all Mishella could do to keep her gaze focused on the road in front of them.

Unwillingly she became conscious of his jean-clad thigh so near her own. Thank God for the cellular phone mounted on the console between them. Otherwise he would be touching her. Her gaze went to his arm atop the armrest barely a fraction of an inch away. He could still touch her if he wanted to....

She cleared her throat. The car suddenly seemed much smaller.

"Speech wasn't my first love fortunately, and no one in Texas notices my twang."

"Which makes you wonder where I'm from that I did?"

"A mind reader," she said, her attention drawn to the large hand that held the steering wheel. A silver ring set with a sapphire stone adorned one of his lean fingers. Mesmerized, she watched as the blue jewel caught the light through the windshield and glittered with the brilliance of an open flame.

"Among other things." His deep voice broke her temporary fascination.

She cut a sideways glance at him, only to have her unease subside when he flashed her a wicked grin.

"So?" she prompted.

"I'm from New York."

"That makes sense."

"Did my accent give me away?"

"No, you don't have much of an accent. You said you felt me when I made the first touch. I was in New York...close by. That's probably why."

"I would have felt you had you been on another continent, Mishella," he said, turning into her drive and braking to a stop in front of the farmhouse.

"But I still don't understand how you knew my name."

I've always known you, a voice whispered in her ear. His voice, yet she hadn't seen his lips move.

He turned, his gaze locking with hers. "The hospital gave me your name," he stated matter-of-factly, "but even if they hadn't, I still would have known who you were. I feel you, Mishella. The power doesn't know distance. I would have found you no matter how far or how close. No matter if I knew your name or not."

When he touched her cheek, she wanted to pull away, yet she couldn't. His eyes entranced her with their intensity and she found herself absorbed in the dark depths, in the strength that drew her like a bee to a flower's sweet nectar.

He trailed his fingertips down the curve of her face to the smooth column of her neck. She closed her eyes to avoid his encompassing stare. That didn't lessen the sensation that spiraled in the pit of her stomach, shooting red-hot flame through her veins.

Stacey... Stacey... Stacey, her subconscious chanted.

Mishella forced her eyes open to find Raphael watching her, his face inches from hers. She'd have sworn he could see deep inside her, knew her most secret thoughts. Quickly she pulled away.

Sensing her unease, he dropped his hand to the seat and leaned back, allowing them both some much needed space.

"I'll be back later," he finally said, reaching over to open her door. One muscled arm brushed her thigh and she flinched as if he'd burned her. Yet his touch felt unnervingly cool, testament to the crazy weather and her even crazier feelings.

"Where are you going?"

"Back to meet the tow truck. The man at the garage said he'd send someone out right away. I'll go and see that they get your car towed and repaired."

"And then?"

"Then I've got some business to take care of. I'm staying in town if you need me, and you have my car-phone number. I'll stop by this evening. Nights can be the worst," he said, leveling a knowing look at her.

She nodded and climbed out of the car. Nights *were* the worst. The visions were more frequent, the fear more consuming. But with his reassurance and a smile that made her melt, she felt as if she could face the darkness.

"Don't forget these," he said, reaching behind her seat for the grocery sack and the largest box of light bulbs she'd ever seen. "I don't intend to go creeping around tonight."

She took the sack and the box and smiled. "With this many bulbs, I don't think I'll have any night creepers for a while."

She pushed the door closed and watched as he backed out of the driveway. Plopping the light bulbs into the grocery sack, she crossed the yard. The car angled from the driveway and disappeared down the road.

Mishella took a deep breath, feeling calmer and more in control than she had in a long time. Her sister would be all right. *She* would be all right, and somehow everything would work out.

Raphael stood, arms folded, as a huge man named Buddy, who wore grease-stained overalls and an even dirtier baseball cap, hooked the last chain to the rear bumper of Mishella's Mazda. He stepped back and the mechanic stomped past, climbed into the tow truck and gunned the engine.

As the car was dragged from the ditch, Raphael turned away. The car's twisted front end stirred his guilt. Guilt he shouldn't feel in the first place. He had no room for guilt. No room for any of the damnable emotions he'd begun to feel lately.

Satisfaction. That should be the only thing he felt. With her car wrecked, she couldn't run again. He'd almost caught up to her in New York, but she'd gotten away. He couldn't let her get away now that they were finally together. He had to be her only support, her only strength. She had to see that the future rested in his hands. Then he would have the control he needed—and she would remember.

Satisfaction and anticipation.

He touched the sapphire stone of his ring and closed his eyes for a moment. Soon, Mishella would be his, as she was always meant to be....

Esteban Malvado touched the flickering candle flame to each taper in the candelabra. A faint glow illuminated the room—the only light in the dark sanctuary beneath the castle.

The walls glittered black onyx in the flamelight. He closed his eyes, feeling the presence surround him, fill him, as it always did here in this room.

Malvado. His name stood for the very evil he wielded. A curse of powers passed down from his grandfather to his father, then to him. The damned power of Belial himself, Satan's most evil and deceptive henchman. The next angel created after Lucifer before the fall from heaven. An all-powerful demon who personified evil, and lived and breathed within Esteban.

Footsteps sounded in the stairwell, followed by the creak of the door. Esteban opened his eyes to the vision in the doorway. As if from a dream she appeared, dressed in rich gold brocade, piles of ebony curls swept high to reveal ivory shoulders and a dangerous display of skin that caused a painful tightening in his groin.

He stared into her eyes, alight with fear, worry and ultimately, though she would be aghast to admit it, intrigue.

"You wish to call upon my powers, Señora de Ruiz. Here—" he motioned around him "—you may call. For here I will listen to your demands, and possibly meet them, if you in turn meet mine.''

"Please. You must!" Her urgent words echoed through the room and Esteban smiled.

"Come to the light." He fixed the intensity of his stare on her, his gaze beckoning, entrancing until she stepped down from the last step and walked across the stone floor toward him.

She stopped just within his reach, her head bowed as if studying the faint discoloration of the ancient rocks that supported them.

"Such innocence," he murmured, lifting her chin and forcing her to meet his gaze.

"I am no innocent, señor," she whispered. "Do you forget I am a married woman?"

"In *my* way you are innocent, Maricela. An untainted woman who comes willingly to me. For that is my price," he said. "Your emotions...your body..." He let his fingers drift down her neck to rest near her collarbone. Her pulse beat an insistent rhythm that matched his own. "Your soul," he added, circling her neck to wind his fingers in the silky black curls at her nape. With a small tug, he pulled the lustrous strands free from their confining combs.

When he moved to touch the swell of her breasts, she placed her hand atop his and halted his movements. Their eyes met.

"You will save my husband?" she entreated, as if to reassure herself the sacrifice she was about to make was worthy.

"Not I, but you, *querida*," he replied, resuming his exploration of her soft skin, her hand still resting on his. "With my power, *you* will heal him. Then you will return to me."

"How can I do such a thing? I know nothing of the darkness. I—"

"You know nothing now, but you will. You will see with my eyes, have my blood pound through your veins, feel my power—all very soon. And soon you will give me what I want most. What I must have."

"Which is?"

"In time," he said, dismissing her question. "Now you must kneel."

In the circle inscribed on the stone floor, she knelt before him. The three flames flickered, glinting off the large dagger Esteban pulled from the crimson velvet wrapping.

He held the blade, his eyes closed, his spirit gaining strength. With a vicious tug, he ripped the white tunic he wore from neck to waist.

Opening his eyes, he trailed the tip of the blade across his muscled shoulder three times, watching as three red lines appeared and his lifeblood traced a path down his chest.

"Look at me, Maricela. Look into my eyes. See my strength."

She glanced up. The moment she caught sight of the dagger, fear etched her flawless face. Esteban captured her gaze with his and willed the emotion away, until he held only her fascination.

With a sweep of his hand, he lifted her dark curls and touched the blade to her exposed shoulder three times. Three times to match his own, three times to transfer the power. Once to link them emotionally, twice to bond them physically, and thrice to unite their souls.

"Now you are mine, Maricela." He caught several crimson drops that trickled down the slope of her breast and touched the blood to his lips. He tasted her essence—warm and bittersweet, lingering on his tongue like the taste of wild, ripe berries freshly plucked and savored.

Sliding his fingers across his own chest, he gathered the tiny rivulets trailing down his skin. "Taste of me, Maricela," he commanded, holding his hand out to her.

She hesitated, her lips parted, her eyes brilliant blue jewels in the candlelight. A moment crept by before she pushed aside her hesitation and reached up to take his hand between her trembling ones. Closing her eyes, she slipped first one of his fingers, then another into the warm velvet of her mouth, suckling and sampling. Only when she had laved every drop from him, did she release his hand.

"We will be one, Maricela, you and I," he said, his voice raspy, his fingers glistening from the moistness of her mouth—a mouth he longed to kiss, to devour....

Esteban felt the blackness threaten him as always when the evil within him was roused. Belial was hungry. So very, very hungry.

Control, he told himself, his fingers still tingling from the satin feel of her tongue.

Her chest rose and fell with each erratic breath. Trickles of red marred her pale skin to disappear into the low neckline of her dress. Esteban felt the clenching in his stomach, his craving for her nearly overwhelming.

Slamming the dagger back down on the table, he forced himself to turn away. *Not yet.*

"Go," he growled. "Deliver the three touches to Miguel. When he lives again, you must return to me. The power is not yours to keep. It is mine, just as you are mine now. Go," he repeated. "I will be waiting, Maricela. I will be waiting."

Slow, agonizing seconds passed, and Esteban resisted the urge to turn and pull her into his embrace. Every nerve in his body screamed with wanting, but he couldn't disrupt the way of things. He would possess her only when the time arrived. First she had to use the power. Then she would truly belong to him.

The first time would join them emotionally.

The second physically.

The third spiritually.

Then they would be one.

He listened to the rustle of fabric as she got to her feet. Her soft footsteps beat a frantic path across the stone floor to the door. A slow, nerve-wrenching creak signaled her final departure, and he turned, staring at the empty room. Now, he would wait. The time would come soon. Very soon....

"You gonna be paying cash?"

The mechanic's voice pulled Raphael from his thoughts. "What?" He unclenched his fist and concentrated on the man in front of him.

"I asked how you plan on paying today, mister. Cash? I got me one of them credit-card machines if you wanna use plastic. You look like one of them credit-card fellas that moseys through here every now and again on his way to someplace else."

"Cash," Raphael grumbled. He retrieved his wallet and counted out several twenty-dollar bills. "Will that cover it?"

"Depends on how fast you want me to get her up and running."

"I'm in no hurry."

"Then that oughtta do it." Buddy licked his thumb and began fingering the bills. "This ain't much of a tourist area. What brings you to these parts?"

"Friends. Speaking of which, I'm looking for an old friend by the name of Domingo Santibanez. Do you know where I can find him?"

"Old Mexican fella? White hair, real dark skin?"

"That's him."

"He works a coupla blocks over. Got a boy about the same age as mine. Ain't never seen a Mexican couple with a white boy, but he's as light as my oldest. My boy tells me Thomas ain't really theirs, though. He's adopted. He'd have to be with all that light-colored—"

"Do you have an address for the old man?" Raphael interrupted, his tone impatient.

"I s'pose." With oil-caked fingers, Buddy shoved the money into his pocket and retrieved a pen. "Here," he said, handing Raphael the torn edge of a receipt with an address scribbled across it. "You oughtta find him there. Your car," he said, motioning behind him, "oughtta be ready in a coupla days or so."

"Like I said, I'm in no hurry. Take your time. I'll check back with you later." And with that, Raphael clutched the paper, turned and walked out into the sunlight.

He wasn't as concerned about the old woman as he was about the man. He could sense the man's power, not as strong as his own, but strong nonetheless. Strong and caring and protective. He would have to keep the old man away from Mishella.

Mishella. Her name was a whisper in his head, her image appearing before him in a vivid blend of ebony hair, ivory skin and deep blue eyes. She was even more beautiful than he remembered. Her skin softer somehow, her eyes brighter.

A few weeks should give him enough time. Mishella would come to him of her own free will. Then the bargain would be complete. They would be together—their minds, their bodies, their souls. She wouldn't escape him this time.

"Inez, I can't believe this is the same room." Mishella glanced around the living room, from the gleaming mahogany bookshelf that spanned the length of one wall, the polished coffee and end tables, the flawless black leather sofa, to the fluffy rug beneath her feet. "You really outdid yourself. It even smells good in here." Mishella inhaled the fragrance, unfamiliar but tantalizingly sweet.

"Herbs," Inez explained. "From my very own garden. Do you like them?"

"Oh, yes. They smell wonderful. Much better than that old musky stench."

"I know. My herbs are good for everything. Whatever ails you, including stubborn smells." Inez wrinkled her nose. "The whole house stank after an entire summer with no fresh air, clear down through the furniture cushions." She untied the apron at her waist. "This whole place was in worse shape than I thought. I still didn't get to those last two bedrooms." With the corner of the apron, she dabbed at the sweat that beaded her forehead.

"That's all right. You did the main rooms," Mishella said, a delighted smile lifting the corners of her mouth. "You have no idea how much I'm going to enjoy walking in here and seeing real furniture, instead of dusty sheets. And I can't thank you enough for getting rid of those horrible cobwebs." Her smile disappeared as she eyed one corner of the room and gave a slight shudder.

Inez grinned. "Them spiders are nasty little critters. When I have Domingo out here tomorrow to look at the washing machine, I'll have him go over the rooms with some spray. That ought to keep the little buggers from coming back."

"That idea is tempting, but you've done so much already, Inez. Take tomorrow off and rest. There's no need for you and Domingo to be out here on a Saturday."

"Saturday's just like any other day when there's work to be done. I still need to get those kitchen curtains washed. Then there's the back bedrooms..."

"I can do a little housework myself." It'll keep my mind off things, Mishella added silently. She welcomed any distraction that would help the days pass faster.

"Put that notion right out of your head, *mija*. That attorney of yours is paying me good money to get this place into shape. I'll not accept pay for work that you did."

"If I know Mr. Morris," Mishella said, "what he's paying you can't be much. He's forever trying to save a dollar. Besides, I'd also be willing to bet he has no idea how rundown things have gotten. I'll see that he gives you extra for all the trouble you've gone to, Inez."

"*Gracias,* but I'm just doing my job, and I'm not finished yet."

"Still," Mishella argued, "I can't let you drag your husband all the way out here on a Saturday. That doesn't seem fair."

"Your mama was my friend. Domingo will be glad to come out here and help me."

"But I can do a little cleaning myself and call a repairman for the wash—"

"Nonsense, *mija.*" Inez dismissed Mishella's objection with a wave of her hand. "I'll do the cleaning, and there's no need to call somebody when my Domingo is more than able to fix that machine. The hot water heater, too. He's real good with his tools. Him and my boy, Thomas, do a lot of repair work for folks in town."

"You're sure?" Mishella asked, all the while wishing she could refuse the Mexican woman's offer, at least the part about Domingo. She couldn't forget him—his features frightening with their severity. Most of all, she couldn't forget the chill she'd felt in his presence.

Stop being foolish. It was dark and cold last night. Who wouldn't seem frightening under those conditions?

Maybe she had misjudged him. In the light of day, he might appear as ordinary as any other man. Her misgivings could be the result of her overactive imagination, or so she desperately hoped, because Inez didn't look as if she intended to leave Domingo home when she came back.

"I'm positive," Inez assured her.

Mishella watched Inez stuff her apron into her sacklike purse. She wondered if Inez would be hurt if she called a repairman, anyway. Then again, she didn't have a phone or a car. Unless she intended to walk to town, she'd have to settle for Domingo's help.

The honk of a horn jolted the silence.

"That must be my Mingo." Inez grabbed her coat from the hand-carved coat tree and opened the front door. "Why in the world he's out there sitting on the horn, instead of coming to the door, I don't know," she muttered, squinting out into the moonlit yard at the truck.

Mishella didn't miss the sudden frown that creased the woman's face.

"It's my boy, Thomas," Inez said, her tone almost disbelieving.

"Is everything all right, Inez?"

"Uh, fine, fine," she murmured after a few seconds. The smile she gave Mishella seemed forced. "I was just expecting Mingo to pick me up, that's all. He must be working late." Still, she didn't appear as at ease as she pretended. "I'll see you tomorrow, *mija*."

"Thanks, Inez. For everything."

"Glad to help. You get some rest."

Mishella nodded, then watched Inez hurry across the porch.

Closing the door, Mishella slid the bolt into place and moved to the window to push the curtains aside. She peered out at the battered pickup parked in the driveway, its engine idling.

The moment Inez pulled open the passenger-side door, the overhead light flicked on, bathing the interior in a yellowish glow.

The driver sat with both arms folded on top of the steering wheel, his long blond hair hanging well past his shoulders, a stark contrast to the black T-shirt he wore. The shirt proved an even greater contrast to his fair skin. He glanced at Inez as she climbed in beside him.

Blond hair? Fair skin? Mishella blinked, wondering if she was seeing things. She'd heard Inez as plain as day. "My boy, Thomas," she'd said.

He must be adopted, Mishella decided. That thought fed her already growing admiration for Inez. She could picture the woman taking in some poor homeless child, rearing him as her own.

When Thomas turned his head in Mishella's direction, she focused her attention on his eyes. He stared across the yard to the window where she watched.

Her gaze locked with his and she felt the rough brush of callused fingers on her face, her neck.

Impossible, her conscience reminded her. Still, she snatched her hand from the draperies, letting them swish back into place. She inched backward, pressing her palms to her cold cheeks, desperate to erase the unnerving sensations.

Even though she knew Thomas could no longer see her, she felt as if he pierced the heavy curtains with his unnatural stare to study her as she moved away from the window.

Now you are being silly.

Still, the feeling didn't subside until she heard the grumble of the pickup as it backed out of the driveway, then the crunch of gravel as Thomas and Inez headed down the road for town.

You're imagining things, Mishella. She had to be. That could be the only explanation. She crossed the living room and walked down the hall. The only plausible explanation.

After much coaxing, her heartbeat returned to normal. She eased open the bedroom door and peeked in on her sleeping stepsister.

"Stacey was right all those years," Mishella whispered to herself. "You are a big fraidy cat."

Fraidy cat. Stacey had nicknamed her that the summer before Mishella had gone away to college. A lover of horror films, Stacey had begged Mishella to rent every horror film the video store had on the shelf. Mishella had told her stepsister a solid no. Stacey had teased her mercilessly after that.

Mishella smiled. She'd gladly sit through every horror film ever made if it would see Stacey well again. She'd do anything to see that.

You're doing all you can, Mishella assured herself. Yet the waiting for the next touch played on her nerves. She wanted it all to be over. But she still needed time, time to gain her strength and build her courage for that last touch.

It'll come soon, and you'll be strong, she told herself, refusing to buckle under to her doubts. Still, the doubt was always there, and the fear.

I can save you, Mishella. And you can save me. Raphael's words replayed in her mind. *Together.* She had to believe him. She had nothing else in which to put her trust.

And if he was wrong? She'd been prepared from the start to make the ultimate sacrifice for Stacey. She still was.

Mishella forced the thoughts aside and went to the window to check the latch. Locked. Then, leaving the bedroom door ajar, she headed back down the hallway.

In the living room, Mishella grabbed her sketch pad and settled on the couch. She took Stacey's radio headphones from the coffee table, tuned in an FM station, adjusted the volume and hooked the headset over her ears.

Music. Now that was one thing Mishella had a fondness for. A surefire distraction, not to mention inspiration.

"It's Friday night and we're rolling right into a block-party weekend with a set of classic Beatle hits," the DJ's silky voice purred in her ears.

Mishella took a deep breath, willed herself to relax and reached for a package of colored pencils. She'd promised Stacey sunshine and flowers.

A good half hour later, she sat on the edge of the sofa, tears trickling down her cheeks as she studied the finished picture.

"It's very beautiful." The deep male voice barely penetrated the strum of an acoustic guitar. "A definite reflection of the artist."

Mishella twisted around, the sketch pad falling at her feet. The headset slipped past her ears. Her heart leapt to her throat.

Relief swept over her the moment she saw Raphael, dressed in faded jeans and a white button-down shirt, his hair pulled back in a ponytail, his arms folded across his chest. He looked so relaxed lounging against the sofa back, studying her with his midnight gaze. A slight smile lifted the corners of his mouth.

"You startled me," she said, touching a hand to her pounding heart.

"Sorry."

"I didn't hear you knock."

He raised one black brow. "And how could you have with those things pasted over your ears?" He eyed the headset hanging about her neck.

"Oh," she murmured, pulling the contraption off as a wave of heat rushed to her cheeks. "I guess I couldn't hear much of anything except the music. I hope you didn't knock for very long."

"Not too long. I went around back when I didn't get an answer. You really should lock the kitchen door."

Her cheeks burned even hotter. "I must've forgotten. I lived in an apartment in Dallas. No back door to worry about..." Her words faded. Why did he have to keep staring at her with those fathomless eyes?

"So tell me," he said, "is it the music or the drawing that made you cry?"

Suddenly self-conscious, Mishella wiped at the moisture on her cheeks. "I wasn't actually crying," she said. "I think I got some dust in my eyes." She gave him a suspicious look. "How long have you been standing there?"

"Long enough to know that you have a very beautiful voice and you like to sing old Beatle songs. But I don't think the lyrics are what brought the tears to your eyes."

He rounded the sofa, coming to stand in front of her. Clasping both her hands, he pulled her to her feet. She felt the chilliness of his grasp. Only the heated look he gave her belied his cool exterior and spoke of the fire smoldering just beneath the surface.

"Tell me what really made you cry." The rich timbre of his voice filled her ears, compelling her to talk to him.

"Not the Beatles," she admitted. "It was the picture. I always get a little misty when I draw something for someone close to me. I try to put everything I feel into my art." She paused. "That probably sounds a little silly."

"No," he said softly, a wealth of meaning in the one word. "Not silly at all. You're really good." He glanced down at the sketch pad. A colorful blend of yellows and oranges caressed a landscape of bright fuchsia flowers. "For your stepsister?"

"I promised her sunshine." Mishella felt the tears in her eyes again, but she blinked them back. She really was silly at times, especially to cry in front of a stranger.

Not a stranger, a voice whispered in her head.

"Do you always keep your promises, Mishella Kirkland?" he asked, his tone like velvet, yet there was an edge of steel to his words she found vaguely disconcerting.

"I try. Promises are made to be kept."

"That they are," he remarked, his grip on her hands increasing slightly.

She wanted to pull away, to tell him that he was hurting her, but she couldn't move. His stare rendered her motionless. Speechless. She felt the unusual tightening in her stomach as he pressed one of her palms to his lips.

Tiny shocks rushed the length of her arm, winding the coil in her stomach even tighter.

Mine, she heard his voice, but his lips never formed the word. *You are mine, Mishella.*

His gaze drew her deeper and the breath caught in her throat. His eyes were so familiar, so utterly disturbing.

Remember me, Mishella. Remember me! She heard the silent command, sensed his raw urgency, yet as much as she tried, she couldn't seem to conjure up any real memory. No recollection that would make sense out of the pull she felt toward him. Still, the connection between them was unmistakable, baffling and very real.

"You seem very familiar to me." Mishella saw something flicker in his eyes and she realized she'd spoken the words aloud. "I guess that probably sounds silly, too."

"Not at all."

"But I'm sure I would remember if we had met before. I'm sure."

His eyes grew darker, more unnerving, more demanding, as if his fate rested on her answer to his next question. "Are you, *querida?*"

CHAPTER FIVE

"I'm positive," Mishella replied without hesitation. She'd never been more certain of anything.

"I'm that memorable, am I?" He smiled, but no softness touched his eyes. "Maybe I remind you of someone," he said, an expectancy in his voice.

"Maybe."

At that moment, the clock struck the first of nine gongs, disrupting her search for some memory of him.

Raphael dropped her hands with a suddenness that startled her and left her oddly disappointed.

"I just stopped by to see if you were all right."

"I'm fine," she mumbled, clasping her hands in front of her. She tried to step away, to give herself a blessed inch of distance from him, but the edge of the sofa jabbed the backs of her legs. "Inez left over an hour ago," she continued, desperate for a distraction from his unnerving presence. "I didn't think you were coming."

"I told you I would. I keep my promises." He said the words as if insulted that she doubted him. Mishella's irritation rose.

"And I'm supposed to know that? You show up, then disappear, and I haven't the foggiest idea where you go. You've vanished three times in the past twenty-four hours. Where do you go, Raphael?" It seemed as if her breathing stopped in the next instant as she waited for his reply.

"Never far," came his evasive answer.

"And what does that mean?"

"It means I'm never far from you. I can feel you—all the time. No matter where I go. We're linked emotionally."

"That's not a straight answer. I want to know *where* you go. Do you have a house near here? Are you camping out? What?"

"I'm not the camping sort," he said, giving her a smile so seductive and disarming her heart slammed against her ribs. "I'm staying in town at the motel."

"Three Rivers is a good drive from here. Wouldn't it be better if you were closer to me?" she asked, fear prompting her question. Fear of the dark, the demon, the time she was away from Raphael. *Together.* The word replayed in her mind. "You said that together we can fight the demon. If so, then the closer we are, the better, right?"

"The distance between us is irrelevant. But I think you've got a point. Together is definitely better," he replied, his voice suddenly low and husky.

For Mishella, *together* meant fusing their powers, but for him, the term held an altogether different meaning. One that sent alarm bells clanging in her head, the warnings quickly drowned out by the beat of her heart as he leaned toward her.

He touched his lips to her forehead, one strong hand easing around her waist.

Mishella closed her eyes, relishing the feel of his lips. She placed her hand on his upper arm, felt the muscles flex beneath her fingers. God, how she needed his closeness.

She trailed her hand over the sinewy curve of his shoulder to slip around his neck. His smooth flesh felt cool, but inviting, as well. She found herself powerless and unwilling to resist.

Never before had touching anyone felt so right. In fact, she'd never actually wanted to touch anyone the way she wanted to touch him. He stirred a desire within her that spiraled from her very soul.

"You taste so sweet," he murmured against her skin.

She opened her eyes the moment she felt his hand cup her chin. He lifted her gaze to his, and she licked her suddenly dry lips. Lips that tingled in remembrance of...of what? Of the feel of his mouth on hers?

The thought sent her senses reeling.

No! She couldn't remember something that hadn't happened. He hadn't kissed her. Not yet, anyway.

A strange surge of longing swept through her, as old as time itself and very frightening. She barely knew him, yet she responded to his touch with an undeniable hunger, as if she was about to feast on a forbidden fruit she'd only been allowed to sample.

And the eyes that held hers mirrored the same craving—a craving he was about to satisfy as he bent his head toward her.

"Shelly!" Stacey's voice rang out.

Mishella jerked her head toward the hallway, the spell she'd been under broken.

"I need a glass of water!"

"I—I'll be right there," Mishella called, her voice shaky—and a little guilty. Guilty because she'd forgotten everything for those few seconds, even Stacey.

"I'd better go see about her," she said, pulling away from him.

"And I'd better be leaving," he said, his tone harsh and clipped.

She glanced up at him. His gaze was once again dark and unreadable, but the stern set of his jaw betrayed his anger.

"Maybe you'd better," she snapped. Damn him for distracting her. Stacey came first, and if he didn't like it—

"I know she comes first," he said, disrupting her thoughts. "No offense. I'm only sorry we were interrupted."

His soft words quelled her anger like water on an open flame.

"You'd better leave," she repeated, her voice quiet, soft now. He had to leave for her to keep her sanity. If only saying the words didn't make her chest ache so badly.

Think only of Stacey, a voice told her. Yes, he had to leave so she could concentrate.

She watched him walk to the door, all the while resisting the urge to stop him. He had to leave. He had to.

Still, she stepped forward and opened her mouth.

"Shell! What's taking you so long?" Once again, Stacey's voice saved her.

Or doomed her. For watching Raphael open the door felt like doom. Damn, why did his leaving bother her so much? Distance was irrelevant. He'd said so himself. They connected emotionally. That should be enough. She didn't need him near her physically. That was much too distracting.

"I'm coming, Stacey."

He paused in the doorway. "The engine block is cracked on your car. They'll have to order some parts."

"The damage is that bad?" She'd already forgotten about the car.

He nodded, his face void of emotion. "You're lucky you weren't hurt. It'll be at least three weeks before they can finish the repairs."

"What am I supposed to do for transportation until then?"

"I'll take you anywhere you want to go and bring you whatever you need. Do you need anything?"

She shook her head.

"Then I'll see you tomorrow. You have my phone number if you—"

"The phone here isn't hooked up," she cut in.

"Then think of me, and I'll feel you. The power we share is much better than technology." He smiled as if teasing, but she knew he was serious. Dead serious.

"Shelly!" Stacey's voice rang out again.

"Rest, Mishella," he said before disappearing outside. The door slammed shut.

Rest and remember, a voice whispered in her head.

She walked stiffly to the door and slid the bolt into place.

The roar of Raphael's sports car filled her ears, then drifted away.

Silence followed. Cold, lonely silence, far worse than the fear that had become her constant companion. She suddenly realized she didn't feel half as afraid as she felt empty. Empty and confused.

Remember me. She could hear his silent plea even now, and how she wanted to remember. Remembering could fill the emptiness and make some sense of her feelings.

If there was anything to remember, reason reminded her. There had to be. She felt it every time she looked at him. That strange familiarity, as if she knew him from somewhere that existed just beyond the realm of conscious thought.

She squeezed her eyes shut, searching her brain for the truth. Why had she been cursed with the touch? Why had Raphael? Were their powers truly one and the same? In his dreams, he'd seen her, but she'd never even glimpsed him in hers. Never.

Did she feel the connection with him, the familiarity, because they shared the same power, or was there some other reason? Maybe she had met him before and forgotten. Her life had become so confusing. Their paths might have crossed before. If so, why wouldn't he remind her of their previous meeting? He acted as if they knew one another, yet he refused to give her any straight answers that would make sense of her feelings. Feelings that told her she *did* know him. Quite well, in fact.

Once again, she searched her mind, praying for a clear recollection. She had to understand. If only Raphael wasn't so evasive. If only the truth wasn't so deeply buried inside of her, for she felt it there, so close, yet so far.

Remember. God, how she wanted to.

"That ought to do it, Miss Kirkland." Thomas Santibanez stood in the kitchen doorway the following evening, his long blond hair tucked behind his ears. With his shy grin and easygoing nature, he had turned out to be quite different from what Mishella had first imagined.

That morning when he had shown up on her doorstep, the sun lighting his features, she had quickly realized his eyes, a pale sky blue, were very friendly.

I told you it was your overactive imagination. She could have laughed at the strange fears that had assailed her last night. The darkness definitely fed her nervousness. And Domingo's impending visit had made her all the more jumpy. Fortunately, his son had come in his place.

"Mishella," she said. "Call me Mishella."

"Mishella," he echoed. "The washing machine's working good." He shifted his toolbox to one hand and hooked the other on the waistband of his faded jeans. "But that hot-water heater..." He shook his head. "That thing was pretty rusted out. One of the worst ones I ever seen. It should last you a few more weeks, but you ought to give some serious thought to getting a new one, what with winter coming and all. Especially if you plan on staying here any length of time."

Mishella recognized the questioning note in his voice, not to mention the glimmer in his eyes. He'd been stealing glances at her all day long.

"My sister and I are just here for a little vacation." Mishella turned the knob on the faucet and let the warmth spill over her fingers. "I was beginning to think I'd forgotten what warm water felt like," she said, smiling gratefully at him. "You did a terrific job."

"Thanks," he said. "It's a shame you won't be here for very long. I'd like to show you around."

Mishella met his gaze and he shifted, obviously awkward when it came to the opposite sex.

Awkward, but certainly not timid, she reminded herself as he plowed on with his next question.

"The VFW Hall puts on a pretty good dance every Friday night. Maybe we could check it out next week? That is, if you're not doing anything." He stared at the worn tips of his boots as he waited for her reply.

"Thomas, I really appreciate your offer," she began, choosing her words carefully. "But... I'm afraid I'll have to decline. I'd planned on spending as much time as I can with my sister. We don't see each other very often with her away at school most of the year."

"It's just a couple of hours," he persisted, his head bobbing up to direct a pleading gaze at her. "Maybe you could bring her with us." New hope leapt into his eyes.

No, nothing timid about him at all, she thought.

"I'm sure Stacey would love for us to go, but she has this bad case of the flu..." Mishella let her words fade, hoping he wouldn't push the date further.

"Maybe another time then," he mumbled, brushing at a lock of blond hair that had fallen into his eyes.

Mishella fought back the pang of guilt that shot through her. She hated to turn him down. Then again, her circumstances hardly warranted a friendly night on the town. That was the last reason she'd come to Three Rivers. On top of everything, she didn't find herself the least bit attracted to Thomas. Better to turn him down now than to encourage his unwanted attention.

"I guess I ought to be going." He shrugged. "My ma said she'll be back out here tomorrow after church if Dad is feeling better. If you need anything else, I'm pretty handy with this thing," he said, holding up the toolbox. "Just give me a holler."

"Thanks, Thomas. Tell your mother not to worry about tomorrow. She can take all the time she needs until Domingo feels better. This old house isn't going anywhere."

"If she ain't back tomorrow, I'll come look in on you."

"I appreciate the offer, but I've wasted your whole Saturday already. There's no need for me to ruin your Sunday, as well."

"Tomorrow," he repeated. "My ma won't be able to keep from worrying otherwise, and neither will I." He stared at Mishella now and she turned her attention to the sink. Unease crept up her spine.

There goes your imagination again. She shook the sensation away.

"Tomorrow then," Mishella reluctantly agreed, concluding from the firm nod of his head that arguing would do no good. He had a stubborn streak that rivaled his mother's. "Tell her I hope your father starts feeling better. Has he seen a doctor?"

"No need for a doctor," Thomas said, shaking his head. "The moment he took to his bed with a fever this morning, my ma was in the kitchen complaining about the weather and cooking up some of her herbs to make him feel better. Her and that garden." He grinned. "I know it sounds kind of old-fashioned, but usually her stuff works."

Mishella met his grin with one of her own. The unease disappeared. "Old-fashioned or not, that's all that counts." The room grew quiet, the silence awkward again.

"Uh, take care," he finally said. Shoving one hand in his pocket, he gave her a quick nod, turned and disappeared through the back door into the last light of evening.

Closing and locking the kitchen door behind him, Mishella leaned against the cool wood and shut her eyes. Raphael's image appeared in her mind, his eyes entrancing her with their intensity. Now if he'd been the one to ask her out . . .

She forced the thought away. She'd decided his abrupt departure last night proved he didn't return the crazy feelings he stirred in her. Had he wanted to, he could have stayed while she looked in on Stacey, and then . . .

Possibilities swirled in her head and she gave herself a mental shake. He wasn't interested. Bottom line. If only his eyes didn't tell another story, a story of hunger, of wanting, then maybe she could get him out of her mind. Forget. Then again, those dark eyes urged her to remember. *Remember.*

Stop it, she told herself. There was nothing to remember. He just had a familiar face. People everywhere experienced déjà vu. He probably only reminded her of someone she'd met in the past. At school, maybe, or an art museum.

Even as she tried to convince herself, deep down inside, Mishella knew she would never have forgotten someone like him. That was the thought that had plagued her all night. She hadn't slept a wink. Wide-eyed now, she had the strong suspicion that tonight would be no different.

A few minutes later, Mishella gathered up her robe and headed for the bathroom. A shower might relax her enough to fall asleep. Anything was worth a try. She felt stiff, her eyes heavy, her head pounding. Her body definitely needed to sleep, even if her mind refused to cooperate.

She turned the chrome knob and tested the warm water cascading from the shower head. In a short time, the porcelain tub filled with a thick, inviting steam that rose above the top of the shower curtain and filled the entire bathroom.

Bless Thomas.

Mishella hooked her robe on the back of the door and grabbed a towel. Pulling her sweater over her head, she dropped the cashmere in a heap on the rose-tiled floor. The pile grew as her jeans followed, then her bra and panties, until she stood naked, her body a blurry ivory reflection in the mist-covered mirror.

Pulling back the curtain, she stepped inside the shower and lifted her face. Like warm rain, the water flowed over her skin, loosening her muscles and calming her nerves. Yes, maybe tonight she would be able to sleep.

Just a moment's peace, she begged, needing desperately to renew her failing strength. She turned, letting the water massage her back, her buttocks, streaming in tiny, tickling rivulets down the backs of her legs.

With the steam rising in her nostrils, clearing her thoughts, she tried to forget the world outside and pretend just for the smallest fragment of time that all was well.

"Pretending will do no good, Mishella."

"Leave me alone," she pleaded, shutting her hands over her ears, desperate to block out the distinctive voice of the burned man. But his voice came from within, inside her head, like a demon inhabiting her soul.

"I am close, Mishella. So close. We will be together again. You will not escape this time."

Then she saw him, the maniacal grin creasing his charred face. His eyes glowed a vivid orange—the orange of the flames surrounding him.

I did not try to escape, her subconscious answered. She shook her head. She had to be losing her grip on reality. How could she answer him when she didn't know what he was talking about?

Or was it the blue-eyed woman who answered? At times, Mishella couldn't discern her own voice, her own thoughts even, from the woman's. It had to be the blue-eyed woman responding to him. Yet, Mishella heard the words in her own voice, as clear as day. *You had a choice,* she told the burned man. *A choice . . . I did not escape you.*

He seemed to ignore her reply.

"This time you will not leave me, Mishella. We are destined to be together. You and I. You will feel the agony of the flames just as I did. The agony of the darkness just as I have all these years."

"No!" she shouted, her voice echoing off the tiled walls, thundering in her ears. She opened her eyes, but tears blinded her.

With trembling hands, she groped for the shower curtain. Then she felt the heat. Like a thousand blazing needles, the scalding water pierced her bare skin.

"Please!" she cried, fumbling for the knob, but she couldn't see. The steam blinded her. Her own tears blinded her.

She grabbed at the shower curtain. The plastic seemed to twist around her arm, barring her way, trapping her in the slippery tub.

"I'll never stop. Not until you are mine!"

"No!" She lost her footing as she clutched the shower curtain.

"Leave me alone!" The frantic plea caught in her throat as she slammed against the bottom of the tub, falling victim to the hot water.

She clawed at the slick edges of the tub, her eyes squeezed shut against the onslaught of liquid fire. Then a hand closed around her wrist. She found herself pulled upright and out of the blistering shower into a pair of muscular arms.

"Mishella." It was Raphael's deep voice that rumbled in her ear, his cool touch that traveled the length of her spine and smoothed the strands of wet hair from her face. "Don't cry," he whispered, holding her protectively to him. "Don't cry, *querida.*"

She snaked her arms around his neck, clinging to him, her eyes clamped tight as she fought to regain some semblance of control. Burying her face in the cool curve of his neck, she willed the violent trembling to leave her. She concentrated on the feel of his pulse beneath her cheek, the beat of his heart, so steady and calm against her own, the scent of soap and maleness that filled her senses.

Calm, she told herself.

"What happened?" he asked after several moments, his voice a soft, soothing murmur against her ear.

"I...I..." a sob caught in her throat as another shudder went through her. "The water," she managed to whisper. "Too hot..."

"It's okay," he assured her, cradling her with one arm and reaching for the shower knob with the other. The spray of water fell silent. "The water isn't too hot now."

He gently pried her arms from around his neck and held her away from him just enough to look into her eyes.

"The water felt fine. Are you sure it was too hot?"

"It wasn't—I mean...not the water," she said between big gulps of air. "Not just—" another big gulp "—the water."

"Then tell me what happened," he urged, his strong hands on her shoulders, his gaze penetrating the veil of shock that hung over her.

"I—I had...a dream." She took a deep breath. The words came a little easier. "No. More of a vision. Then the water started to get hot and—" she took another breath "—I guess it scared me."

He lifted his fingers to wipe away the drops of moisture that trickled down her cheeks. "It's over," he said, drawing her into the depths of his eyes, willing her fear away. "Don't be frightened."

"But the vision was so real," she said. "The man..." She stopped, but his gaze compelled her to finish. "He's the demon. I see him. He speaks to me."

He loosened his grip on her shoulders and slid his hands down her arms. He slipped his hands around her waist and drew her closer.

"He won't leave me alone," she went on. "Ever since that first time..." She caught her bottom lip between her teeth to stifle its tremble.

"When you first discovered your power?" Raphael asked, but she could tell he already knew the answer.

She saw the understanding in his dark eyes and she sensed the compassion. Her heart told her to talk to someone. No, not just someone. Him. She needed to talk to him, more than she'd ever needed to do anything before.

Together. The word echoed in her head.

"I never knew what I could do," she explained, leaning into the comfort of his arms, needing his strength to continue. "Not until my twelfth birthday. I'd always been crazy about cats, but there had been one in particular—Millie. That was her name, and she was the best birthday gift ever." She smiled a small, sad smile at the memory.

"It was late afternoon. I looked all over the house for Millie, but I couldn't find her anywhere. I went outside, crawled through bushes, looked under cars, but she was nowhere. By the time the sun started to set, I'd begun to cry.

My parents joined the search, but nobody could find her.'' Mishella felt the tears in her eyes spill over, glide down her cheeks, but she couldn't lift a hand to wipe them. She was twelve again, searching for the lost Millie, heartbroken at losing the most precious of her gifts.

''My mom told me she would buy me another kitten. A dozen if I wanted. She only wanted me to stop crying. But I couldn't. Everybody went back inside, but I stayed in the front yard in case Millie found her way home.''

''I was bent down behind one of the hedges when I heard the car. Even before I reached the street, I knew something bad had happened. I'd felt it coming all evening, ever since she'd been missing. Then I saw her by the curb, lifeless.'' Mishella stopped for a moment, gathering her courage to face the dreaded memory.

''I picked her up. There wasn't very much blood, but still, she didn't move.'' Mishella clutched the edges of Raphael's jean jacket, staring up at him but not really seeing him. ''That's when I felt the tingling in my hands, almost like a burning. I blacked out then. When I came to, Millie was breathing. She still didn't move, but I could feel the slight thump of her heart. She was *alive*.''

''The vet said by all rights she should have been dead. I knew she would have been if I hadn't touched her. I made her breathe again. Me. My touch.''

''I saw the burned man that night,'' she added. ''That's when the dreams started.''

''You saw him?'' Raphael seemed to tense.

''Not clearly. The flames distorted his face. He looked evil. He *is* evil. I knew it then, and I know it now.'' Beneath the open edge of his jacket, she spread her hand against the soft cotton of his T-shirt, felt the reassuring drum of his heart beneath her fingers.

"I saw the blue-eyed woman, too," she went on. "But she didn't scare me, not like the burned man."

"I had similar dreams," Raphael said softly. "They started when I was very young. On my seventh birthday, to be exact."

"It happened on your birthday, like it happened on mine," she said. "Maybe that has some significance." She glanced into his eyes. "My birthday is February twenty-seventh. When is yours?"

"February fifth."

"Twenty-two days," she said, searching her brain for some significance. Only she found none. No connection. Nothing special that might put things into perspective. "I guess it's not our birthdays, then." Regret filled her voice. She wanted so much to understand why the touch belonged to the two of them. Why them, of all the people in the world. "If we were born on the same day, that could have meant something."

"Perhaps," he replied, his voice noncommittal, yet she saw the gleam that lit his eyes, as if she'd snatched a carrot that he'd dangled in front of her.

She tried to analyze the thought further, but his voice, almost hypnotic, filled her ears, pushing everything from her mind save the smooth, rich baritone.

"The dreams showed me my power, Mishella, and helped me see what I could do. What I am . . ." He paused, indecision flickering in his eyes, as if he wondered whether or not he should continue. "I see the demon, Mishella. I feel him. Like you."

"The burned man is the demon," she said, compelled by his deep gaze to speak her thoughts. "But I still don't know who the blue-eyed woman is. She looks familiar—what I can see of her. Do you see her?"

"No," he replied, his voice taking on a harsh note. "I see only the demon. Feel only him—and you."

"Maybe the woman's an angel, a spirit to counter the demon. She's always been helpful to me, never really frightening, only vague at times. She isn't the evil one. The power comes from the burned man—the demon—doesn't it?"

"Yes, it does."

"I knew," she whispered. "I've always known. The day after I touched Millie, my mother started to get really sick. No one knew why. The blue-eyed woman told me it was because I had used the touch. She said the healing wasn't finished, that I would have to do it twice more in order to save Millie. If I did, she said my mother would . . ." Her words faded. "'A life for a life,' she said. That life would be the closest person to me, the one I loved the most. My mother."

Mishella shook her head. "I was scared. I didn't make the second touch. I couldn't. Instead, I let Millie die."

"Better your kitten than your mother." His voice sounded colder now. She lifted her gaze to search his face. She could've sworn she saw a flicker of torment in his eyes, regret even, as if he, too, had faced a similar decision.

"I always thought it strange how Millie disappeared and I found her at just the right moment for the touch. Almost as if some force intervened in my life to make sure I discovered the power on that day, at that time. Otherwise, I might never have known." She shook her head. "Sometimes I wish I didn't know. I never wanted this power," she said, desperation creeping into her voice. "He has to know I never wanted it."

"It doesn't matter, Mishella. All that matters is that you are using it, and he won't leave you alone until you give him something in return." Raphael touched his fingers to her cheek.

"This is all so crazy!" she exclaimed, not wanting to hear the truth of his words, as if denial could erase what she already knew in her heart. *A life for a life.*

"Not crazy, Mishella. You're alone now. There's no one close to you except your stepsister, and you're using the touch on her. That means the life the demon requires must be your own." He spoke the words softly as he let his fingers slip to the curve of her jaw to tilt her face toward his. "He wants you, Mishella, almost as badly as I want you." The murmured words sent a surge of panic through her.

She became instantly aware of her nakedness, of the hand pressing forcefully against the small of her back. *I want you,* she heard the voice in her head again. Raphael's voice, but his lips didn't move. Only his fingers, trailing lower, over her collarbone, to the hollow between her breasts.

I want you, querida.

"No—" The denial was lost in a sharp intake of breath as he brushed the tip of one breast.

Pull away! She wanted to, but as quickly as she'd felt the panic, it subsided. Longing stole through her as he cupped the fullness of her breast and the cool pad of his thumb found her turgid nipple. The same longing she'd felt last night when she'd waited for his kiss. A kiss she'd been denied for much too long, for ages it seemed. But no more.

He bent his head toward her and she closed her eyes, her lips parting, trembling as he pressed her even closer, crushing her fully against his hard length.

He captured her mouth with his, trailing his tongue across her bottom lip before sucking its fullness into his mouth. He slipped his tongue inside to tangle with hers, to savor, to stroke.

Mishella had participated in her share of kisses, but never one as sinful as the one she experienced now. Her tender breasts swelled against the roughness of his jacket. One of his hands held her bare hips tightly to his. Through the tautly stretched denim at his groin, she felt his arousal, prominent, demanding against her softness.

He nibbled and tasted her mouth with his. His scent filled her nostrils, primitive, male and so intoxicating. He drew the very breath from her, drained her strength, until she sagged in his embrace—an embrace that felt more right than anything should.

"This *is* right," he whispered against her lips, as if in reassurance to her thoughts. Lifting his head, he added, "So very right."

And this time she saw the torment in his eyes, the indecision, and something else, as well—nothing less than his very soul. A soul haunted by love and violence and death— the three so closely intertwined that it frightened her, almost as much as she knew it frightened him.

In the next instant, she saw the tightening of his jaw, the hardening of his eyes, as if he struggled to recover from his momentary loss of control. "No, not yet," he growled. "Not us. Not yet."

With his words came the awareness of his cold hands gripping her flesh. What had felt soothing only seconds before now felt chilling.

She stared up at him, desperate to make some sense of his words and her own reactions. The fire in his dark eyes had died. A guarded look came over his face, leaving no trace of desire, warmth, not even the torment. No emotion of any kind.

He pulled her hands from around his neck and stepped away from her. She felt a draft then and folded her arms across her chest, totally bewildered by his abrupt mood change.

"Here," he said, his voice low, and as emotionless as the rest of him. He snatched up the towel and draped it around her shoulders.

She pulled it tightly around her. The cover did little to dispel the coldness that gripped her, though. Turning away from him, she blinked back the tears and fought for control as emotions warred within her.

"Mishella." His voice sounded almost regretful. He placed his hands on her shoulders and leaned down until his lips brushed her ear.

"There's more to our relationship than just the power we have in common," she whispered. "I know you, Raphael. From somewhere I know you. Tell me the truth," she said. "Tell me why I feel the way I do with you."

"The power is our only link," he replied. "That's it." Even as he said the words, she knew he lied. She sensed it in the coolness of his touch, the banked tension in his powerful body so close behind her, yet at the same time, so far away. "We share the healing, Mishella. That's why you feel connected to me. That's the only reason."

"There's more," she persisted. "Something else you're not telling me."

"I'm telling you all I can."

"I don't believe that. You have to help me remember," she begged, frustration fueling her voice. *"Please."*

"I can't."

"You mean you won't," she corrected, grasping the towel tighter. "Go, Raphael." Her voice broke on his name, but she managed to whisper, "Just go and leave me alone."

Never! The word thundered in her head.

His breath was cool against her ear, unusually so, his voice soft when he spoke. "Listen to the visions. Don't fight them. Understand. Then you and I . . ." His words died. Silence followed. "Just listen, *querida,*" he added.

And remember. She heard the same silent, frustrating plea.

He tugged the edge of the towel past her right shoulder and pressed his lips to the three tiny lines that marred her flesh—marks she'd had since birth. Then he tore his mouth away to kiss her temple.

"Remember what?" she asked again, but he simply shook his head, her words falling on deaf ears.

"I'll see you tomorrow. It's late. Try to get some rest." And with that, he turned and left, leaving her cold and alone and filled with dozens of maddening questions he had no intention of answering.

"Damn you," she whispered as the door closed behind him. And as much as she damned him, she wanted him. Despite the unanswered questions and the secrets she knew he was keeping.

Moments later, she pushed the living room curtains aside to catch a glimpse of his car as it sped off. Her anger slipped away and the emptiness returned, consuming, until she was sure she'd never felt so alone. Or had she?

Forcing aside the disturbing question, she hurried to her bedroom, desperate to put on some warm clothes and crawl beneath the covers.

Damn him again for distracting her, for making her feel things she could make no sense of, for leaving her.

"There's nothing to remember," she tried to convince herself as she burrowed beneath the quilts. Nothing.

"Remember, damn it!" Raphael cursed as he gripped the steering wheel and did his best to keep from turning the car around. It had taken every ounce of strength he had and then some to leave her. To resist her when she wanted him as much as he wanted her. They were linked emotionally. The first touch had seen to that.

The second touch provided a physical connection. They were together now. Mating would complete the physical union. Their bodies and their emotions would be joined then. They would be ready for the last and final connection.

The third touch.

Time for their spirits to entwine, for his to conquer, and then he would have her soul as he was always meant to.

For now, she still had to give of her body willingly. She would, of that he felt certain. Her response proved it. Their pasts proved it. Now she only had to realize it. To remember as he did. Then she would come to him again.

Esteban reined in his mount as he reached the top of the rise. The sun was a trace of burnt orange brushing the surrounding countryside, which spread before him like a lush green blanket as far as the eye could see.

His horse danced nervously, then settled beneath Esteban's soothing hand as he scanned the horizon in what had become a daily ritual for him over the past two weeks.

Two weeks.

Anger made his hands tremble. He clenched his fists and took a deep breath. Studying the landscape, he riveted his attention on a slight movement in the far distance.

Even in the last light of dusk, he could discern the outline of a carriage. The lamps on either side rocked violently back and forth, like two eyes not quite certain where to focus.

The carriage wound onward. Finally Esteban could see the tiny figure of a driver as he cracked his whip above the team of horses. They thundered forward at a gallop along the narrow road. Their destination could only be the Castillo de Malvado.

He surveyed the distance between the carriage and the great stone fortress that was his home. Then, shifting forward in the saddle, Esteban signaled his mount and charged down the rise, straight for the path the carriage traveled, a mixture of anger and excitement heightening with every stride of his horse.

Breathless moments later, he slowed the horse to a walk, then stopped in the middle of the dirt path. The carriage rumbled toward him.

"Whoa!" the driver called, slowing the team the moment he spotted Esteban. The carriage rocked to a dead halt as he tightened the reins.

"Señor, you are blocking the way," he shouted, his beady black gaze suspicious.

"What business have you traveling across my land, to my castle?" Esteban demanded.

The man opened his mouth, but the creak of the carriage door killed his reply.

Even before she stepped out, he felt her. Then she appeared, wrapped in a blue velvet cape, her face hidden in the shadow of her hood.

"Señora, you must get back inside. This stranger—"

"Is no stranger," she finished, stepping forward despite the worried look on the driver's face. She eased the hood back from her face. "My driver takes this route at my instruction," she said, directing her statement at Esteban. "I believe the last time I was here, you bid me a quick return."

"Three months," Esteban said, his voice deadly cold and calm. Three months had passed. The three months required for her to administer the healing. Three months that had seemed like three years, and then he'd had to wait even longer. "You are late, señora."

"Only two weeks," she replied as if the time was nothing compared to the eternity she'd pledged to him.

But the time had passed with agonizing slowness for him, a man unaccustomed to patience. "*Sí,* only two," came his reply which revealed nothing of the turmoil inside him. Elation that she'd returned. Fury that he'd had to wait. Anticipation of what would now come.

Their gazes locked and for a moment it felt as if he actually touched her.

"Señora?" The driver's voice intruded on the silent communication. "Darkness comes. This is no place to be once darkness comes."

"You fear the darkness?" Esteban sneered at the wide-eyed stare the driver gave him. Then his face grew somber. "You should. The darkness swallows your soul."

"We...we really should be on our way," the driver stammered. "Señora?"

"Do not let his words frighten you, Pedro," Maricela said, her gaze still fused with Esteban's.

"And you, Maricela?" He delved into the dark blue depths of her eyes. "Do I frighten you?"

"Is that your intention?"

Despite her bold stance, he didn't miss the slight quiver of her lips. He did frighten her. In that instant, he should have felt satisfied. "I am a man who strikes fear into the hearts of many, sometimes by choice, but sometimes not. I have a reputation, as you well know."

"*Sí,* Señor Malvado. I do know."

"Esteban Malvado," the driver gasped, the name sounding like a whispered indecency. "You are Esteban Malvado?"

"*Sí,*" Esteban admitted with a reluctance that surprised him.

Remember what you are, a voice—the voice of Belial, the demon who made him what he was, what his father and grandfather before him had been—whispered in his ear. *You are no mere man. You are a Malvado. One of my own. A Malvado.*

"See her to the castle," Esteban growled, reining his horse around and spurring the animal to a gallop. Bitter rage at the evil that flowed through his veins overpowered him. He pushed his horse faster as the blackness threatened him. A blackness meant to swallow one's soul.

Raphael eased up on the accelerator enough to maneuver the car onto the main strip through town. He tried to slow his breathing a few seconds later as he brought the car to a skidding halt in the parking lot of the town's only hotel.

In his room, he rushed into the bathroom and began splashing cold water onto his face. Ripping off his jacket and tearing off his shirt, he splashed more water, until icy droplets covered his face, neck and chest.

He stared at his reflection—the wildness in his eyes, the harsh line of his jaw, the veins protruding from his tightly flexed muscles. He looked as out of control as he was starting to feel.

He needed to fill her, to possess her until he felt only the hot warmth of her body wrapped around him, sucking at him, pulling him deeper, making him forget who and what he was.

But he couldn't forget. Even now he felt the rage deep inside. The hatred. The torment. The demon.

There is no escape.

He wanted to believe that. He wanted to welcome the cold, the numbing possession where he no longer felt or thought for himself. Where he became nothing but a shell to house a five-hundred-year-old curse.

But Mishella Kirkland had started to crumble that shell with the raw hunger she stirred. Hunger and something else . . .

An emotion that should have disintegrated into the thick, black smoke and the putrid smell of burning flesh centuries ago.

But he felt it now. Hell, he'd never stopped feeling it. And the stronger it grew, the angrier Belial became and the fiercer the battle waged, with Raphael serving as the battleground, torn between the cold and the heat—her heat.

With a violent oath, he slammed his fist against the marble vanity top. No pain. That was good. If only he was as immune to her.

He stared at his reflection again, hating himself, who he was, what he was, and all because of her. "Damn you!" he swore, smashing his fist into the mirror. The glass cracked. Blood trickled down his arm.

He'd never warred with the demon. He'd never wanted to—until her. Until he'd begun to feel what he wasn't supposed to.

Slamming his other fist against the broken mirror, he damned her for making him wait, for making him want her so badly. Most of all, however, he damned her for making him feel the cold again. The miserable, god-awful cold.

CHAPTER SIX

"You owe me two thousand dollars," Stacey declared. She gave a satisfied smile as she pulled a pale hand from beneath the coverlet. "Pay up, Shell."

"Haven't you punished me enough for one night?" Mishella asked. Actually Stacey had punished her since she'd started to feel well enough to sit up. Three weeks, to be exact, since the second touch.

Only five more days, Mishella's conscience reminded her. Five more days...

Mishella fought back the sliver of fear that eased up her spine. She had nothing to be afraid of. Nothing and no one. The night of the full moon would arrive. At the exact moment the sun caressed the horizon to make way for darkness, she would make the third and final touch, and it would all be over. Stacey would be well again and Mishella would survive the ordeal, thanks to Raphael. They would merge their powers and beat the demon. *Together.*

"Shell?"

"Hmm?" Mishella forced her attention back to her stepsister.

"I'm waiting." Stacey held out her open palm. "Pay up."

"I'm broke, little sister. You wiped me out the last time I landed on Boardwalk."

"You don't look broke to me," Stacey said, studying Mishella's stack of Monopoly property cards spread out across the cover. "Seeing as how you're my sister, I'll have a little mercy on you. Instead of money, I'll take your railroads," she graciously offered. "And your utilities. And the green properties." She looked thoughtful for a moment. "Oh, and I'll take those red ones, too."

"And you're showing mercy?" Mishella cocked an eyebrow and gathered the cards. She dropped them into her stepsister's waiting hand.

"Thank you very much, big sister, dear." Stacey added the cards to her already substantial pile and settled back against the pillow to count her money. "Let's see," she mused. "Maybe I'll buy another hotel."

"I'm retiring for tonight," Mishella said, scooping the dice and the game trinkets from the board. "Your show of mercy left me with exactly five dollars and Baltic Avenue."

"You shouldn't have wasted your money on that cheap property. Daddy always used to say you have to spend money to make money." Stacey fanned the money out on top of her blanket. "I guess he was right, and I guess I win. Again." She grinned.

"I should never have bought this game," Mishella said, a smile on her face. She'd been desperate for a diversion for Stacey when the days in the hospital had seemed endless. Except that chemotherapy had kept her stepsister too ill to do much of anything. Mishella had packed the unwrapped game into her suitcase in the hope that Stacey might eventually be well enough to sit up, maybe roll the dice a few times and play.

Since the second touch, the fever had subsided. Stacey had started sitting up, eating more, even laughing. The dark circles under her eyes gave the only indication that the illness still fought for control of her frail body.

"You're a party pooper," Stacey informed her, brushing a wispy blond bang from her forehead.

"Pooped is right, and you should be, too. And since when did you get so good at Monopoly?"

"I played all the time at school. I was the best player on my floor." Stacey's smile disappeared as she leaned her head back against the pillow and closed her eyes. "I wish I was back at school, Shell," she whispered.

"Now that's a first," Mishella said, trying to ease the sudden gloom that surrounded them. "I seem to recall that your favorite part of the school year was vacation. In fact," she went on, "I recall you threatening to burn your uniforms a time or two."

Stacey opened her eyes, her smile wistful. "I almost did when Miss Margaret made me wear cuffed socks, instead of the tube socks Daddy bought me Christmas before last."

"He went to five stores before he found those socks." Mishella laughed. "Imagine yellow-and-white-striped socks with a blue plaid skirt. I bet they looked terrible with your uniforms."

"Did not! Those were the official socks worn by Britain's soccer team. They brought me good luck before my games. I had to wear them. That's why Daddy bought them. He knew."

"He knew it was better to buy them than to see you mope while you were home for vacation," Mishella teased.

Stacey didn't smile. Instead, she sighed. "I miss Mom and Dad," she said. "Do you miss them, Shelly?"

Mishella nodded.

"When I went back to school after the accident, I felt so lonely," Stacey said. "I could be in the middle of the soccer field surrounded by other girls and still feel lonely. I guess it was knowing I wouldn't ever see them again." She gathered up the red plastic hotels and dropped them into a small bag. "I'm just glad I still have you, Shell. That's one reason I always liked vacations. I got to see you, even if you did hate my socks."

Now they both smiled.

"Not that I didn't like school," Stacey continued. "I did, more than I knew. I only wished you could have been in New York with me."

Mishella managed to find her voice. "We're together now."

"I know, but for how long?" Stacey's question caught Mishella off guard. "I mean, after I get better, I want to go back to school. I miss my friends and stuff. But when I think about not seeing you every day, I feel sad. So—" she paused to take a deep breath "—I've been thinking about what we could do."

"And what's that?" Mishella asked. Stacey had the same look as the time she'd asked for the tube socks.

"I've been thinking that when we leave here, you could come back to New York with me." As if afraid Mishella might object, Stacey rushed on. "As good an artist as you are, I'm sure you could find work. Even if you couldn't, Mom and Dad left plenty of money. I could go to school, and you could draw. You could even come to my soccer games," Stacey finished, her voice anxious. "It would be great, Shell. Really it would."

For the first time, Mishella dared to look past the third touch, to really envision a future.

When she'd first touched Stacey, she'd resigned herself to her own death, knowing she would have to sacrifice herself to save Stacey. She'd made arrangements with her attorney to provide for Stacey's well-being, preparing for the worst even though, at first, she hadn't been completely certain she would die. By the time she'd made the second touch, however, she'd been convinced. The power was draining. *Was*—until Raphael had shown up.

Now Mishella had a chance. A future.

"If you want me in New York with you, then wild horses couldn't keep me away," Mishella said, watching the smile that lit Stacey's pale features.

"Great!" Stacey clasped Mishella's hand. "You'll love it. I promise!"

"Where did you get that?" Mishella asked, her attention going to a glint of silver that peeked from beneath the edge of the blanket near Stacey's pillow. Her thoughts fled as she stared at the crucifix Stacey held out.

"This?" Stacey asked. "Inez gave it to me last week. I really like seeing her every day, Shell. I'm glad she's been coming out here even though I know she ought to be home with Domingo since he's still sick."

Mishella took the worn-looking cross. Years of handling had smoothed the ornate carving. The metal had long since dulled, but she could see the beauty it must have had at one time. It felt warm in her grasp.

"Inez said that when I'm feeling sick, I should keep it nearby," Stacey went on. "That it'll make me feel better. She keeps one at home just like it. She said when she goes to mass, she takes it with her and the padre blesses it. She said the padre blessed mine." Stacey smiled as if tremendously pleased. "I tried to get her to take it back home and give it to Domingo to make him feel better, but she said he doesn't have anything a little chicken soup can't cure." She paused. "Inez said I need it more than Domingo."

"She's very kind to think of you." Mishella made a mental note to thank the old woman the next time she saw her, which should be first thing in the morning. Inez had been coming in every day for the past two weeks despite her husband's illness and Mishella's urging to stay home and nurse him back to health. The woman seemed to have an abundance of energy that would put Florence Nightingale to shame.

"Inez told me this crazy weather has a lot to do with Domingo being sick. That's why he can't seem to get better." Stacey shivered and pulled the blanket up to her chin. "But she said I'll get better."

"She did, did she?"

"She tells me so every time she makes me sit up and eat my lunch." Stacey shook her head. "I've never seen anybody so happy to see someone else eat."

"Then you haven't been paying any attention to me when I pick up your empty dinner tray. Inez isn't the only one who likes to see you eat."

"I'll get fat if I keep eating all the stuff you fix for me."

"You could use a little fattening up," Mishella said, feeling a tightness in her chest at Stacey's still-hollow cheeks.

"When I played soccer I used to eat two desserts every night, and I never gained an ounce," Stacey announced. "But now—" she closed her eyes "—I can't play anymore."

"You'll be back at school in no time, baby. I promise you that." And Mishella meant it, more than she'd ever meant anything in her life.

"We both will," Stacey declared. "Don't you think it'll be just great for you and I to be together?" Stacey settled back against the pillow with a heavy sigh. "You'll love New York."

"I'll love it because I'll be with you." She would love the very fires of hell as long as Stacey was happy and healthy and smiling.

Silence surrounded them, disrupted only by the soft rustle of paper as Mishella sorted the Monopoly money and placed it in the tray.

"You'll be with me and...Raphael," Stacey finally said. "He's from New York. Did you know that?" She grinned now, her eyes alight with mischief, as if she knew a secret that Mishella didn't.

"And what makes you so sure I want to be anywhere near Raphael?"

"I see the way you look when he's around, and I still don't believe you two were just friends."

"And how is it I look?"

"You know—nervous and stuff," Stacey replied. "And how come you never mentioned him when you were in college, anyway? You told Mom and Dad about all your boyfriends, but you never said one single word about him."

"I never told you about him because he wasn't my boyfriend, nosy. We were and are only friends."

"You don't have to be embarrassed, Shelly." Stacey patted her hand. "Raphael's a real hunk. The girls on my floor would die if they saw him. He looks like one of those male models. Janie Beard's brother is a model and he's not nearly as good-looking. Though, you'd think he was Mr. America or something from the way Janie goes on and on about him. She makes the rest of us sick!" Stacey sighed.

"Anyway," she continued, "they'd all flip if they got a glimpse of Raphael. Don't you think he's simply gorgeous, Shell?"

"I haven't really noticed," Mishella said. *Liar!* She'd been painfully aware of exactly how gorgeous he was each and every night when he dropped by to check on them. Lucky for her peace of mind, he had kept his distance. He stared at her endlessly, but he hadn't tried to touch her again, not after the night he had rescued her from the shower two weeks ago. The longest two weeks of Mishella's life.

She found herself almost regretting that he didn't come near her. *Stop it. Distance is better. Safer.* She should feel relieved. She *did* feel relieved, she told herself.

"Enough talk about—"

"Who won?" Raphael's familiar voice caressed Mishella's ears.

She turned to see him standing in the doorway, and her heart skipped a beat. Clad in snug-fitting black jeans and a long-sleeved black shirt that accented the deep tan of his skin, he leaned against the doorjamb, his stance casual as he studied her.

Mishella fought for a calming breath, disturbed more by her reaction to him than his sudden appearance. He had a knack for showing up in the evening just when she least expected him. And he also had a knack for making her very, very nervous.

"Are you all right?" He searched her face with a thoroughness that made her swallow.

"Fine," she murmured, barely resisting the urge to lick her suddenly dry lips.

"Shelley's just nursing a wounded ego," Stacey chimed in. "Because I won again, of course."

"Of course," he agreed. "But I bet your sister played a good game."

"Nope, she lost her shirt."

"Really?" Raphael swept his gaze over Mishella, seeming sorely disappointed to find that she still wore her shirt. "Too bad I got here late."

Stacey giggled, Mishella felt her face flame, and Raphael simply smiled, still staring at her with those damnable dark eyes that made her more than nervous. They fired her blood. Filled her with longing.

"Bedtime," Mishella declared, tearing her gaze from his to scoop up the Monopoly board and shove it back into the box.

"He is a hunk," Stacey whispered a moment later as Mishella leaned over her to kiss her slightly warm forehead.

"Janie Beard would be green," Mishella said. Stacey smiled and closed her eyes.

Game in hand, Mishella turned toward the door. Raphael had disappeared. She found him in the living room, bent down in front of the fireplace stacking kindling on the stone hearth.

"I brought her some chocolate ice cream," he said.

"If you're trying to win her over, you already have," Mishella replied, placing the game on the coffee table.

"She likes ice cream that much?"

"And candy and all the other goodies you've been showering her with."

"I hope you don't mind."

"Not at all. She usually doesn't feel like eating anything, even chocolate. When this is all over, we'll spend a few weeks in the dentist's office, but for now, she loves sweets, and I like to see her happy."

"And what about you, Mishella?" He paused in his task. "Are you happy?"

"I will be," she replied, "when I make the last touch and Stacey is well again."

He reached for a log. "You're almost out of wood."

Mishella stared at his back, fascinated by the ripple of muscles beneath the material of his shirt as he placed the iron grate in place.

She shook her head and wondered how one look at him could make her feel so jittery. True, he was a "hunk," but Mishella knew her reaction to him had more to do with the entire man than just his appearance. Despite the nightmare she found herself in, he could make her feel safe. She never felt the tears when he was near, or the fear, only a strange sort of contentment. And a huge amount of frustration, her conscience added, the quivering in her stomach refusing to be ignored.

More than anything, however, he made her feel stronger. With the third and final touch approaching, she needed strength. Then again, she also needed to keep her mind focused, which was why she tried to ignore the feelings he stirred in her. She wanted his nearness, his strength, yet she didn't want to be attracted to him.

"She seems to be doing better every day," he remarked without looking up.

"Yes. That's the way it was with the first touch. Afterward, for a few weeks, anyway, she seemed to get better. She still had the pain in her legs, but it wasn't so bad. Then the fever returned. And the pain. In fact, they both got worse. That's probably the way it'll be this time, too," she said, her words sounding more like a question.

"Maybe, maybe not," he said.

"I know your being here has something to do with her feeling better. You not only strengthen me, but Stacey, as well."

"I came only for you, Mishella." There was a thread of coldness in his voice as he added, "And for myself."

She might've been put off by his words, but he'd already told her as much. He'd been drawn to her, driven to help her in order to save himself from the demon. And self-preservation she could understand. She'd grasped the hope he'd brought, desperate to save her own life and her stepsister's any way she could. "Thank you for coming." For whatever reason, she finished silently, whether selfish or otherwise.

He tensed, the material of his shirt stretching tautly across the rigid muscles of his back.

"I haven't seen her smile very much since all this started," she continued, undaunted by his reaction. "She almost seems her old self."

Seconds crept by before he stood. Turning to face her, he said, "She smiles for you, Mishella. You're stronger than you think. *You* make Stacey smile, not me." He closed the distance between them until he stood close enough for her to feel his breath fan her face.

"Maybe, maybe not." She found herself echoing his words. She wanted with all her heart to believe what he said. But before he'd come, she hadn't been very strong. She'd felt weak, defeated, destined to lose at times. He made her feel as if she could actually win against the evil. She could. *They* could. *Together.*

"Have you ever had to use your power to help someone you loved?" Her question appeared to catch him off guard. She saw a spark in his eyes as if he wanted to say something.

As quickly as the spark flared, however, it died. His eyes grew dark, turbulent, unsettling as he let the silence linger between them for an infinite moment.

"Once," he began, putting his back to her as he faced the fire. She saw the faint trembling of his shoulders, the goose bumps that rose on his forearms. "A long, long time ago. But my reasons were selfish. Not the same as what you're doing."

"Mine aren't so unselfish. My mother and stepfather are gone. They married when Stacey was two years old. She's like my own flesh and blood. I don't have anyone except her."

"It's still not the same." He shook his head, but he didn't say more, and Mishella was left to wonder what secret he kept from her.

"I was always so afraid to use the power," she heard herself say. "Because of what happened the first time."

"Yet you used it, anyway, even when you thought you would die. Weren't you afraid?"

"Terrified," she replied honestly. "The only difference was that I was more frightened of losing Stacey than of what could happen to me. I didn't care what happened to me. As long as Stacey lived." Raphael turned to face her again.

"As long as she lives," she managed to find her voice, "nothing else matters. Whatever happens to me doesn't matter."

"But you don't want to die, do you?"

"Who does? I want to grow old, to see my sister grow up. But if that's the only choice I have, I would make the sacrifice. I still will if I have to," she said, the possibility that all that he'd told her was a lie continuing to plague her.

"Such a willing sacrifice," he remarked, yet his voice held none of the sarcasm his words implied. "Would you really make the final touch, even if it killed you?"

"I told you I would. Stacey is young. She deserves a chance at life. If my life can give her that chance..."

"And your soul, Mishella? Is her life worth the price of your soul, as well?"

Soul. She contemplated the word as the enormity of what she was doing for Stacey crystallized in her mind. Icy rivulets of fear ran down her spine, making her hands tremble. "What does my soul have to do with giving Stacey life?" She knew. Somewhere in the dark recesses of her mind, she knew the answer to her question, yet she felt compelled to ask him.

"That's what the demon seeks in return for use of the power," he answered. "For the use of *his* power. He will settle for nothing less. He won't only take your life, he'll take your spirit, your essence, your very soul, do you understand? Is Stacey's life worth that to you?"

She fought back the doubts, the near paralyzing fear, and without even a moment's hesitation, replied, "It's worth more."

"There isn't more."

"There is," she insisted. "There's love. Love has to figure in somehow." She shook her head. "But all this talk is crazy. You're here. We'll deliver the third touch and everything will be fine again. It will," she added, more for her own reassurance than his. "You said it would. As long as we join powers. Together."

Raphael regarded her for what seemed like an eternity. He stood so close she could feel his coolness, prickling the sensitive skin of her neck, her arms.

"Do you need anything?" He asked her the same question he asked every night before he disappeared.

She shook her head.

"Then I'll see you tomorrow."

"Tomorrow," she whispered, watching him stride to the door. The urge to stop him, to beg him to stay, came close to overwhelming her. She wanted him to tell her more about the demon. All he knew. Fear kept her from calling out.

The old saying about ignorance being bliss came to mind. A part of her wanted to know, yet she feared what the knowledge would do to her newfound courage. She'd started the healing and she had to finish.

The door closed, reverberating with a finality that sent a shiver through her. She sank to the sofa and stared into the crackling blaze. She feared the vision would come as she watched the flames lick at the wrought-iron grate, but she couldn't look away. Compelled, she could only stare and wonder if Raphael had gone back to town.

A long while later, she leaned her head against the sofa back and closed her eyes. No visions tonight, she pleaded, feeling suddenly exhausted. As if in answer to her prayers, no visions came. Only blackness.

The creak of the door brought her wide-awake. Her eyes snapped open as a rush of cold air filled the room.

And there he stood in the doorway, bare-chested, his dark hair falling in disarray over his heavily muscled shoulders, jeans hugging the lean curves of his hips and thighs. A cloud of frigid mist surrounded him, giving the room a dreamlike aura.

She felt a presence surround her like a strong embrace, and pull her to her feet to face him. The hunger that burned in his eyes transcended the space separating them, and in that instant, as their gazes locked, she felt the unmistakable familiarity, as if they had played this scene together before.

Impossible, she thought as she dismissed the feeling and dared to stare into the eyes of the man in front of her.

Eyes that entranced with their intensity.

Eyes that reflected the brilliant orange of the fire raging on the hearth.

Eyes that mirrored the desire that unfurled inside her.

She watched, mesmerized, as he stepped into the room, bringing with him a gust of wind that lashed at the flames, fueling them higher.

The door banged against its hinges, rocked with the force of the violent wind. The windows flew open. The curtains billowed, but Mishella paid little attention. She saw only him. She *felt* only him.

Invisible fingers played at the buttons of her blouse, then pushed the edges aside. She gasped for air, her breasts pressing against the lace of the flimsy bra she wore. The front clasp popped open. She felt cool hands on her skin, pushing the material from her shoulders. She wanted to stop them, to stop *him,* but he stood motionless across the room from her, his arms at his sides. His eyes followed the path of the unseen force that slid the material down over her shoulders, her arms, until the blouse and bra fell in a creamy heap of silk at her feet.

She closed her eyes, thinking once again she had to be dreaming... or maybe her sanity had snapped. There had to be some explanation. This couldn't be happening to her. Not really. Yet the cool hands that cupped her breasts and caressed her swollen nipples felt so very real. Opening her eyes, she let the rush of heat rippling through her body override her doubts.

Raphael still watched her, touching every inch of her with his eyes. She felt the snap on her jeans pop open. The material glided down her legs. Her panties followed, until she stood naked before him.

He stepped forward and she reeled backward. The floor fell away as a soft mattress came up to meet her. She found herself lying in a white cloud of cool linen sheets, in an enormous room with a ceiling so high that darkness enshrouded it. The only light came from the flickering candles that surrounded the bed and illuminated the man poised above her.

She blinked her eyes, temporarily taken aback at the change in Raphael. Now a beard covered his firm jaw. His hair was slightly shorter, but his eyes held the same intensity, the same deep hunger that forced all speculation from her mind.

He touched his hand to her face, the silver of his ring catching the flicker of one of the candles. She flinched beneath the contact, like ice against her heated flesh. Still he didn't pull away. He trailed his hand down her throat to the swell of her breasts, across her abdomen, down her thighs, until no part of her body escaped his exploration.

She shivered as fear gripped her. This didn't feel right. It felt unnatural. Cold, emotionless.

"Please stop," she murmured. He didn't. Instead, he touched his lips to the hollow of her throat and she instantly warmed. His tongue stroked the three lines on her shoulder. Then his mouth followed the trail of his hand, heating her skin, making her burn with need until the cold was a memory and she whimpered with the wondrous longing only he could satisfy.

She ran her palms over the taut muscles of his shoulders, awed by the strength beneath her fingertips. As his tongue found one swollen nipple, she closed her eyes and arched her back, eager for the wet heat of his mouth.

Her heart thundered, pumping desire through her veins until the ache between her thighs was so fierce she knew she would die. Eager to feel the satisfaction, which had always been a mystery to her, she opened to him, easing her legs up on either side of him.

She felt him hard and rigid at the entrance to her heat. But he didn't thrust forward and fill her as she so desperately wanted.

"*I win,*" he whispered, then he pulled away.

"No!" she cried, the sound of her voice almost alien to her.

She opened her eyes to find herself stretched out on the familiar leather sofa back in the living room. Her gaze flew to the door. Closed. She glanced at the windows. All closed. Not even a draft filtered into the room. The fire crackled on the hearth, emanating a comforting warmth.

She touched a hand to her pounding heart. The contact of flesh against flesh startled her, and she glanced down at her flushed body. Her blouse, her jeans, her underclothes lay in a heap beside the sofa. Mortified, she scooped up the clothes and began pulling on each piece.

What was wrong with her? Had she lost her mind? Naked on the sofa? Alone? Maybe the stress was getting to her. Yes, that had to be it. She refused to acknowledge the small voice that told her Raphael and his lovemaking were real. She'd had a dream, a rather vivid dream, but a dream nonetheless. She'd simply undressed in her sleep. That was all. That had to be all.

Fully clothed, she hurried from the room, anxious to leave the fresh memories of Raphael behind. Moments later, as she lowered herself onto the bed next to Stacey, she blinked back a sudden well of tears—tears of frustration, confusion and loneliness, for she'd never felt the way he'd made her feel only minutes ago. Dream or not.

Stop it. You're a grown woman. He's only a man, a rather good-looking one, but a man just the same. Your reaction is normal. Everybody has erotic dreams now and then.

Feeling little comfort at her thoughts, Mishella clasped her hands around Stacey's, which held tight to the old crucifix.

Closing her eyes, she prayed for sleep to come. And surprisingly it did.

Raphael opened his eyes. The candles, which formed the circle around him, had all but burned out. Only one or two flames remained, dribbling wax onto the dirt floor and doing little to dispel the darkness that filled the barn.

He took a deep breath and let the cold air rush into his lungs. Despite the past hour spent in a trance, he shivered. He closed his eyes again, willing the cold away and the numbness in its place. If only he didn't still feel her beneath him, touching him.

He shivered again.

I win. The words echoed in his mind. He *had* won. She had surrendered to him, and for a brief moment, he'd seen the recollection in her eyes. She remembered. Somewhere in the back of her mind, she remembered. She didn't want to, however, and that kept her from acknowledging the past. But in time, she would face it. Embrace it even, just as he did, and the physical union would be complete.

He tightened his fist, feeling the sharp edge of the ring against his palm. She would embrace the past—who she was, who he was, and soon.

Esteban leaned against the doorjamb and stared across the room to the woman who stood gazing out the window into the blackness of the night.

"So Miguel has recovered?" he asked.

Maricela's head snapped around and the velvet drapery swished back into place. She looked startled, fearful even.

"Completely," she said, her voice slightly nervous. She cleared her throat. "The servants are calling it a miracle from God."

"From an angel," he corrected, his gaze fixed on her. She looked tired, as if the past three months had drained her. Still, her eyes sparkled with blue splendor in the light from the candelabra.

"Angel? A fallen angel, like you, Señor Malvado," she quietly informed him. "Fallen and cast out."

"Esteban. The time for formality has passed," he said, ignoring her last statement.

"As you wish...Esteban." She clasped her hands.

"What did you tell Miguel?"

"Nothing." She shook her head. "I left a note telling him not to look for me. That I have contracted a deadly disease

and I fear that in his weakened state he will be too susceptible. I wished him a long and happy life.''

"And you think he will believe such a story?"

"The carriage driver was a very loyal servant of my
mother's before her death. He will take back my crucifix
and tell Miguel that I fell desperately ill on the way to Ma-
drid. That I passed away in the refuge of a church and was
buried nearby. Miguel will believe him. The crucifix will be
proof enough.''

"Why is that?"

"My mother gave the crucifix to me on her deathbed. I
have never taken it off. Miguel knows I never would for any
reason, unless..."

"Unless you had no choice, like in death," he said, "or
now.''

"*Sí.*" She put her back to him and swept the draperies
aside once again. The faint glow of moonlight illuminated
her figure.

"Disappointed that Miguel will not be coming for you,
Maricela?" Esteban's tone was bitter. "Even if he did, I
would not let you go. I will never let you go." He needed to
say the words, to reassure himself that he held her completely. She exuded a strength he found very challenging.

"I knew that when I came."

"Yet you still chose to doom yourself and leave the man
you love?"

"I did not leave the man I love."

"Oh? You sold your soul to heal a man you have no love
for?" His voice was stern, demanding an answer. "I am no
fool, Maricela. You were desperate."

"*Sí,* but not for love."

"Then why?" Suddenly he had to know. "Tell me what
brought you here seeking the powers of darkness and what
prompted you to sell yourself.''

"Loyalty," she replied, her voice small, faraway. "I owe Miguel a great deal. Saving his life was the least I could do. He saved mine not very long ago, though it seems like forever." She spoke more to herself than to him. "He made me his wife though he never loved me. An act of mercy, you might say. I would have died had he not saved me from..." Her voice faded.

"From who?" He felt the blood pound through his veins. The thought of someone touching her, hurting her, stoked the fire that always burned within him, the rage he managed to keep just below the surface.

"My father. My own father." She paused as if deciding exactly how much to tell him. When she spoke, her voice was small again as she relived a horror only she could see. "He would come into my bedchamber at night...late...after everyone had retired."

He saw the shimmer of tears in her eyes. The unfamiliar tightening about his heart not only surprised him, but angered him. He should feel nothing for her. He *must* feel nothing. She was his possession like everything else—bought with the evil to satisfy his cravings, be it for pleasure or power. In this instance, both.

She wiped at her tears as if disgusted with her show of weakness. "Miguel knew my father, what kind of man he was. When he met me, I guess he felt pity."

Had Esteban not been so angry, he might have laughed at her assessment of Miguel's feelings. The last thing any man could feel for her was pity. To look at her and not feel the uncontrollable stirrings of lust would take a strong man, indeed. Much stronger than any mortal.

"He asked for my hand. My father refused. Miguel knew my father very well, so he threatened to report him as a heretic. As powerful as Miguel was, the authorities were sure to believe him. My father had no choice. I thought Miguel

a gallant knight come to rescue me.'' She shook her head.
''But he, too, wanted only to control me. Miguel was demanding, but never cruel. I was thankful for that.

''So you see—'' she turned to him ''—I owed Miguel my
life.''

''Now you owe me,'' Esteban reminded her, stepping into
the room and pulling the door closed behind him. She
inched back, a wild look in her eyes, like that of an animal
sensing imminent danger.

He stopped a few feet from her.

''Do not fear me, Maricela.''

She laughed, a nervous, hollow sound that even she noticed. Tearing her eyes from his, she bowed her head. ''I
suppose the time for fear has passed, as well.''

She took a deep breath. Her chest heaved, then quivered
from the effort, and Esteban felt a fist clench in his stomach. Her beauty had stayed vivid in his mind, yet the mental picture of her had been nothing compared to the woman
before him now. Pale, almost translucent skin, eyes like
bright jewels, silken hair as black as the darkest night. She
would bear him the most exquisite child.

She turned, letting her gaze sweep the massive room, from
the imported carpets gracing the floor to the hand-carved
bed swathed in white linen.

''This room is yours. Is it to your liking?'' he asked,
quirking one brow, the need for her approval another surprise to him. It should have mattered little what she thought,
yet it suddenly mattered a great deal.

''*Sí*, but I thought I was to be...''

''My whore?'' he asked. Her head came up, her eyes
blazing now. ''Are you so eager to fulfill your part of our
bargain, Maricela?''

"Of course not," she sputtered. Her face flamed and he smiled. "I—I just did not expect to have my own bedchamber, that is all."

"I am a man of patience, *querida*." He touched a black curl that fell near her cheek. "We will fulfill our bargain in due time. But we will share dinner before we share anything else. Though, I must say, you are quite tempting. More so than the most succulent leg of lamb." He trailed his finger down the slope of her jaw, expecting her to flinch from the coolness of his touch. He used no seductive trance on her.

Yet she didn't pull away. She closed her eyes, her chin trembling ever so slightly, almost in anticipation. The thought stirred his lust. But more than anything, it sent a thrill racing through his blood the likes of which he'd never experienced before.

Suddenly angry, he dropped his hand and turned on his heel, desperate to put some distance between them. They were linked emotionally, the bond already strong, gaining strength with each day that passed. The physical union would come next.

"We will partake of dinner, and soon, *querida,* I will partake of you," he growled.

Confusion flashed in her eyes for a moment. Then she nodded, her eyes narrow, slicing the distance between them.

He felt a moment of reluctance that he'd angered her. Then again, he didn't want her cooperation, her warmth or her understanding.

"Pray your carriage driver follows your instructions. If Miguel comes for you, he will die. I do not intend to relinquish the woman carrying my child."

"What?" The word was a gasp.

"You will give me a child. A son. *My* son," he said, ignoring her startled expression.

"As you wish," she finally whispered a moment before he slammed the door shut.

Raphael realized he was shaking. He stiffened his spine, determined to withstand the cold. He was the cold—fierce, biting, destroying the warmth. Slowly his muscles relaxed. The shaking ceased. Peace settled over him as the last flame dwindled down. *I win.* The words sang out in his head. *I win.*

"And you, my dear Mishella, lose," he growled. "To me. Your mind, your body, your soul . . ."

CHAPTER SEVEN

The next day, with her sketch pad in hand, Mishella entered the dense patch of forest that bordered a small pasture in back of the house. The afternoon sun hung high in the sky, yet a thick overlay of branches forced the light to fight its way to the ground. Mishella hugged the paper to her chest and stepped over gnarled roots and fallen limbs, guided only by a fond memory and a desperate need to escape, if only for a little while.

She'd been to the stream only once before, with her mother nearly five years ago when she'd graduated from college. Coming to the farmhouse had been a long-awaited treat after years spent living in the dorms at the University of Texas, spending even her summers taking classes in order to graduate with a degree in art history and gain a fellowship at the Museum of Fine Arts in Dallas. She'd felt isolated while away at school, and so the three weeks she'd spent with her mother and stepfather were among her fondest memories. They were heartbreaking memories, too, because of the special closeness she and her mother had begun to share that summer, when they had become more like friends than mother and daughter. It had ended less than a year ago when a drunk driver had crashed into her parents' car, killing them both.

The day before Mishella had packed for Dallas, her mother had pulled her aside and suggested a walk. Together, they had followed this very path. They had talked, laughed, even cried their goodbyes, holding hands and strolling through the trees, which now seemed thicker and more ominous than Mishella remembered.

Frigid air surrounded her, seeping through her jean jacket to prickle her arms and remind her of last night.

Last night. She glanced at the faint spot of red that marred the flesh on the back of one hand. It hadn't been there before her dream, she was certain. What caused it? A shiver went through her as she remembered the iciness of Raphael's ring. *It was only a dream,* she told herself again. As wintry as the weather had been, she could have gotten the mark from any number of sources.

"A dream," she whispered, reassuring herself. Last night had been a product of her sleep-fed imagination.

The crunch of leaves echoed, the only sound disrupting the stillness and penetrating her thoughts. She walked for endless minutes, driven by the need to see something familiar from her past.

The trees grew thick, the shadows more disturbing, and her uneasiness mounted. At the faintest brush against her shoulder, panic gripped her and she jerked around.

It's only a tree, silly. She closed her eyes and took a deep breath, shoving the branch away. *The stream can't be more than a few feet ahead.*

She started walking again, her heart still pounding, her senses alert to danger. If she didn't find the blasted water soon, she'd turn around and go back.

She had just decided to give up when she spotted a break in the trees. Relief washed over her as she parted a cluster of branches and stepped into daylight once again.

Sunlight filled the clearing, casting shimmering rays on the stream. On the opposite bank, the forest grew thick again, creating a nearly impenetrable wall of twisted brown tree trunks and foliage. But in the spot where she stood, a stretch of grass crept all the way to the edge of the crystal stream. Rocks glistened as the water rippled around them, over them. She felt herself snatched back in time.

Mishella pushed a strand of hair from her face and took a few slow, steady breaths. The moist air tickled her nostrils and sent a purifying rush of cold through her. Her heartbeat instinctively calmed. Peace enveloped her, guiding her to the stream's edge, urging her to sit down on the grass and savor this moment when not even the demon seemed able to touch her. The place was too remote. Fear became a bad nightmare she'd left in the forest. Here, only the stream, the grass, the sunlight existed. No unseen enemies and no haunting visions.

She splayed her fingers on the ground and felt the grass, cool from the weather despite the warming rays of the sun. Mishella plucked a few blades, grateful to touch something real when everything in her life had become so unreal.

Hugging her knees to her chest, she rested her chin on her hands and stared at a smooth, brown rock half-submerged in the middle of the stream. The rock stood undisturbed. Here, no misery existed, no pain, just peace. If only Mishella could feel the same complete peace. Instead, her heart felt heavy—overwrought with misery and anger at having to wrestle fate for her sister's life with a power she'd never asked for in the first place.

Stop feeling sorry for yourself. She didn't have time for self-pity. Her thoughts went to Stacey who napped back at the house, watched over by an attentive Inez.

Stacey needs your strength, your optimism. She needs you, Mishella. You can't let her down. Mishella took a deep breath. She had no intention of failing her stepsister. She knew what had to be done. And at least she wasn't alone in her struggle. She had Raphael....

His image lingered in front of her—the firm set of his jaw, his full, sensuous lips, the intensity of his midnight eyes. When he looked at her, she could feel him delve into her mind, reading her every thought, touching her every emotion. His gaze unnerved her, yet thrilled her, too, in a way that felt strangely familiar. Maybe because no man had ever touched her as she had imagined last night. The way she wanted him to touch her now.

Mishella shook her head. Now where had that thought come from? *From the knot in your stomach, the pounding in your chest, the wanting inside of you.*

Wanting? She'd never wanted anything in her life save solitude and time to pursue her one passion—art. Having always felt so different from everyone, Mishella had become accustomed to being alone. Her talent had set her apart, and her power had made her feel even further removed.

Despite the closeness that had begun to develop between her and her parents that summer five years ago, there had never been a real sharing of confidences. The power had formed a wall around Mishella, setting her apart, isolating her. Her parents didn't know what she could do, and she'd been afraid to tell them. Afraid for them. Afraid for herself.

She'd never felt connected to anyone. Until now. Until Raphael had come to her and she'd discovered someone else cursed with the power. They shared a special bond, perhaps one that went deeper than the power, she wasn't sure. Certainly the touch could account for the familiarity she felt with him. But could it account for the strange feelings he stirred inside her? The ache? The wanting?

Too many questions taunted her, threatening the small amount of tranquility she'd found. She forced them aside and picked up her sketch pad. She had so little time before she had to return to the house. Inez would be leaving at sundown.

Propping the pad on her knees, she made the first of a series of careful strokes, her attention riveted on the half-submerged rock. But she didn't draw the rock. Instead, she outlined a vivid pair of eyes, a bearded jawline, a mane of jet black hair. A perfect likeness of Raphael.

This wasn't the first likeness of him she'd put to paper, but certainly the best, she admitted a good while later as she set the charcoal down and surveyed her work. Engrossed in her sketching, she barely heard the crunch of grass behind her.

"It's getting late."

His deep voice startled her. The sketch pad fell to the ground as she twisted, her heart pounding. He stood only a few feet from her, a dark figure that almost blended into the murky shadows of the trees behind him.

"You scared me," she breathed, reaching for her pad and willing her heartbeat to return to normal.

"Sorry," he apologized, yet he didn't sound the least bit apologetic.

"It's all right." She prayed he didn't notice the shakiness in her voice. Clearing her throat, she glanced at the barest hint of sun visible above the trees. "I came out here to sketch a little. I must have forgotten the time. The..." She paused, wishing he wasn't staring so intently at her. "The water's beautiful," she finished, closing the sketch pad, not ready for him to see she'd been drawing him and not the scenery.

He covered the distance between them in a few swift strides, his gaze never leaving her face. "Beautiful," he agreed, yet Mishella got the distinct impression he wasn't talking about the stream.

She scrambled to her feet, unwilling to sit and have him tower over her. Still, she had to look up to see his face, to stare into those damnable eyes.

"You're early," she said, her voice softer than she'd intended.

"You're out of wood," he remarked. "The fire last night took the last of it."

She noticed the small ax in his hand.

"You came out here to chop wood?" Visions of the past night flashed in her mind. She wanted to believe he came in search of her. Then again, that thought was most unsettling. Downright distracting, and she didn't need any more distractions right now.

"If you want a fire tonight," he said, pulling his jacket tighter, "then we need some wood. With it so cold and all, there's none left to buy in town. But it doesn't matter." He shook his head. "There looks to be plenty around here," he motioned at the surrounding trees. "Give me a hand and then I'll walk you back. It'll be dark soon."

For a fleeting moment, she thought she would rather face the night alone, demon and all, than be so close to this man who conjured the most wicked dreams and set her blood on fire. One look at the stern set of his jaw, however, and she knew he didn't intend to have his offer refused.

Stop letting your imagination get the best of you. He's here to help you, silly. Last night wasn't real.

Dismissing her uncertainties, she murmured, "Thanks," and let him take her hand.

"Been playing too close to the fire, Mishella?" he asked, studying the red mark on the back of her hand. A smile curved his sensuous lips, but didn't quite touch his eyes.

"Not fire," she said. "I think it's a cold burn. Like frostbite or something." She tried to keep her voice steady and her mind off the strong fingers that trailed over the mark in a caressing, almost possessive gesture.

"The Devil's mark," he said, his voice suddenly thick. His eyes took on an unusual light.

"Devil's mark?" She wanted to snatch her hand from his, but his grip remained firm.

"Haven't you ever heard of the Devil's mark?" He sounded surprised.

"Well, yes, but it wasn't real," she said. "During the seventeenth century, the authorities used any mark on the skin, a birthmark, a blemish, to prove someone a witch. They were only excuses to burn innocent people."

"So you have heard of the mark." He looked almost pleased with her recitation.

"From school," she went on. "We spent a few days on the Salem witch trials in senior history." She didn't tell him the chill that worked its way up her back had nothing to do with what she'd read in books. *Devil's mark.* Her fear came from within, as if some past experience provided the knowledge.

Nonsense. She dismissed the disturbing notion. Especially now, standing in the twilight facing a man as dark as the Devil himself, and certainly as disconcerting. It didn't seem right to speak of such evil things. Evil was too much a part of her life already. An unwanted part she hoped to outdistance and overcome.

He smiled, the unusual gleam in his eyes even brighter. "So you know about witches and devils and things that go bump in the night?"

"Unfortunately. Can we talk about something else?" she asked, hoping to shake the sudden cold.

"Of course," he replied, glancing at her hand again, the subject obviously forgotten. "Be careful what you touch, Mishella, or rather what touches you. It's a shame to see such skin flawed." He glanced away for a brief moment. Then when his gaze met hers, his eyes were once again guarded, the gleam gone, and she found herself wondering if she'd only imagined the strange light.

Another shiver inched up her spine. "Thanks for the warning."

"The least I can do," he replied. Instead of loosening his hold on her hand as she'd hoped, he laced his fingers through hers. His grip, cool and firm and so very reassuring, forced her to relax. Thoughts of Devil's marks and witches left her as she let his strength fuel her own.

"Do you know how to use one of those?" She gestured to the ax, suddenly anxious to keep them both talking and her mind off his nearness.

"I'm from New York, remember? With the crime rate rising, we law-abiding citizens have to know how to defend ourselves." His smile widened.

Mishella couldn't help the laugh that burst from her lips. Raphael needed no ax to defend himself. As well-muscled and as foreboding a figure as he presented, she knew anyone who bothered him had to be a fool. She had to be a fool for being so close to him. For holding the hand of a man who seemed the very essence of danger.

He's a guardian, she reminded herself. *Your guardian. A man come to join powers and save you, and himself, from the demon.*

Still, guardian or not, he was dangerous to her sanity. He inspired thoughts she'd never had before. Erotic, forbidden thoughts that unnerved her.

"Kidding aside," she said, the need to keep them talking growing with every moment. "Where did you learn to use an ax? My stepfather used to tell me there's a definite art to splitting wood."

"My parents had a cabin in Colorado. I've done my share of wood splitting."

"Your family lives in Colorado?" she asked, suddenly eager to know some bit of personal information about him. He was still a virtual mystery to her.

"No."

"But you said—"

"My mother and father are dead." His words were clipped, meant to silence any further inquiry.

For a fleeting second, Mishella could feel his pain, so similar to her own it brought a tightening to her chest. Ignoring the inner voice that told her not to get close to him, she squeezed his fingers in a comforting gesture. "I'm sorry," she said. "I lost my parents barely over a year ago. It's rough."

"It's not so rough for me," he replied. "Mine have been dead a long time." Mishella sensed a hesitancy despite his words.

"What about the rest of your family? Do you have any brothers and sisters?"

"I'm an only child. I have no family."

"No aunts or uncles?"

"No one," he said, "now that my parents are gone." His words were abrupt, obviously intended to halt her questions about his family.

"So you've lived in Colorado?" she asked, her voice light, meant to ease the tension.

He stayed silent a moment longer, as if contemplating how much he wanted to reveal of himself.

"Off and on," he finally said. "My parents kept a home there, as well as in California, New York, Mexico and Spain."

"Spain?" She found herself intrigued.

"An estate near Barcelona."

"What did your father do for a living?"

"Shipping," Raphael replied. "My great-grandfather started the company when he came over from England. The Dalton heirs continued after his death."

"Including you?"

"I see that the company runs well now that my father's gone."

"How many ships do you have?"

"Fifty, plus two hundred warehouses and a trucking line here in the States. We have similar setups in two different countries."

"So that's why you spend so much time in town." Suddenly everything fell into place. His absence during the day, the late-evening visits. She could picture him holed up in his hotel room, his cellular phone in one hand, a laptop computer in front of him and a portable fax machine humming away in the corner.

"What do you ship?" she asked.

"Large freight for the most part, but we have no specific size limit."

"It must be a horrendous job. I bet you rarely see daylight."

"The company runs well without my overseeing every detail. I have loyal employees who look after things in my absence."

"Still, your coming here must have been a very big decision. To abandon your life and your business for an indefinite period of time..."

"A month isn't indefinite. Besides, I might be absent, but I'm very much aware of everything that goes on," he replied.

Mishella got the distinct impression he not only referred to his business but the situation at hand. Even when he wasn't with her during the days, she felt him. He felt her, too. Or so she hoped.

"Don't see me as the overworked businessman, Mishella. When I'm home, I have other interests, as well."

"Like what?" she asked, wanting to know what a man like Raphael Dalton did with his time when he wasn't roaming the country playing guardian.

He smiled as if hearing her thoughts. "I spend a great deal of my time running an antique gallery."

"Antique gallery," Mishella echoed, unable to ignore the small thrill that shot through her to find they had something in common besides the touch. "Your ring is an antique," she said, glancing at the sapphire. "How old?"

"Over five hundred years."

"You must be kidding!" she gasped, grabbing his hand to gaze into the brilliant stone. "That's ancient. How did you come across it?"

"Why the sudden interest?" he asked, pulling his hand away.

She ignored the tension that erupted, anxious for the camaraderie they'd shared moments before. "I just love antiques, that's all. That's one of the reasons I switched my major to art history. The past fascinates me."

"Does it, Mishella?" She sensed an expectancy in him as he waited for her answer.

"Yes," she replied, then said, "you said you lived in Spain. Are you Spanish?"

"On my mother's side."

"My mother had some Spanish blood," Mishella said.

"Of that I had no doubt, *querida*. Your coloring proves your ancestry."

The next few minutes passed in silence as they walked into the forest. The trees grew thicker, enshrouding them as the afternoon gave way to dusk.

"This looks like a good piece," he said as he dropped her hand to reach for a fallen tree branch.

Mishella stooped to pick up a small chunk of wood.

"Ouch!" she cried, jerking her hand back. The sketch pad tumbled to the ground, momentarily forgotten as she stared at the splinter that had pierced her finger.

Raphael turned, his face hidden in shadows. Yet she could sense his frown, his concern. "What's wrong?"

"Just a splinter."

"Let me see." He reached for her hand, pulling her closer to him until she felt the length of his thigh against her own. His unique fragrance—wild, untamed, almost savage—intoxicated her, stirring fresh feelings of desire.

With a careful touch, he forced the splinter partially out. Mishella's eyes watered, her desire instantly quelled by the pain.

"I'm sorry," he said. "I know it hurts, but this is a big splinter. Just hold still."

Pressing again, he managed to squeeze the wood the rest of the way out. Mishella shut her eyes and took a deep breath.

"It's bleeding," he commented a second later.

Her eyes opened.

"I'm sorry," he whispered again, a moment before he touched her injured finger to the warmth of his lips.

"It's all right," she murmured, unable to think clearly as he laved the wound with his tongue until her entire finger tingled. No pain remained, only tiny shocks that traveled up her arm.

The air between them was charged with an electricity that roused her every nerve and traveled through her body like a live current.

"It doesn't hurt anymore," she managed to say. Her finger might not have hurt any longer, but God how *she* hurt.

All over, but with a pleasurable sort of pain. "You're very resourceful."

"And you, Mishella, are very beautiful." She saw the hunger in his eyes and sensed his need.

Raphael touched his lips to her temple. The drumming in her ears increased.

"I've waited so long to touch you, Mishella." One hand went to the small of her back, drawing her even closer until she was pressed fully against him. "So long to feel you," he murmured, kissing the sensitive hollow of her ear. His breath tickled her, sending a shiver that started in her hands and ended in the tips of her toes.

"Can you feel me, Mishella? Can you feel how badly I want you?"

Undeniably, she could feel every inch of him hard against her body. The sensation both frightened her and thrilled her, pumping her blood even faster.

She tilted her head back to gaze up into his eyes, to lose herself in their midnight depths. For a moment, everything seemed to stop—her heart, her breathing, the buzz of night insects—everything. Absolute silence descended. Then he captured her parted lips with his.

He stroked the inside of her mouth with his tongue, the corners of her lips, tasting and touching every inch of her in a kiss that felt so right—so familiar, as if she'd always been meant to touch him and him only.

No. No. No! Warning signals flashed in her brain, quickly overcome as he ran his hand down the length of her back, then up again to wind his fingers in the hair at her nape. She trembled as he pressed her closer, his mouth harder, insistent in a kiss that bordered on savage.

Finally he tore his lips from hers to savor the length of her neck. "I feel your blood pound," he whispered, his lips at the base of her neck where her pulse beat a frantic rhythm.

She sagged against him, her legs weak, her senses overwhelmed. "The blood is part of what makes us who we are," he whispered. "Blood descendants."

"What do you mean?" she asked, only to have him swallow her question as he devoured her mouth for another exquisite moment.

"Touch me, Mishella," he said when he finally managed to pull away from her, his command a throaty growl she dared not ignore.

She placed her hands on his shoulders, then trailed her fingers down the length of his muscled arms. So much power beneath her fingertips. She brought her hands to his chest, moving them over every ripple, every bulge that confirmed his strength.

His hold on her eased as she felt a small shudder seize him. She almost smiled with the knowledge that she could affect him so.

Driven by the need to give back the same delicious sensations he gave her, she moved her hands lower to the waistband of his jeans. He instantly tensed.

She hesitated. But only for a moment, for his very presence compelled her to touch, to feel, to do all he wanted. All *she* wanted.

She touched the prominent bulge in his jeans. He groaned, moving one hand between them to cover hers. He guided her movements, back and forth, until his breathing grew even more ragged and every muscle in his body taut.

"You're so warm," he said, cupping her bottom with his large hands and closing the fraction of distance between them. He pressed her against him in a slow circular motion that took their breaths away.

"I need your warmth, Mishella," he said. "To lose myself inside you." His voice was an agonized plea that begged to be heard and satisfied.

As much as she wanted to deny, she needed him. The cool fingers she remembered from last night were now like firebrands, burning through her clothing and singeing her with an intensity that not only frightened her, but stoked the fire raging within. The sudden change in him was unnerving, and wondrous, as well. How she needed his heat.

She felt him pull her shirt loose from her jeans. With the briefest of movements, he undid her buttons. Then she felt his hands on her bare skin, pushing the edges of her jacket and shirt aside. She closed her eyes and relished the feel of one of his hands on her breast as he circled her nipple until the turgid peak pressed painfully against his palm.

The instant she felt the touch of metal on her heated flesh, she stilled. The ring . . .

The memory of their last encounter, of the icelike touch, the red mark on the back of her hand, flashed in her mind. *Devil's mark.* Her eyes snapped open. Fear jarred her from hazy pleasure back to the earthy smell of the forest. She couldn't let this happen. Not here. Not now. And not with him. She'd lose her sanity for sure.

"Stop," she whispered, pushing at his hands. "Please!"

She felt him stiffen. She felt the disturbing silence that followed and then she felt regret when he finally stepped away from her.

She couldn't see his eyes, but she knew his gaze was on her. It seemed to slice through her like a freshly sharpened knife. She snatched the edges of her jacket and shirt together and focused on the black shadows that were her boots.

"I—I'm sorry," she murmured. "This just doesn't feel right." *Liar,* she chided herself. It had felt too right. That was what bothered her so much. The first time wasn't meant to be like this. Thank God for the ring, or else . . .

Heat crept up her neck and she said another silent thanks for the darkness. She didn't want him to see how he affected her.

"This *is* right," he said. "More right than anything either of us has ever felt before." A pause followed. "We'll be together, Mishella. You want me as much as I want you." His voice rang with a confidence that unnerved her. "You didn't really want to stop me. Not really, no matter how much you try to convince yourself otherwise."

As he snatched up the ax, then turned and strode ahead of her, she felt her fear subside. The ache of wanting him returned in full force, so strong she wondered if she could resist him again. He was right. Damn him, he was right.

She wiped at her tears, grabbed her fallen sketch pad and hurried after him. He walked so fast she lost sight of him. Determined, she dodged branches and rushed forward. When she broke free of the trees into the field surrounding the house, she glanced around. He was nowhere in sight. Gone, as if he had blended into the darkness and become a part of it.

She held the sketch pad to her chest and headed for the house. A gust of wind lashed at her, lifting and whipping her hair into a tangled mass. She closed her eyes and stumbled forward.

Maybe he wouldn't come back to the house tonight.

That thought should have been reassuring, only it brought with it an undeniable disappointment. Despite all her mixed feelings—the strange connection between them, the fear and desire that seemed intertwined—she wanted to see him again. And that realization disturbed her more than the visions of the burned man.

Inside the decaying interior of the barn, the smell of rotting wood and damp earth pungent around him, Raphael touched a nearly burned-down match to the last candle. His gaze fixed on the sudden flicker of the flame that grew a brilliant white, the center as sapphire blue as the ring he wore. As radiant as her eyes . . .

Esteban stared out at the black, moonless sky. He felt the pounding in his temples. The same damnable headache, which had tortured him since she'd arrived, beat an insistent tattoo in his skull.

But the headache would soon leave him. Tonight his waiting would end and she would come to him. They would join physically. He had exercised a great amount of patience. But no more. Fate could no longer be put off. He wanted her. All of her. Mind, body, soul. They were connected mentally. Now he needed her body. Her soul would soon follow.

Thoughts of her had tormented him far too long. The drink did nothing but cloud his senses, not render him unconscious, as it had before. He had no relief from Belial, from the demon's damned domination of his soul. For now she would give him at least a few moments of peace. He would lose himself inside her, in her warmth, over and over, until he burst and spilled his seed deep within.

The slow creak of hinges disrupted his erotic thoughts. Turning from his place at the window, he stared across his bedchamber to the vision in the doorway. Only a few candles had been lit, but still he saw every exquisite detail of her, exactly as he had pictured her night after sleepless night.

Her eyes were wide, her cheeks slightly flushed. Black curls cascaded past her shoulders, a stark contrast to the ivory nightdress she wore. The lace bodice plunged low, hugging her full breasts to perfection. He felt himself harden and swell all the more at the sight of her dark, erect nipples visible through the sheer material. No woman had a right to be so beautiful. To have such an effect on him.

The urge to cover the distance between them, throw her to the bed and take her nearly overwhelmed him. But tonight was the first of many. Tonight she would offer herself to him, and the second union would be complete.

"Come here," he said, his voice gruff, raw with need.

She hesitated, still staring at him. He could feel his skin tingle as her gaze swept from his face to his bare chest to the waistband of his breeches. He knew she noticed his erection, barely contained beneath the fabric. He watched her swallow nervously. She would turn and run now.

She stepped forward.

With her came the incredible heat, warming his icy skin, firing his blood.

"The time has come, *querida,*" he murmured as she stopped inches from him. He reached out and traced one dark nipple through the lace.

"Yes." Her breath caught on the word. "Esteban," she whispered, her full lips parted as if begging for his.

Esteban accepted the invitation and drew her fully against him. "Tonight and every night you will be mine," he whispered, claiming her mouth, drinking in the sweetness he'd longed to taste. The waiting was over.

Raphael loosened his clenched fist and stared at the crushed box of matches in his palm. He inhaled, then watched the expelled breath meet the air and form a crystalline mist.

Sinking to his knees, he closed his eyes. He had been patient once before, and for that she had been taken from him and his soul had spent five hundred years alone in the darkness. But no more, Mishella, no more. The waiting was over.

CHAPTER EIGHT

"Where on earth have you been?" Inez exclaimed, throwing open the door as Mishella stepped onto the porch. "I was worried sick! The sun set nearly an hour ago."

"I—I lost track of the time," Mishella said, still trying to piece together her shattered resolve.

Worry lit the Mexican woman's eyes and Mishella felt a wave of panic. "Is Stacey all right? Has something happened?" The questions tumbled from her lips.

"Stacey?" The woman looked puzzled. "No. No." Inez shook her head. "The child has been asleep for the past hour. I was only worried for you, *mija*. The wind picked up so suddenly it blew the shutters off the back windows and gave me an awful scare. Then my foot started to ache, and that's a sure sign of trouble."

The panic subsided and Mishella grinned. "That's what had you so worked up? An aching foot?"

Inez frowned a full second before she gave in to her own smile. "I know I sound foolish," she said, cupping Mishella's cheek. "I shouldn't worry so much. I'm just an old woman letting her imagination get the best of her. But when I have a feeling—"

"You're usually right," Mishella finished, tossing her sketch pad onto a nearby table and clasping the old woman's hand. "But not this time. I'm fine." Mishella sighed. "You don't know how glad I am to be inside. The wind is blowing like there's no tomorrow." She shrugged out of her jacket and rubbed her hands together.

Inez continued to study her. "Are you sure you're all right?" she asked again, her frown returning. "You look a little pale, and my foot was hurting something terrible."

"I'm fine," Mishella assured her, carefully avoiding the woman's intense black eyes. "I guess the wind spooked me a little, too." She shivered. The wind hadn't spooked her. Raphael had. Or rather, her own reaction to him had. She shouldn't allow such intense feelings, not now when she had to keep her mind on Stacey.

She took a deep breath and hooked her jacket on the coat tree near the door. "I'm sorry I'm late, Inez. I was out by the stream and the time slipped away. I hope I didn't keep you too long."

"No, no. Thomas isn't here yet."

"Thank him again for fixing the washer and the hot-water heater. I wouldn't have made it through these past few weeks without them."

"No trouble. I hope he didn't surprise you. I know I told you Mingo would come...."

"It was nice of Thomas to take his place. It must have taken a great deal of talking to convince him to spend an entire Saturday out here working."

"I didn't do any talking. He got up and left the house before I even knew Mingo was sick."

"Really?"

Inez turned away as if she'd said too much. "He must have gotten up early and seen that Mingo felt bad. Thomas is a good boy." When she faced Mishella again, her smile once again in place, worry still filled her eyes. "He really is," she repeated. "I told Mingo that."

"What do you mean—" Mishella began, only to have her question cut short by a knock at the door.

As if on cue, Thomas Santibanez opened the front door, letting in more of the cold wind.

"Thomas, why didn't you honk?" Inez seemed startled. She hurried past Mishella, to stand in front of her son. "I told you just to honk."

"I know, but I thought I'd come to the door." Thomas peered over his mother's shoulder, his gaze finding Mishella. "Evening," he said, giving her a lopsided grin.

"It's certainly a cold one." Mishella folded her arms in front of her, trying to erase the goose bumps on her flesh.

"It's supposed to get colder." His voice held none of the warmth of his smile.

Unease settled in the pit of Mishella's stomach and set her nerves on edge. Another shiver worked its way up her spine. *You feel uncomfortable because you know he likes you,* she told herself.

Thomas continued to stare at her. His eyes were a shade darker, harder even, than their usual pale blue, and Mishella looked away, her unease growing. *Maybe he's upset because you wouldn't go out with him.*

As if sensing the sudden tension, Inez cleared her throat and fastened the hooks on her coat. "Thomas, you should have honked. Let's get going."

"How is Mingo doing?" Mishella asked, grateful for any distraction from Thomas and his scrutiny. She directed her question at Inez, but he answered.

"Dad's . . . still sick." He seemed to search for the words. "The doc can't seem to find what's wrong with him. The symptoms aren't normal. The fever comes and goes, up and down like a yo-yo. Even Ma's herbs don't work. Nothing does."

"Fever?" Mishella frowned. "Inez, I thought you said he felt better. How high is his fever?"

"Not very high anymore," Inez replied, her voice small, distant. "Don't worry about him. Can we go, Thomas?" The wary look the woman gave her son was unmistakable.

The uneasiness Mishella had felt the first night Inez and Domingo had come to her door returned in full force. She glanced at Inez, silently begging the woman to smile and calm her sudden fear.

Inez simply busied herself with her coat while Thomas kept his gaze fixed on Mishella, and the tension in the room mounted.

"You shouldn't be out here if Domingo is still sick. Take tomorrow off. A week . . . however long you need."

"That's what I told her," Thomas said. "I can check in on you and your sister while she stays home."

"That's not necessary," Mishella said.

"Nonsense," Inez argued. "Mingo doesn't need me anymore. There's no need to worry about him now."

"But you shouldn't be worrying about me," Mishella said. "Or Stacey, either. Don't stress yourself because of us. We can look after ourselves."

"And I can help them out," Thomas added.

"Stacey and I don't need—"

"There's plenty of me to go around." Inez waved Mishella to silence. "There's no reason I can't help out here. It's late, Thomas. Please, let's go." She tried to push him through the doorway in front of her, but he stepped to the side and she had no choice but to precede him.

"Thomas?" Inez called over her shoulder, but he didn't move. He leaned against the doorjamb, his attention on Mishella.

"The truck's running. You go on. I'll be there in a minute."

"But—"

"I'll be right there. Go on." There was an edge to his voice.

Inez looked uncertain for a moment, then she hurried across the porch.

"Buddy says your car's ready," Thomas said when Inez had stepped down off the porch.

"Buddy?"

"The guy who owns the auto repair. He said your car's been ready for the past week."

"But I thought it would take longer..." Her words died. "Didn't they have to order a special part?"

"A drive shaft?" He shook his head. "Yours was messed up, but Buddy managed to fix it. If you need a ride to town to pick it up, I can give you a lift day after tomorrow. Buddy's closed tomorrow, it being Sunday and all."

"I...that would be nice," she sputtered. *Raphael made a mistake about the damage. That's all. A simple mistake.* Dread settled in the pit of her stomach.

"Buddy says a friend of yours brought the car in." Thomas's statement seemed more of a question.

"I...yes," she stammered. "A friend of mine from...from college."

"A boyfriend?" Thomas asked, blond brows raised. "I thought you didn't know too many folks around these parts."

"Just him, and he's not my boyfriend. He's an old friend." She felt a pang of guilt about lying, but somehow her words didn't seem like a lie. At times, she felt as if she'd known Raphael a long, long time. Then of course, there were moments when she realized what a stranger he really was.

It'll take three weeks to fix. The words replayed over and over in her mind like a broken record.

"Has he been here recently?"

"I beg your pardon?"

"Your friend. When was the last time he visited?"

"I don't think that's any of your business," Mishella replied.

Thomas frowned. He seemed different tonight—hard and not very friendly.

Friendly? Staring into his glassy blue eyes, she wondered how she could ever have thought them friendly. "I think you'd better leave," she told him. "Your mother's waiting, and my personal life is none of your concern."

He didn't budge. Instead, he continued to stare at her.

After several seconds, his face split into a slow, easy smile. "I guess not. I didn't mean to sound nosy. I was just concerned." His gaze softened. "Sorry if I came on a little strong."

Suddenly his prying made sense. He'd made no attempt to hide his attraction to her. He was jealous. She relaxed. "You did, but it's all right."

"My offer still stands. Monday I can take you to get the car."

"Thanks, I'd appreciate that."

The blare of the truck's horn reminded them of Inez.

"I'd better go," he said, glancing over his shoulder. "I'll see you around noon. Stay inside and keep warm. The night looks like it's going to be a cold one." He pulled his battered leather jacket tighter, shoving his hands into his pockets. "Is your friend coming tonight?"

"Nosy again," Mishella reminded him. He colored, and she added, "But for the record, no." She wondered why that knowledge filled her with such regret.

"Good." He looked relieved. "It's not a night for visitors. I'll see ya." He turned and disappeared onto the porch.

The wind whipped through the doorway, billowing the curtains and blowing a few magazines onto the floor. Mishella forced the door shut and slid the bolt into place.

You cracked the engine block. The car will take at least three weeks to fix.

The car has been ready for the past week.

She touched trembling fingers to her temple. Monday she would go into town with Thomas and pick up her car. When she saw Raphael again, she would confront him with what she'd learned. He would explain to her that he had made a mistake about the extent of the damage. A simple mistake.

A mistake or a lie?

The blood makes us who we are. Blood descendants. His words echoed in her head. She'd asked him for an explanation many times, yet he'd declined to give her one. He'd said he didn't know. *Blood descendants.*

As she turned and started toward the bathroom, desperate for a hot shower, she tried to ignore the fear that settled in the pit of her stomach. He was her guardian...sent to help her. He had no reason to lie to her. No reason at all. Or did he?

Later that evening, Mishella hugged her arms, still unable to shake the chill that had gripped her on her way back to the house. Several hours and a hot shower had done nothing to dispel the cold or ease the terrible suspicions swimming in her mind.

Several hours.

The murky shadows of dusk had long since given way to night. Raphael hadn't come to the house. Not that she'd thought he would after the way things had ended between them. She'd felt his anger when he'd turned away from her.

We'll be together. His words magnified the chill she already felt.

Don't be such a wimp, she told herself. She wanted him. He wanted her. Sex was the natural result when two people felt such strong attraction.

Two people who cared for one another. Who'd been honest with one another. Raphael had lied to her. Why? Was he really who he said he was?

She closed her eyes, hating him for lying and hating herself even more for wanting him despite everything.

The sound of the clock startled her. She swung around in a swirl of white cotton robe. Staring at the gold pendulum rocking back and forth, she flinched with each chime until the twelfth sounded. Midnight.

You're better off that he didn't come back, she tried to convince herself, though disappointment swirled, turbulent and fierce inside her. She wanted him to come back so that she could question him. Demand some straight answers. But that wasn't the only reason. Her body screamed for him, for his fingers drifting over her skin, for his lips whispering across hers.

If only she didn't feel him close by, beyond her reach but near enough to stimulate her senses. Tonight, however, the feeling seemed stronger, as if their touching, their kissing, had bonded them in some inseparable way that even distance didn't sever.

She glanced at the blackened ashes in the cold, lifeless fireplace.

No wood. No fire. No heat. No Raphael.

Visions of him filled her head—from the warmth of his mouth, the intensity of his gaze, to that small instant of familiarity. Mishella shook her head and tried to hold on to her self-control, only to feel it slip away as she contemplated what would have happened had she not pulled away from him in the woods.

You had to pull away. Nothing can happen between the two of you. Not with Stacey still sick. She needs all your strength.

Mishella touched a trembling hand to her forehead, damning herself for being so weak. She had to forget his touch, the feel of his lips—

"Stop it!" she whispered, the sound of her own voice echoing off the living room walls and returning some semblance of control.

She snatched her sketch pad from the coffee table, grabbed a piece of charcoal and walked down the hall to Stacey's room.

Pausing, she leaned against the doorjamb for a full moment and observed her stepsister. Her face was a smooth, peaceful mask as she slept, her breathing only slightly labored, her snores faint, comforting in their steadfast rhythm.

"Soon, Stacey," she whispered. "No more pain. Just four more days." She swallowed at the sudden lump in her throat. Barefoot, she walked across the hardwood floor, the soles of her feet silent on the cool surface. She placed a gentle kiss on the girl's forehead, smoothed several strands of tousled blond hair, then straightened and turned toward the window.

Outside, tree branches swayed, casting dancing silhouettes into the otherwise dark room. Wind hissed through the crannies of the house, sending trembles dancing up her spine. She felt something strange in the air. An expectancy almost, but of what, she had no idea.

For the past two weeks, the air had been cold but still. Tonight, however, the wind had picked up as if stirred from a peaceful rest to lend an almost eerie quality to the night, to set it apart from the others.

She moved closer to the window, drawn to the pale sliver of moon visible through the trees. Desperate to focus the anxious energy that flowed through her, she flipped open the sketch pad. Leaning against the windowsill, she stared past the flailing branches out into the yard illuminated in an almost ethereal glow of moonlight.

She didn't mean to draw him, but her hand seemed to move of its own volition. Touching the charcoal to the page in front of her, she put another image of Raphael to paper, this one similar to the one with the beard and the shorter hair she'd done down by the stream.

The vivid eyes came to life beneath her strokes. Deep, intense and so very bewitching, they stared straight through her, rousing an ache deep inside until she felt her heart beat faster.

It's a picture. Just paper and charcoal. Yet the fluttering in her stomach, the catch of breath in her throat, couldn't be ignored.

She tore her gaze away and closed the book with a slap. *He's not here,* she told herself. If only she could believe it. *You must. You must.*

With a firm shake of her head, she tossed the sketch pad onto a chair and stared out the window again. That was when she saw the light filtering through the cracks of the barn door.

She knew she should have been frightened, but she wasn't. Across the expanse of crisp grass and dew-iced earth, she felt him. He beckoned to her, and she could no more resist than she could deny the sudden draft that seeped around the edges of the window and swirled around her, licking at her heated flesh.

Moments later she stepped off the porch and walked across the yard, her movements slow and steady, trance-like. Yet she didn't feel the calming effects induced by a trance. Her heart pounded, shooting white-hot flames through her veins. Even the cold wind did nothing to soothe her. There was only one source of relief.

She spread her palm against the rough, decomposing wood of the barn door. As she pushed the door open, the slow creak grated on her nerves and made her heart beat faster. She stepped inside.

Mishella had never seen so many candles. They were everywhere—lining the dirt floor, sitting atop the fencing surrounding the abandoned stalls, even on the broken-down tractor parked in one corner. The flickering flames bathed the interior in a strange sort of light. A light that glowed with vigor and charged the air with anticipation. And in the midst of the light, he stood.

His profile reflected power and ageless strength, as if he knew and controlled everything around him. His eyes were closed, his head tilted slightly back, his thick, black hair flowing past his shoulders. A fine crystal mist surrounded him, a thin sheen of perspiration glistening on his bare torso. He was perfection in a dark sort of way that captivated, as well as frightened. And again, she knew she should be afraid, but she wasn't. Far greater than her fear was her desire to touch him. To have him touch her.

A current of air circled her, sneaking beneath the hem of her robe, and she shivered.

She studied the flame-cast shadows on his sinewy shoulders, like the last rays of sun flickering on the smooth waters of a mysterious ocean. She found herself wondering why he didn't feel the cold as she did.

"I've been waiting for you," he said, his voice deep, laced with the sexual hunger she saw the moment he opened his eyes.

"Last night wasn't a dream, was it?" She already knew the answer, felt it in her heightened awareness, the strange, nervous quiver in her stomach.

He shook his head and faced her. "No, it wasn't."

She trembled as visions of the experience came flooding back. She could almost feel the heat of his lips....

"You know you weren't dreaming," he said. His eyes turned a shade darker, if that was possible, for they already resembled glittering chips of black onyx.

"But it seemed so...so *unreal.*" She sensed the truth, but to accept it meant surrendering to him. And how could she give in to a man so complex and so unsettling? A man who kept so many secrets? She didn't know him, not really.

You know me well, Mishella, a voice seemed to whisper in her ear, *his* voice, yet it couldn't be. He hadn't said the words out loud.

"It was real, Mishella. The way you felt. The desire." He lifted his hand and trailed his fingers in midair. "Just as real as it is right now. As real as this."

Shock jolted through her when she felt the delicate touch along her cheekbone. The space that separated them ceased to exist.

"This can't be happening," she whispered, shutting her eyes to break his hold. Her imagination had to be playing tricks on her. He couldn't stand across the room and actually touch her. Last night had to be a dream. This had to be a dream. Everything was too impossible!

Not impossible, Mishella, his voice whispered again.

She felt the roughened tips of his fingers as he slid them around the slope of her jaw, down the sensitive column of her neck. Her skin tingled and rose in gooseflesh, testament to the contact.

Impossible! her mind screamed over and over, battling with his voice that told her the opposite. She took a deep breath. The wild fragrance of him filled her nostrils and snapped the small thread of denial. The strange tightening in her stomach increased. Then heat rushed through her, until she ached and burned with the same lustful craving she'd had the night before.

This is meant to be. She heard his voice, sneaking into her mind, refusing to be ignored.

She should turn and run from the barn, far from this man who seemed more than a man. He possessed a dangerous strength that set him apart, that drew her to him despite the loud voice of reason that told her to stay away. But the invisible ties that bound them were powerful. The moment held a certain inevitability. *This is meant to be.* His words rang once again, this time with an irrefutable truth.

"There's a fine line between real and unreal," he said, his voice smooth, hypnotic. "Between past and present, pain and pleasure, need and want. Quit denying me and yourself. Open your eyes."

She did as he commanded. "This is a dream," she whispered, as if saying the words would make them true. "A dream. Unreal."

But in his eyes everything unreal seemed very real. And the moment her stare locked with his she knew on which side of the line she stood. Her need for him was real, all consuming, painful.

"Forget your doubts," he urged, as if sensing the turmoil that raged within her. "Feel only me, Mishella. No doubts, no fear. Only me and how much I want you."

Her heart beat to a frantic rhythm that increased as he invaded her mind. He reached across the space between them to caress her ears with his words, her body with his touch, weaving his spell even tighter until all hope of escape seemed futile.

It was as if he knew when the last doubt left her. But he wanted more than silent acquiescence. He wanted to hear her say the words of surrender.

"Why did you come out here?"

"I felt you," she admitted. "I wanted to come. I wanted what almost happened last night." She paused, but only briefly, for his gaze compelled her to speak. "I want tonight," she said, surprised at the thickness in her voice. "I— I want you so much it hurts."

She saw the tensing of his muscles and knew her words had affected him. "It doesn't have to hurt," he said, his voice gruff. "The time for us has come."

He made a slight motion with his hands and her belt came loose. She felt the pressure of his palms on her shoulders. Then the robe glided down her arms and pooled at her feet.

He studied her for an endless moment and his eyes took on a strange light. They seemed to glow with the same brilliant intensity as an open flame, filled with heat and mystery.

The breath caught in her chest. Her nipples rose, pressing against the thin silk of her nightgown. The bodice felt tight, confining, as her breasts swelled, eager for his touch.

His stance was rigid, every muscle in his body taut as he waited. His gaze revealed an all-consuming desire that promised the most exquisite pleasure, should she answer his silent call.

Come to me, querida.

She took a step forward, then another, until she entered the circle of candlelight.

He towered over her, barely a fraction of space between them. She closed her eyes to the feel of flesh meeting flesh.

The hands and lips that claimed her were merciless in their possession. Mishella felt the breath sucked from her body and her vitality drained as he crushed her against his unyielding strength. A growl rumbled from his throat and she stiffened. Afraid, yet eager.

When she felt his desire, rock-hard against the softness of her stomach, sanity intruded for a brief moment. Long enough for fear to take root. The roughness of his hands, the hard pressure of his lips, fed that fear. Panic welled up in her.

She balled her fists and pushed against his chest, but he seemed undaunted. His hold tightened. Futilely she struggled, her fear growing, outdistancing the need that had consumed her only moments before. Fear at the relentless hands of a man so powerful, a strength so overwhelming.

She finally managed to twist her face away. "Please!" she gasped, her voice bordering on a sob.

Where all her struggles had been useless, the one word, or maybe the tears that blinded her, stopped him cold. He let go of her with a suddenness that surprised them both.

She blinked, staring at him as he raked his hands through his hair, his mouth set in a severe line. A muscle in his jaw flicked angrily.

What drew her attention more than anything, however, were his eyes, eyes that had been aglow with an almost brutal force mere seconds ago. Now his gaze was once again as fathomless as a starless sky in the black of night.

"Go," he ordered, his voice harsh. He turned away, massaging the muscles of his neck. "Get out of here, Mishella. Now . . . while you can."

She watched his back, knowing she should do as he said. She wanted to but she couldn't make herself turn and leave. She'd pulled away just now because he'd frightened her with his savage touch, but as much as he'd frightened her, he'd intrigued her, as well. Even more, perhaps.

She wanted him—the man from her dream, the man who touched her and fired her blood. She remained absolutely motionless for a moment. Then she touched his shoulder.

He flinched, but didn't pull away. "You wanted me to stop. I did." His voice held a note of defeat. "Damn it, I did!" He sounded almost disbelieving and extremely angry with himself, as if he had battled some unseen power and lost.

"You were hurting me."

He stayed silent for a long moment. "I know," he replied, turning back to her, his face a mask of severity, unabated by softness.

A shiver of apprehension eased up her spine, but she paid little attention. It was only a shiver, not the terror she'd felt a moment before.

She let herself be pulled into his gaze. A rush of heat surged through her, and she marveled at the sudden breathless fear, or maybe it was excitement, he incited with just one look. At the moment, lost in the depths of his eyes, overwhelmed by this compelling man, she couldn't discern between the two. Nor did she want to. She only wanted him, and that wanting took control and prompted her to reach out.

He locked his fingers around her wrist before she could touch him again. She saw a flicker in his black eyes, and for a fraction of a second, she regretted not having fled when he gave her the chance. She froze, feeling her heart hammer in her chest as she watched emotions, raw and painful, war in his eyes. Then his grip tightened and he jerked her roughly, almost violently, to him.

The strange light returned to his eyes as he studied her, then it disappeared, lost in the smoldering blackness. He loosened his grip to slide his hand up her arm and over her shoulder, while his other encircled her waist and pressed insistently at the hollow of her back.

The lips that touched hers this time were like a whisper, soft and teasing and so very tender. Doubt and fear dissolved as he nibbled her bottom lip, coaxed her mouth open and slipped his tongue inside. He stroked the interior of her mouth until she seemed to melt against the hard contours of his body.

She felt the fingers that slipped beneath the strap of her nightgown—fingers that lingered at the three lines on her shoulder—but she didn't think to resist. She thought only of the warm lips that became increasingly more demanding, matching the eagerness of her own.

He slipped first one strap down her arm, then the other, before tugging the bodice to her waist. Tearing his lips from hers, he lifted his head and stared into her eyes before letting his gaze drift down to her throbbing breasts.

"So beautiful," he murmured, touching one taut peak with his fingers.

The hand at the small of her back pressed her closer, arching her against him, urging her breast upward into the moist heat of his mouth. His lips closed over her nipple, nibbling and suckling as she whimpered from the exquisite torture. She buried her hands in the silky thickness of his hair when he delivered the same delicious assault to her other breast.

Eyes closed, chest heaving, she clung to him, afraid to let go, afraid to lose him to the angry violence she'd been given a glimpse of.

But the hands that slid down the curve of her back to push the nightgown past her hips were slow and gentle, despite their heated insistence. There was no violence now.

She ran her hands over the rippling muscles of his back and locked her fingers around his corded neck.

He cupped the rounded swell of her bottom and drew her against him until they touched thigh to thigh, chest to chest. She felt his heart beat a rapid tempo in time with her own. His breath was hot against her ear, his lips brushing the curve of her jaw while his hands kneaded the sensitive flesh of her buttocks.

Warm hands. Hot, even. A change that both thrilled and baffled her. She wanted to understand what the warmth meant, but the sensations flooding through her demanded her full attention.

She felt him hard beneath his jeans, stretching the material until she thought the fibers would give way. He rubbed against her most sensitive spot, the roughness of the fabric creating decadent spirals of heat that wound their way through her to stoke the already raging fire of need.

"Would you give up your reality to join me, Mishella?" he breathed, sending shivers down her spine.

"Reality?" she gasped.

"Yes. Come with me to my reality. Let me show you what is meant to be. What *was* meant to be."

"Yes," she heard herself whisper.

"Feel what I feel." He scooped her up into his arms and she felt herself being lowered. But instead of feeling the biting cold of the ground in that next instant, she felt a soft, cushioned warmth, as if she'd fallen into a cloud.

"See what I see," he said.

Her eyes fluttered open. Candles still surrounded them, only she lay in the familiar bed of her dream. Darkness loomed above her—impenetrable and threatening—beyond the reach of candlelight. Then Raphael lowered his body over hers, blocking out the darkness. She saw only him, felt only his bare skin against hers.

"Where are we—"

Her question was cut short by the cool press of his finger to her slightly parted lips.

"In my reality, *querida*. You see through my eyes now."

She stared up at him, at the raven black hair that fell slightly past his jaw, the lines of which were lost beneath the covering of his beard. Thick, black lashes framed his eyes, which mirrored her own hunger—a hunger so fierce she knew it would consume them both.

Surely her sanity had snapped. She had to be hallucinating. She couldn't be here in a room straight out of the fantastic musings of her mind with a man who seemed so much a part of her that he felt her every need, knew her every thought. She couldn't . . . but she was.

When he touched the inside of one of her thighs, she caught her bottom lip between her teeth. Her breathing all but stopped as he stroked and caressed, his movements going higher until he found the throbbing heat between her legs.

A sob tore from her throat, only to be silenced by his mouth claiming hers. She met his kiss with an urgency that betrayed the tightening in her stomach. Thrust for thrust, her tongue tangled with his, until her senses were alive with the feel, the touch, the taste of him.

When he slipped a finger inside her, she arched, drawing him deeper, shocked at the intrusion, yet desperate for it. Then he dipped another into her warmth, and she moaned over and over as he moved deep within her, touching her very essence.

She tightened around him in a painful but delicious rhythm. The coil inside her wound tighter until her body turned to liquid—a white-hot liquid that bubbled and rippled with each rush of mind-blowing sensation. Heaven could have been no sweeter.

"Ah, but there is more heaven," he assured her, reading her thoughts. "You're wet for me. I can feel you . . . so hot, so ready. I'll show you much more of heaven." His words held a promise that stoked the flames of passion shooting through her veins.

She became acutely aware of his arousal hard against her hip. He moved over her, opening her legs with an intimate touch of his hand that sent a shudder through her. Easing her legs up on either side of him, he probed her moistness with the tip of his manhood, a low groan rumbling from his throat.

"So long," he whispered, his voice hoarse, almost pained, as his gaze captured hers. "I've waited so long to feel you. A dozen lifetimes."

She, too, felt as if she'd waited an eternity for what was about to happen. She touched her hand to his face and felt the softness of his beard before running her palm over his roughened cheek, her fingers through his thick hair.

Tears brimmed in her eyes, as she remembered a past of loneliness and longing for a man she could never have. A man strong enough to endure the very fires of hell but not strong enough to admit his love.

"I'll wait no longer, *querida,* to claim what is mine." His eyes held hers as he plunged into her, filling her, possessing her as he was always meant to.

The tears spilled over to run down her cheeks.

"No tears," he said, his voice soft, soothing. His movements stilled. He brushed the wetness away with a tenderness she remembered so well.

She wanted to see his eyes, to see what he was thinking, but the pain was overwhelming. Pain between her legs for the virginity lost and pain in her heart for the man she'd lost.

The man who had finally returned to her. The man whose voice and touch came to her in a flood of memories that rendered her paralyzed.

"Esteban," she sobbed. "Esteban . . ."

CHAPTER NINE

The memories came like a steadily increasing storm—soft at first, bringing only a hint of recollection. Then the heavens opened and she felt the downpour of emotions, the thunder of her heart, as if she was not only remembering, but living a distinct moment from the past.

But the moment was new, a chance to complete what had been left unfinished. She'd found him again and never would she relinquish her hold.

Now there would be no intrusion as there had been that night so long ago. No one to stop her from joining with this man. Esteban. Raphael. One and the same spirit.

He waited, poised above her, his body tense, as if he expected to be ripped from her as he had been before.

She delved into his gaze, reading the question in the simmering midnight depths. He hesitated, his muscles tightening, his powerful shoulders shaking with each ragged breath he took.

She knew he waited—for her to resist him, to beg him to stop. But she wouldn't. She hadn't then and she wouldn't now. Not ever. She wanted him as much as he wanted her. Maybe even more.

"A dozen lifetimes I've waited," she murmured, remembering his words. "I can't wait any longer."

Surprise registered on his face, only to disappear when she arched against him, drawing him deeper and gasping at the sweet pain that filled her. A fire ignited in his eyes, flaring like a spark in the dry heat of summer.

"No more waiting, *querida*," he groaned, sheathing himself within her until a cry burst from her lips.

She clutched at his sinewy back and lifted her hips to take all he could give.

He withdrew, only to glide back into her wetness, this time driving farther, stretching and filling her, until she felt as if he'd touched her very soul.

He plunged into her over and over until she knew sensations so exquisite that nothing could ever compare. But the feeling intensified. With each swift motion, he sent her senses soaring higher, until she felt her body shatter into thousands of tiny, weightless specks, as light as stardust drifting in a night breeze. She bucked against him, exploding into a wave of violent trembles, lost in the throes of the sweetest misery.

Capturing her lips with his, Raphael held her in a deep, demanding kiss. Only when her shaking subsided did he make one final thrust. A deep groan rumbled from his throat as he shuddered, spilling himself into her.

Mishella wrapped her arms around him, feeling the liquid warmth deep within where his rigid shaft still pulsed.

I've waited so long, love. She heard the words in her head, feeling his satisfaction as deeply as she felt her own.

I, too, have waited a long time, her mind answered.

"A long, long time to love you," she added aloud, holding his face with her hands, gazing deep into his eyes. She needed to be sure he heard. "Centuries to say how much I love you."

For the briefest moment, his muscles tensed. The eerie glow returned to his eyes, and Mishella glimpsed the violence inside him. The evil . . .

A cold fist of fear tightened in her chest and she regretted her words. Still, prompted by centuries of longing, she said them again. "I love you," and in her mind the phrase played over and over, feeding her courage, despite the clenching of his jaw and the narrowing of his eyes.

She held his gaze, knowing she had to face the same horror he faced if she intended to save him this time. Together, they could overcome the evil.

Together. That's what he'd told her.

Yes, together they could win, *if* that part of him that once loved her still existed, lost somewhere inside the powerful man who looked ready to strangle her.

"I love you," she whispered again, feeling his fingers at the base of her throat. "I always have. Always."

Slowly the strange light faded until she saw only his dark, smoldering eyes. Then he gathered her in his arms and held her close. Her fears subsided and she felt only him, not the cold ground beneath them, nor the frigid air that swirled about. His warmth closed around her—a warmth that had been denied her for five hundred years.

"Sleep, Mishella," she heard him say.

"No. If I do, you'll leave me. I know it," she said, her voice bordering on a sob.

He touched his lips to her temple, letting them linger in a soothing caress that calmed her doubts and her racing heart.

"Sleep, Mishella," he whispered again, the warmth of his words lulling and so very entrancing.

Unwillingly she closed her eyes as the exhaustion of the past few weeks took hold. She marveled at how her body tingled from his nearness, feeling alive yet heavy at the same time. Movement was impossible. Not that she wanted to move. She wanted to stay in his arms forever. To have him deep inside her, filling her for eternity and then some.

He eased away from her.

Stop him, her mind cried, but the blackness held her in its grasp, pulling her in.

He lifted her in his arms.

Sleep, she heard again, the word pushing her into unconsciousness. But Mishella fought with all her strength.

When she felt the warm bed beneath her, the quilts that he placed on top of her, she struggled to lift her hand, to touch him one last time. He was leaving her. She knew even before she heard his whispered command.

"Sleep, love." He feathered his lips across hers, trailed his fingers over her cheek as if memorizing the curve of her face. Then he moved away, and the fear and loneliness and emptiness closed in.

Come back! her mind screamed, but her lips wouldn't form the words. *Please don't leave me! Please!* she called to him. He didn't answer. He was gone, and she was left to journey through the dark maze of her past alone. To relive who she'd once been.

Fear snaked through her body, gripping every nerve until she lay frozen, barely breathing, afraid of the past and the future and what truth waited for her in her dreams.

She wanted to open her eyes to reality, go to Stacey, hold her and forget the past. She needed to think of the future and of what tonight's revelation would mean. Only the memories called to her, reminding her of the woman she'd once been.

"No!" Mishella managed to cry. She didn't want to know the same agony of that night, a night filled with darkness and despair, instead of the love that should have been. A night of pleasure that had ended in pain, sealing both Maricela and Esteban's fates and separating them forever.

He should have stopped the men, but he'd been powerless. Because of her, he'd been powerless.

Remember, his voice echoed in her mind, draining Mishella's last ounce of resistance.

She opened her mind, powerless herself to keep the memories at bay a moment longer. Fear slipped away and suddenly she found herself anxious. Eager to embrace who she'd once been and learn from the mistakes she'd made. Now that she'd found him, she had no intention of letting him go again. She'd fight Satan himself.

As she walked the dark tunnel, back through the centuries, across time and space, she realized she just might have to.

"I've waited my entire life for this," Esteban said, his voice ragged. "A lifetime filled with misery. But I would gladly spend a dozen more for one moment with you," he said, allowing himself the smallest bit of penetration. "For one moment of this."

Maricela felt her body pull at his, greedy, ready to suck him in, but he held his control as if determined to relish every moment, every sensation.

"Please, Esteban," she begged. "I, too," she panted, "have waited . . . a lifetime." She stared up into his eyes and saw herself mirrored in their dark depths. At that moment she knew he restrained himself for another reason. He wanted her words. Her thoughts. He wanted to know that she felt what he felt.

"I've waited a lifetime for *you,*" she admitted. "I knew the first moment I saw you. I knew you were the one. I knew that I—"

A loud banging silenced her.

"Open in the name of the Holy Office!"

"The Holy Office?" she gasped, her glance flying from Esteban to the door, then back. Desire subsided as panic streaked up her spine.

Esteban didn't move. "Finish, Maricela. Say the words." His gaze held hers with such intensity she felt her fear subside. In that instant, locked in his embrace, her body melting into his, the threat of the intruders paled in comparison to the desperation in his voice.

"Tell me," he demanded again.

"Open this door!" The pounding continued.

"I knew then—" she began.

"Please, señor!" It was one of Esteban's servants. "Do as they command. They've killed some of the others!"

"—and I know now—" she continued.

"Break down the door!"

"—that I love you."

The sound of splitting wood echoed through the room.

But for Maricela, time stood still as Esteban held her immobile with his eyes. Her heart catapulted at the raw emotion she saw there. She knew then, whether he said the words or not, he felt the same.

The door crashed open. Dozens of men pushed their way inside.

Esteban tore his gaze from hers, his face a mask of sheer rage as he reached for his sword.

"Stay put, Devil!" a voice shouted, but Esteban had already locked his fingers around the handle.

"Esteban!" Maricela screamed, seeing the man behind him, the steel blade flashing in the candlelight a second before the man plunged it down into Esteban's shoulder.

He merely flinched, his face registering no expression other than the same cold fury. Blood ran in rivulets down his arm and chest. Determined, he reached for his sword again.

Hands grabbed for him, wrenching him from her.

"Maricela!" she heard his voice as the men closed in around him.

"Esteban!" she cried, scrambling to the edge of the bed, struggling to catch a glimpse of him before the men hauled him through the door, his blood leaving a trail across the rug.

"Get up, woman!"

She clutched the bloodied sheet, still straining to see him. "Esteban!" she wailed, her voice like the cry of a wounded animal.

"Get her up!"

More hands reached out, closing over her shoulders, only to be jerked away.

"*Dios mio,* she carries the Devil's mark," came the startled gasp.

"Impossible. Señor de Ruiz himself says that she has only been bewitched. She does not carry the mark."

"Look. She does, I tell you! She carries the mark—the same as *his.*"

"Seize her! The Inquisitor must know."

"But what about her husband? He will be very angered that we have disobeyed his orders."

"He can take his grievance to the Inquisitor."

This time when the hands reached for her, Maricela couldn't pull away. There were too many of them.

"No!" she screamed, feeling the sheet ripped away, her heart along with it. "Noooo!"

Mishella shot straight up in bed, her heart thundering with each labored breath. Her hand went to the three tiny lines at her shoulder. She'd always thought the lines were some sort of birthmark. Only now she knew the truth... they'd been her deathmark. The Devil's mark.

No! her mind screamed. The marks came from Esteban. He might have believed himself possessed by evil, but he had been a man, as well. A flesh-and-blood man, just like Raphael.

She clutched her ice-cold hands together in her lap and glanced at the window. Moonlight still peeked through the tree branches, sending faint shadows dancing across her quilt-covered legs. Raindrops splattered the pane, trickling down the glass like the tears on her cheeks.

Grabbing her pillow, she hugged it to her aching chest and tried to come to grips with the past, the future. Now.

She was a direct descendant of Maricela. That was why the woman's spirit lived inside her. That and the fact that she'd been born on the day of Maricela's death—February twenty-seventh, exactly twenty-two days following Esteban's execution.

Raphael was the reincarnation of Esteban. February sixth—his birthday—had been the day Maricela had lost Esteban. The day she'd lost her heart and her future with the pass of a torch.

The blood makes us who we are. Blood descendants.

The Malvado blood flowed through Raphael's veins. And so did the evil. It lived and breathed and fought for control.

Mishella crumpled to the bed, fear and joy fighting a battle within her. Fear of a man who'd cursed her once, and joy because that same man had shown her life. Love.

But he'd seen only death, known only the fury of the flames.

"Esteban," she whimpered, closing her eyes tightly. "I'm so sorry." Sorry for wasting precious time with her declaration of love. If only he'd reached the sword a second sooner.

But he'd wanted to hear the words I love you.

Despite a lingering sense of regret, she found herself glad she'd told him. Glad he'd known her feelings before he died.

Glad because she knew that, though he shouted words of hatred and thought her a traitor, he loved her, anyway. The same as Raphael loved her now, even though he wouldn't admit it to himself. She knew, just as she'd known then.

She wiped at her cheeks. The time for regret had passed. Esteban had returned. And now she had a second chance to erase the tragedy that never should have been and prevent the tragedy that loomed in front of her.

Death waited—for her, her stepsister and Raphael, too. Mishella wondered if she could save herself and those she loved this time. Or would she lose everything? Would she lose him again for another five hundred years, or for eternity?

Raphael skidded to a stop near the side of the road, the trembling in his hands so severe that he could barely grasp the steering wheel.

Traitor! came the growl.

He shoved open the door and climbed from the seat, desperate to escape the voice that hammered in his head.

Wind lashed at him. Rain pelted him. The trembling became more violent, and the voice more insistent.

Remember who you are. What you are.

Raphael sank to his knees, grasping the edge of the car door as the blackness threatened him.

That was why he'd left her. He couldn't risk the demon seizing control. He couldn't face the thought that he might come to and find Mishella dead at his own hands.

That's the way it should be. She remembered. You possessed her. She must die now. She owes us.

"No!" Raphael lunged to his feet and crashed his fist into the back window, the glass cracking in response. The pain...he needed the pain. He didn't want the blackness or the cold. He wanted to feel.

He leaned against the side of his car, cradling his bleeding hand, the burning a blessed relief from his usual numbness. There was still a human side to him. Just as there had been a human side to Esteban.

"Esteban, you look like hell, but then I guess that's only fitting considering the charges being levied against you." The familiar voice echoed off the stone walls of the prison.

Esteban took a painful breath and forced his eyes open a fraction, only to close them again at the blinding torchlight, which penetrated the pitch-black cell where he slumped against the wall.

"And these quarters," the voice continued. "Such quarters aren't suited for the lowest peasant, much less a man of your distinction. A prince—son of the Evil One himself, or so I'm told."

Esteban willed his eyes open again. Four distinct shadows loomed in front of him. He blinked, watching the four merge into one—one that stepped closer to bend down in front of him.

"Ah, but at least you don't have to share your quarters with the rest of the filth under charge by the Inquisition. You are a true prize, Esteban. All of Spain has been talking of you these past weeks. It is not everyday the Holy Office apprehends such a blasphemer. Rest assured that the Queen herself will attend the auto-da-fé tomorrow."

"Miguel..." Esteban managed to whisper, his throat on fire. "What do you want?"

Miguel de Ruiz smiled, the expression a mockery to the coldness in his eyes. "I have come at the request of the Grand Inquisitor himself. It seems you are a most stubborn man, Esteban. But then, I warned the authorities when I first went to them."

"Maricela..." Esteban closed his eyes. He could still see her, smell her, as if they'd been together only moments ago, instead of weeks, or was it months?

"Ah, my faithful wife," Miguel stated. "She is lovely, isn't she? Bewitching, I'd say, but then she was the one bewitched, was she not? By you and your evil ways. Open your eyes, Malvado!"

Esteban caught his breath when Miguel grabbed a handful of his hair and jerked his head back. His eyes snapped open.

"Did you really think I would just let her go?"

"...supposed to be dead."

Miguel chuckled, releasing his hold to brush at the sleeves of his coat. "A few cracks of my whip had her driver confessing every detail of her *safe* delivery to your castle. You should have disposed of him when you had the chance. But then, we might not be having this conversation had you been so careful."

"Where is she?" Esteban swallowed, the taste of blood bitter on his tongue. He longed to reach up and wipe his mouth, but his arms were heavy, one broken in several places from the strappado he'd been subjected to upon his arrival in the torture chamber. And then there were the manacles....

"I think the Inquisitor's little forms of persuasion are starting to wear on you," Miguel commented, his merciless gaze scouring Esteban's starved and mangled body. "Which, of course, brings me to my business here."

"Maricela," Esteban whispered. He had to know what had become of her.

Esteban! Her screams still rang in his ears, so distinct and heart-wrenching. He had to know.

"Ah, yes. You did inquire about her, didn't you? Well, I expect she's resting comfortably at the moment, maybe even choosing a new gown to attend your tribunal. She does love a celebration. And since she had a hand in bringing the feared Malvado to justice, I'm sure she is all the more excited.''

Esteban opened his eyes wide against the onslaught of light, Miguel's words penetrating the veil of pain that hung over him.

"Shocked, Malvado? I would think a man as brilliant as you would have seen right through her. You have dealt with far more worthy adversaries, but then none quite as beautiful as my wife. She can be very convincing when she puts her mind to it. I bet she even told you the story of her father's abuse.''

"You're lying," Esteban growled, digging his fingers into the dirt floor, flinching at the fire that shot up his arms. "What... did... you... do... to... her?''

"Nothing, I assure you. You, on the other hand, have done a great deal. Then again, Maricela always had a taste for blood, Malvado, even before she met you.''

Esteban stiffened.

"Yes, I know of your little bargain. Maricela filled me in on the interesting details. Which brings me to my business. I've come to give you one last chance to save your soul.''

"I'd rather... die," Esteban mumbled.

"You will. Tomorrow. You are a trophy for the papal authorities—an evil man brought down by the cross—yet they still fear you.'' Miguel chuckled. "That's why they do not intend to wait for a confession. You have managed to withstand even the severest forms of torture. You have the Evil One on your side, Malvado. That's why they intend to burn you tomorrow, with only Maricela's confession as evidence.''

"Confession?''

"Yes, indeed," Miguel said. "The minute the authorities seized her, she confessed your guilt and pleaded her own innocence. I would advise you to stick to making deals with the Devil, Esteban. He is probably more loyal than any woman, especially my dear wife."

"In fact," Miguel continued, "only the Devil himself could have seen you through these past weeks. The Inquisitor is frustrated to no end. Your stubbornness has worn his patience. You are going to die, with or without confessing. But being a faithful supporter of the Church, I have come to offer you one last chance at redemption. Confess your guilt, profess repentance, and face your death tomorrow as a cleansed man."

"Go to hell."

"No, I think you are the one headed there, dear friend. I am on my way home to bed my wife. These past weeks she has been most grateful that I have spared her the horrible torture you've been subjected to. You see, Maricela is a selfish woman. She willingly turned on you, Esteban, in order to save herself."

"No," Esteban whispered. "She...loves..."

"You? A man born of the Devil?" Miguel laughed. "May the Devil save you now, Malvado."

But Esteban knew the Devil wouldn't save him. He had betrayed one of the Devil's own—Belial—by softening to Maricela, and the demon meant to have his soul. Tomorrow.

"So much for love, right, Malvado?" Miguel sneered.

The flames of the candles glowed brighter, blinding, and Esteban felt the tremors in his hands.

"But rest assured," Miguel added, "she will not escape unscathed. I will make her pay for betraying me." Miguel touched the whip at his side. "I might add a few more scars to the ones on her shoulder. Maybe a few on her face..."

The manacles snapped and Esteban reached up, locking his fingers around Miguel's throat. "I'll see you in hell," he hissed, the light blinding, bloodlust tightening his grip.

"Guards," Miguel gurgled, clawing at Esteban's hand. "Help..." His strangled cries filled the dungeon.

The door burst open a moment before Miguel went limp.

"Captain?" a guard cried, rushing forward.

Esteban loosened his hold on Miguel's throat and closed his eyes as the guards moved in and the shaking seized his entire body.

Betrayed. The word echoed in his head, hammering at his temples, stoking the fire raging inside him, feeding the fury of the demon.

He would see Maricela in hell even if it meant waiting a lifetime. A dozen lifetimes. She wouldn't escape him. Not again.

Raphael tilted his face to the downpour of rain, feeling the water stream down his cheeks, his neck, drenching his clothes.

She betrayed you. She betrayed us. Remember your vow.

Still, he couldn't kill her. He, Raphael, couldn't kill her. But Belial...

He closed his eyes.

The demon would settle for nothing less than her soul.

Raphael felt the rain come harder, the wind whip more violently, and then he felt the icy fingers wrap around him, shaking him.

"No," he growled, hauling himself out of the weather and into the car, but the cold followed him, and the tremors. And in the end, as he slumped against the seat, the blackness won—just as it always had in the past.

* * *

"You didn't finish the pancakes." Mishella eyed the half-eaten breakfast on the tray in front of Stacey.

"Aw, Shell, I'm full. Besides, my stomach feels a little funny." Stacey rested back against the pillow and closed her eyes.

Mishella reached down and brushed a few strands of hair away from her stepsister's forehead, her hand visibly trembling. She quickly pulled away and balled her fingers.

Control, she told herself. Think only of Stacey. Not Esteban. Not Raphael. Only Stacey. She had to, or else she would find herself crumpled in a heap, sobbing her head off, and such foolishness she couldn't risk. She had only three days until the third touch.

A touch she would make with or without Raphael.

A life for a life.

If he no longer meant to help her, then she would meet her death willingly. Stacey had to live. She had to!

"Do you want to watch some television?" Mishella managed to ask, hoping her voice didn't sound as hollow as she felt.

"No. I feel a little sleepy. I think I'll just take a nap." Stacey opened one eye and stared at Mishella. "You look like you could use a nap, too. You didn't sleep well last night, did you?"

"I slept plenty," Mishella replied, feeling her cheeks stain. She touched her hand to Stacey's slightly warm forehead. The fever was returning.

Three more days.

"Did Raphael come last night?"

"Y-yes, he did." Mishella averted her gaze to concentrate on tucking the covers around Stacey's legs.

"That's why you didn't get enough sleep." Stacey snuggled down beneath the quilts. "You were probably up late smooching."

"Very funny. You need to rest."

"Yes, boss," Stacey said, a smile lifting the corners of her mouth. "Can we play some cards later?"

"Maybe."

"Then you can tell me if Raphael's a good kisser."

"Funny again," Mishella said, turning and heading for the kitchen, desperate to escape Stacey's innocent prying. The questions brought back the memories, the hurt.

Later, as she sat at the kitchen table, a cold, half-eaten piece of toast on the plate in front of her, images of the past night flashed in her mind. She could see him again, taste him, feel him.

"I told you there would be no escape this time."

Mishella heard the words a split second before the blackness closed in on her. Then she saw the blaze, and in the midst stood the burned man—his voice, his eyes now so familiar.

I never tried to escape, her mind replied. *Never.*

"Liar! You betrayed me, and now you shall die. You will feel the torture of the flames this time."

"I felt the torture before!" Mishella cried, burying her hands in her face. "Like you, Esteban. Like you."

She shoved away from the table and ran down the hall.

In the living room, she grabbed her sketch pad and ripped picture after picture from inside.

Laying the drawings side by side, she compared her pictures of Raphael to those of the burned man. They were the same. The demon had come for her in the guise of the man she loved.

Guardian. She wanted to laugh at the notion. Instead, she closed her eyes as the tears spilled over. Raphael had caused the car accident, the scalding water in the shower, the visions, the fear.

Yet she loved him.

And she could free him—their love could free him, if only he'd let it. But he hadn't been strong before. He'd let doubt override his feelings—and the demon control his heart.

Not again, Mishella vowed, wiping the moisture from her cheeks. Raphael would be stronger than Esteban. Stronger than the demon.

She flipped to a page with vivid blue eyes—the woman she'd seen time and time again in her mind. Trailing her fingers over the colorful sketch, she realized she stared into her own eyes—Maricela's eyes. The blue-eyed woman had been a vision from the past, trying to warn her of who she was, what she was and what waited for her in the future.

Raphael waited for her. Raphael and the demon—one and the same—but not for long. She would free him. This time, if it took all she had, even her life, she would set them both free and save Stacey in the process.

Maricela's love for Esteban had saved her from the demon in the first place. She'd lost her life at the hands of evil men, declaring her love for Esteban even as she'd taken her last breath. That was why her spirit had journeyed into the light rather than the darkness. Love had made the difference then, and it would make the difference now.

She would make Raphael fight this time—for her, himself and their love. No more darkness, no more death and no more demon.

Only light. Blessed, soul-cleansing light.

CHAPTER TEN

Wiping at the tears that streaked her cheeks, Mishella closed her eyes and listened to the rain pounding the roof like an overzealous drummer.

What had started as a drizzle in the early hours of morning had increased throughout the day, falling harder and heavier.

Mishella had waited, hoping and praying Raphael would come. She had to see him.

Not the burned man in the vision, but the living, breathing man who had loved her last night.

Then again, she hadn't even seen the vision since that morning. And she hadn't seen Raphael since last night, either.

"Please let him come," she whispered to herself as she settled onto the couch, her legs curled beneath her as she pulled the blanket tighter. The chill that gripped her seemed almost unbearable.

But she knew he wouldn't come. She felt the cold, the emptiness, as if he had drifted far away from her.

What drove her crazy, however, was wondering what kept him away—his conscience or the evil inside of him? Either way, she still had to see him.

The rain persisted, and without a car or telephone Mishella had no hope of contacting him.

She called to him with her mind. Over and over, all day, and when the murky gray clouds gave way to black, she continued to beckon him.

He wasn't listening. Or he didn't care.

Tomorrow, she promised herself, leaning her head against the sofa arm. Tomorrow she would find him and she would know the truth. For now, if only she could fall asleep and escape the emptiness, morning would come quickly.

But the night proved long, and sleep as elusive as Raphael. Mishella tossed and turned on the sofa, then paced the hall until finally climbing into bed with her stepsister. Closing her fingers around Stacey's, which clutched the crucifix, Mishella felt the worn cross against her palm and remembered another silver cross that had belonged to Maricela.

Peace slipped over her, and for the first time that day, her tears dried. She fell into an exhausted sleep.

"Are you ready? I've got to be back at work in a couple of hours." Thomas ducked his head into the doorway of Stacey's room. Clad in a faded blue jacket pulled tight over his navy work overalls, he looked much older than his twenty-four years. His long, blond hair was tied into a ponytail, away from the wide planes of his jaw. His features seemed harsher than usual.

"Almost," Mishella replied. *Nonsense. He's younger than you,* a voice whispered. She bent down and gave Stacey a quick kiss. "Don't give Inez too much trouble."

Stacey nodded, her eyes closed. "Since when have I ever been any trouble?"

Mishella shook her head, watching Stacey smile at her own words. "You?" She raised her brows. "Never." She smoothed the blond bangs from her stepsister's warm forehead. "How do you feel?" she asked, her voice growing serious.

"Really tired."

And feverish, Mishella added silently. "Rest and I'll bring you some fudge ice cream."

"It's a deal," Stacey mumbled, nuzzling the corner of the pillow and burrowing beneath the blankets.

"Where's your mother?" Mishella asked as she turned toward Thomas.

He seemed oblivious to the question. He leaned against the doorjamb, his stare riveted on Stacey. For a split second, Mishella could have sworn she saw a slight narrowing of his eyes, a tightening of his jaw.

"Thomas?"

"Yeah?" His smile slid back into place as he met her gaze.

"Where's Inez?"

"The kitchen, I think. We'd better get going."

"Let me just say goodbye first," Mishella said, moving past him. She found Inez in the kitchen dicing onions for a pot of chili that simmered on the stove.

"Inez, we're leaving," Mishella said, noting the way the woman's head jerked up, a startled look crossing her face. Her eyes were red-rimmed, her cheeks streaked with wetness. She sniffled and wiped at her face with a handkerchief.

"Inez, are you all right?"

"It's the onions," Thomas cut in.

Mishella met the woman's bloodshot gaze. "Is that why you're crying?"

The woman stayed silent as she glanced from Mishella to Thomas, then back again.

"Isn't that right, Mama?" Thomas asked, crossing the room to place his hands on his mother's shoulders. "The onions and peppers do it to her every time."

Mishella saw something flicker in the sparkling depths of the woman's eyes. Desperation? Fear? Sadness? Mishella shook the thoughts away. Her imagination was definitely working overtime. It was the food, plain and simple. Even standing across the room, she felt her own eyes water.

"Isn't that right?" Thomas asked again. His grip seemed to tighten, his knuckles turning whiter.

Inez opened her mouth, only to snap her jaw shut and nod.

"Are you sure?" Mishella asked, still unconvinced. "If you're upset about something, I'd be glad to listen. Just tell me what's bothering you."

Inez shook her head and mumbled something incoherent.

"Don't mind her," Thomas said. "Right, Mama?"

The woman's head was a frantic bob this time, her son's hands large and pale as they rested against the blue-flower print of her dress.

"Then I guess I'll see you in a few hours," Mishella said, turning to leave. The woman's voice followed her out.

"Be careful, Mishella," came the whisper.

Mishella glanced back at Inez, but the woman wore no expression as she stared silently after Thomas, who had joined Mishella in the doorway. It was as if the words had never been spoken.

Still, they followed Mishella out to the truck.

Be careful, Mishella.

"Don't mind my mother," Thomas told her a few minutes later as he opened the passenger door of the pickup to let her climb in. "She always gets teared up when she chops onions and peppers."

Mishella clutched her hands together in her lap, eager to ignore the uneasiness that had settled in her stomach. Undoubtedly her feelings stemmed from the need to see Raphael. She had to find him, talk to him.

Thomas rounded the front of the pickup to the driver's side, then climbed behind the wheel. Soon they were speeding down the road, spraying gravel. The windshield wipers dragged across the glass, back and forth, erasing the light drizzle, only to have it reappear instantly.

The sky was still dark and overcast, but the rain had calmed some. Now, if Mishella could only quiet the storm that raged inside her.

"Are you all right?"

Mishella forced her attention to Thomas, who directed a concerned frown at her.

"Fine," she said.

"You're sure?" He didn't look convinced. "Because if anything is bothering you, I'd be glad to listen."

"Thanks, but everything is fine. I just have a lot on my mind."

"Sometimes it helps to talk things out."

"Sometimes." But Mishella knew this wasn't one of those times. How could she ever explain her relationship with Raphael? Did she even want to? No. It seemed almost a breach of confidence to talk of him to anyone else, especially after what they'd shared. "Things are very complicated for me right now, Thomas. I don't understand what's going on in my life myself. I doubt I could explain it to you, and I'd rather not try. Not yet, anyway. But thanks for asking." Her voice was soft.

"I'm a pretty understanding guy," he replied, placing his hand over hers and giving her fingers a squeeze, his touch as cold and clammy as the vinyl seat they sat on. "But if you

don't feel like talking, you don't have to. Just remember—
I'm here if you need me.''

"I'll remember,'' she whispered, wishing he'd move his
hand.

He smiled, then to her relief placed both hands on the
steering wheel.

The wipers squeaked back and forth, each sweep grating
on her nerves.

"I can't believe it's still raining,'' she mumbled, desperate to fill the uneasy silence.

Her sentence drew a thoughtful look from Thomas, who
replied, "If it wasn't for this freeze, I'd say the rain came at
a good time.''

"Yes,'' she said mindlessly, her attention going back to
the quick motion of the windshield wipers.

Thomas continued. "Everything around here is always so
dry. Now take those fields for example.'' He pointed across
Mishella at the landscape to her right. "A good rain will
have that grass...''

His words became a monotonous drone as Mishella's
thoughts returned to Raphael. She felt her stomach clench
and her heart drum faster. She took a deep breath, but the
farther they drove, the more heightened her senses became.
She could feel *him*.

Even Thomas's ceaseless talk didn't loosen the knot in her
middle. She nodded a time or two, murmured "uh-huh,''
and kept her gaze fixed in front of her. Only a few more
miles.

Finally they turned onto the main road leading through
town. With the day so dreary, the traffic was sparse, and
they reached the auto-repair shop in a matter of minutes.

The building was a converted barn, a peeling sign hanging out front. Mishella watched as Buddy, a bear of a man

wearing grease-stained overalls and a baseball cap, slammed the hood on her car.

"It's all yours, honey," he said, opening the door for her to slide into the driver's seat.

"How much do I owe you?" She reached into her purse for her wallet.

"That friend of yours that brought her in took care of everything. You just be careful on these roads. I wouldn't want to have to drag this baby back. I hate working on these computerized engines. Dang cars are as temperamental as any woman."

Buddy flashed her a grin and she smiled. Then she stared across the parking lot to where Thomas stood feeding quarters into a soda machine, and her smile slipped away.

"What was wrong with the car?" she asked on some wild hope that Thomas had been the one mistaken.

"Drive shaft," Buddy muttered. "But I fixed it in no time."

Disappointment welled up in her. *Why did you ask? You knew Raphael lied. You knew when you realized who he was. What he was.*

"Thanks, Buddy," Thomas said, coming up beside the man.

"No trouble. Pleasure meeting you," he said to Mishella, then turned and strode into the shop.

"I'll see you later," Thomas said, leaning down to peer inside Mishella's car window. "Are you sure you don't need any company during your shopping? I've got about an hour, and I'd be glad to help."

"You've done too much already, Thomas. I appreciate the ride."

"Then I'll see you later. Tell my mother I'll pick her up around six."

Mishella said goodbye and backed the car out of the parking lot. Steering down the main street through town, she steeled herself for her next task.

She drove slowly, scanning both sides of the street. He'd said he was staying at the motel.

She spotted his car before she saw the half-rusted Vacancy sign hanging in front of the old building. Pulling up next to his Jaguar, she took a deep breath and climbed out.

Paint peeled along the edges of the building, the doors a cracked mass of dingy white. She went to the door directly in front of his car and knocked.

No answer. She knocked again. Then again.

Either she had the wrong room or he wasn't there. Bracing herself, she reached for the doorknob.

The knob turned easily and she found herself peering inside the dark interior.

"Please let this be the right room," she said as a shiver streaked up her spine. She stepped inside, into the dark, into the cold.

The curtains had been drawn, leaving the room in shadows. Only a sliver of light peeked around the edges of a door she guessed connected to the bathroom.

She eased the door closed behind her, letting the darkness swallow her. Her eyes took a second to adjust.

Then she saw him.

Sprawled in the middle of the bed, his back against the headboard, his legs spread before him, he wore only a pair of jeans, his chest bare like his feet. His muscles flexed with each tremor that shook his powerful frame.

"My God, you're going to catch pneumonia!" she gasped, rushing forward to snatch a blanket from the chair beside the bed.

She turned to spread the blanket over him. He shot out a hand and gripped her wrist with icelike fingers. Then his eyes opened, the depths glowing with a strange light—a demonic light.

"No," he growled, tightening his grip until the blanket slipped from her fingers.

"But the cold . . ." she whimpered.

"Comes from within," he finished, his voice harsh. "There's no escaping it." He stared deep into her eyes, into her soul, and she knew he meant to frighten her, but still she didn't look away.

They fought a battle of spirits—a battle Mishella had no intention of losing. She held his gaze for endless seconds, frightened, yet even more determined. Slowly the strange light started to fade. His shaking subsided to a small shudder and he released her.

"Get out of here," he said, leaning his head back against the wall and closing his eyes. "I don't want you here."

Mishella scooped up the blanket and threw it over him before he could stop her. Then she crossed the room and shoved the thermostat up, her gaze never leaving him.

"You know," he said, his eyes still closed. "You finally remembered."

"Yes." Her breath caught on the word.

"Why did you come here, then?"

"I had to see you." She neared the bed, drawn to him despite the anger she could feel boiling in him. "When you didn't come last night, I had no choice."

"You're testing fate, Mishella. You escaped once before, but you might not be so lucky this time. You might find yourself burning right alongside me." A bitterness laced his words, betraying the anger and stinging Mishella with its intensity.

"But I wanted to," she whispered, knowing she sounded crazy, but she was compelled to tell him all she was feeling. She came to stand at the side of the bed. Her attention riveted on the hard lines of his face, the unpleasant twist of his mouth. "I wanted to die with you," she admitted, her voice bordering on a sob. "God, how I wanted to be with you, to stay with you, even in death."

"*You* signed my death sentence!" he exploded, the words erupting like thunder in the chill silence of the room.

"No!" she cried, shaking her head. "They tortured me and—"

"No more than they did me, Mishella," he cut in, his voice cold, furious.

Her heart seemed to stop as she remembered her own pain and that of the man she so desperately wanted to believe her. She had to make him understand. To make him see. "The pain was so bad at times," she whispered, "I don't know what I said or didn't say. I never signed a confession. Miguel forged my signature. I wouldn't have done such a thing. *Never!* I loved you."

The silence lengthened between them for several excruciating moments.

"You came to me willingly," he began, "asking for my help, knowing what I was. The bravest of men feared me, yet you sought me out without a thought for your own safety. You accepted who I was, or so I thought." His mouth lifted in a satanic smirk that iced the blood in her veins.

"In the back of my mind, I expected your betrayal," he went on. "But my heart—my damnable jaded heart— needed to believe that you could love me. Me!"

He slammed a fist against his chest and she flinched. She felt his rage eating away at him, at both of them.

"A man possessed by Satan's own," he went on. "A man who had never felt anything but lust and greed." He laughed then—a hollow, forced sound that sliced through her heart.

"You loved me all right. So much you sent me to the stake without a second thought."

"No!" She dropped to her knees, reaching for his hand. "I didn't forsake you to save myself. I swear!"

She watched emotion war on his face—trust with mistrust, acceptance with contempt. "Let me show you," she pleaded. "See what I see. See what you never had a chance to."

A long, unnerving moment passed, then his fingers tightened around hers and she closed her eyes.

"This is your last chance. Repent, witch!"

Maricela clamped down on her already swollen lip as the hot iron burned into her shoulder where Esteban had made the three marks. She arched up off the trestle, her arms and legs straining against the ropes.

"At least you shall meet your death without the cursed Devil's mark on your body. Repent!" The Inquisitor's voice rang in her head, the word echoing over and over. *Repent! Repent! Repent!*

"Again!" he commanded. She heard the crank of a handle. The ropes tightened. Pulled. Stretched.

White-hot pain wrenched through her body. She tried to scream, but the sound died in her raw throat. She prayed for death to come. In death she could join him.

Esteban! she cried silently, remembering the stench of burning flesh, the expressionless mask of his face as the flames had swallowed him.

His voice had crossed the distance of the courtyard to her. "We will meet again, Maricela. When the time is right, we will meet again. There will be no escape. I will claim what is mine," he'd vowed, his eyes alight with the brilliance of the flame. "*You* are mine—in mind, body and spirit. Always!"

He hadn't uttered another word, nor a scream, even when the blaze had risen higher.

"Repent, witch." The voice seemed to come from far away now. "Repent and beg for mercy on your soul, or you will feel the rack once more."

Her heart beat faster, the only sound except for the pounding in her head.

"Again!" the voice commanded. The ropes tightened.

Pain streaked through her body, exploding into her skull, and she sank into the blessed blackness.

But the relief was short-lived. The moment the guard jerked her to her feet, the soles of which had been burned days, maybe weeks, ago, she regained consciousness.

A scream lodged in her throat. Her legs buckled, but the hands on her arms forced her upright.

"Cover her nakedness," the Inquisitor commanded.

A coarse robe was thrust over her head, then the hands seized her again, half-carrying, half-dragging her through the dungeon, up the stairs, outside.

"Step back!" A guard shouted, shoving past the crowd that closed in on her.

The swarm grew frenzied. Shouts hammered in her head, following, taunting, as the guards hauled her through the street, to the auto-da-fé.

"Back woman!" the guard shouted as someone rushed at Maricela.

"I beg to lay a cross on this condemned woman, that she may know the truth of Christ. That He may protect her in the last moments."

"Then be quick, woman," the guard commanded.

Maricela felt a hand at her neck, then cold metal at the hollow between her breasts. She wanted to open her eyes to see, but she couldn't. Her head rolled to the side.

"Strength, child," a woman's voice whispered.

"Now, out of the way, woman!" And the hands started dragging her again.

Shoved to the ground, Maricela found herself bound once more, her hands above her head. The stake was hoisted upright, the fire stoked.

"For thy sins, you shall pay, Maricela de Ruiz. You are the Devil's own. May your soul burn in hell."

"Esteban!" she cried, the flames licking at the ends of the robe, engulfing her body. Higher, higher. Hotter, hotter. "Esteban!"

Mishella felt the tears on her face. She opened her eyes and found Raphael staring at her, his eyes dark, fathomless.

"I didn't betray you," she whispered, her hands trembling. "Miguel lied. I faced the same death as you. He only wanted to torment you. He was jealous, hurt. He wanted to hurt *you* because he knew I loved you as I never loved him."

Raphael made no response for a long, agonizing moment. Then he muttered, "Get out," and let go of her hand.

"Don't you see?" she demanded. "I didn't betray you! Once they killed you, I signed my own confession about what happened between us, but I didn't repent. Repent," she scoffed, feeling her own bitterness rise to the surface. "I was supposed to repent to men who tortured and killed in the name of mercy. They were the ones who should have repented, the ones who should have burned. Not you..."

Mishella wiped at the tears trickling from her eyes. "I didn't betray you," she added, her voice soft, pleading. "You saw for yourself." She reached for him again, but he shrugged away.

"I wish you *had* betrayed me," he hissed, clenching his hands into fists. "Damn it, I wish you had!"

"But why?" she asked, her voice incredulous.

"Because I feel the cold again, the same as I felt it when I sat in that prison cell week after week waiting for death. I promised myself then that I would find you again somehow and make you pay for betraying me."

"I didn't—"

He lifted a hand to silence her. "I came after you, Mishella," he continued, "to take your soul for cheating me so long ago. I needed to possess you, to spoil you. You should have been frightened by me. When I touched you, you should have fought me, begged for mercy." He pounded his fist on the mattress. "But you didn't. You didn't hate me like you should have."

"I love you," she said, closing her fingers around his fist. "I always have."

"You can't," he spat. "You know what I am. You know—"

"You're a man."

"I'm evil, damn it! Even now, I can feel him inside me battling for control. He wants you, too, Mishella. He's strong."

"You're stronger. *We're* stronger."

"You don't understand how powerful he is."

"I understand I love you and I know you love me."

"No," he growled. "I can't love."

"You did before."

"I wasn't supposed to." His voice softened then, and she knew he remembered the feelings between them, as real as what flowed between them now. "Then you came along. I didn't even realize what was happening to me." He sounded sad, but then his words grew harsher. "But my feelings made him angry. He's angry now...." The glow returned to his eyes, piercing her to pull at her soul. "Get out of here while you still can."

"I want to help you!" she cried, grasping his hand. "Please, let me."

He was on his feet in a second, hauling her upright, his hands clamped on her shoulders as he propelled her toward the door.

"Leave now. Don't you understand that I can't control him? He'll kill you, Mishella. *I'll* kill you!" His voice was a tormented, inhuman growl. He shoved her against the door. "Get the hell out of here!"

She turned and stumbled, blindly searching for the door-knob. Tears poured down her face. Finally her fingers found the knob and she tried to pull.

"Wait!" came his agonized voice. He pinned her to the door, his arms on either side of her, holding her prisoner, his chest pressed against her back. "I'm sorry," he said, his voice softer. "Sorry I couldn't resist you then, and sorry I can't resist you now." He bent his head, his lips near her ear. "Don't cry, Mishella. Please."

"I love you," she murmured again. "I know you love me. I know."

"It's not enough." She felt the shudder that went through him at those sad words.

"It is! I won't let him have you this time," she vowed, twisting around in his embrace to stare up at him, barely a space between them. "I won't."

"You're too late."

"No! There's a part of you that belongs to me," she whispered, touching her fingers to his stubble-roughened jaw. The coldness had disappeared. She felt only the warmth of flesh meeting flesh. Man meeting woman.

"There's nothing for you in loving me, Mishella. Only an eternity of darkness. I have nothing to give you. Only hell."

"You give me heaven, the sweetest I've ever known."

She touched her lips to his neck and rested her palm against the hard wall of his chest, feeling his heart beating the same furious tempo as her own. "Show me heaven, again," she begged. "There doesn't have to be any more hell."

When his gaze met hers, she saw the struggle in him. The strange light that flickered in the midnight depths, the man battling the demon, and she wondered for a moment who would win.

When he grabbed her wrists with his viselike fingers and pinned her arms above her head, she might have thought the demon the victor. But the eyes that met hers were depthless and jet black, and very, very hungry.

He captured her mouth with his, slipping his tongue inside, stroking and tasting until she slumped against the door, only his grip on her wrists holding her up.

She drew a ragged breath when he tore his mouth from hers to leave a fiery trail down the length of her neck to the hollow between her breasts. Then he released her, his hands going to the buttons of her blouse, his movements urgent as if they had not a moment to spare.

He pushed the edges open and unhooked her bra, baring her aching breasts. Dipping his head, he closed his mouth over one swollen nipple and greedily sucked the sensitive flesh.

She matched his urgency with her own lusty, unsated needs as her hands found the waistband of his jeans. She heard the groan that rumbled from his throat as she trailed her fingers over the bulge of the material. Impatiently she tugged at the zipper, then dipped her hands inside.

Hot and hard, his shaft pulsed, swelling even more when she brushed her fingers along its silky length.

He lifted his head and captured her with his heated gaze, stoking the fire already raging inside her. "Don't," he whispered, stilling her hands with one of his own, but he didn't push them away. "Don't do this, Mishella. We can't do this." She knew he fought for his last thread of resolve. But the need that burned between them was much stronger. "I don't know how long I can control what's inside me, and I can't let him have you."

"I *won't* let him have *you,*" she promised, kissing the pulse at the base of his neck, her hands moving up and down his arousal. She rained kisses over his chest, laving his nipples with her tongue.

With a groan of defeat, he pulled her closer, his hands insistent at the small of her back. "I need to feel your heat around me. I need you so bad," he said, his lips a soft vibration on hers.

Then he kissed her again, plunging his tongue inside to explore and savor until she gasped for breath. She felt his erection, hard and hot against her stomach, promising the ecstasy to come, making her painfully aware of the throbbing and the wetness between her own legs.

When he moved his mouth to leave a burning path down her neck, she tilted back her head, pleasure rushing to her brain and building the anticipation. His tongue traced the slope of her breast, down around its fullness, and a cry tore from her lips the moment he found her nipple.

Mishella buried her hands in his hair, holding him close, arching her breast into the moistness of his mouth. She felt the waves of heat build inside her, rising higher like molten lava in a volcano, until she felt ready to erupt.

"Please," she breathed.

In one swift motion, he unzipped her jeans and pushed them down, making quick work of his own. Then he locked her in his powerful arms and lifted her.

She clung to him, wrapping her legs around him as he slid her down onto his rigid length, the delicious friction sending jolts of electricity shooting through her body, singeing every nerve until she burned as hot as the man inside her.

She didn't know when he moved them. She only felt the bed against her back, the pulsing heat between her legs. Lifting her hips, she grasped his muscled buttocks and pulled him closer, deeper, her desire for him overriding all else.

She rose to meet each violent thrust, taking all that he could give and wanting more. They came together in a frenzied, primitive act, lust making them burn, fear like a potent aphrodisiac heightening their senses and their need.

When she felt the waves of pleasure begin, she dug her nails into his flesh, crying his name over and over again. Then every nerve in her body exploded. She heard his groan and felt the spurt of heat deep within. Closing her eyes, she clung to him, feeling each tremble of his muscled strength and relishing the power she held in her arms.

"I love you," she whispered minutes later into the curve of his neck as she reveled in the aftermath of ecstasy. "No matter what you say, I love you."

He rolled off her to sprawl on his back, one arm flung above his head.

"I know you love me, Raphael."

"It doesn't matter." Defeat filled his voice.

"It does!"

"Leave, Mishella. Leave Three Rivers and go far away."

"I can't. I won't!"

"You have to—for Stacey. For both of you. You'll die if you don't."

"How can I make the third touch without you?" she cried. "You said we had to do it together. *Together.*"

"We are together," he replied, touching a hand to her cheek. "Inside, where it counts. So go, love. Go and save yourself."

"No!"

"Don't you understand?" He turned on her then, flinging her to her back, locking her arms on either side of her body as he glared down, cold fury in his eyes. "I don't know how long I can control what's inside me. And when I lose what little hold I have, he'll go after you. He'll kill you—*before* the third touch. If you want to help your stepsister, take her away from here, Mishella. Now!"

"But the third touch means death. I'll die—"

"No!" he blazed, as if the very idea tore at him as fiercely as the demon. "We're joined, *querida*, emotionally, physically. My strength is yours. You won't die with the third touch, not now. But you must leave. Otherwise, you'll die *before* the touch."

"I can't leave you," she sobbed. She wouldn't let him go now that she'd found him again. "I can't!"

"And I'll kill you if you don't leave. Don't you see? There's no way to win. No way." He dug his fingers into her arms. "Do what I say and leave. It's the only chance you have. Please!"

The desperation in his plea tugged at her heart. Slowly she nodded. "I'll leave—for Stacey. But then I'm coming back, and I won't leave you ever again."

He smiled then—a sad, heart-wrenching smile that told of broken promises and forfeited dreams.

"Say you'll still be here when I come back," she entreated.

His only answer was, "Go, Mishella. Save your stepsister and yourself. Do it for me."

"Swear you'll be here," she pleaded. "Swear!"

"If there's any way possible, I'll be here," he said slowly, letting go of her and moving away.

She watched him retrieve her clothes from the floor. "Here," he said, his voice gruff. "You have to hurry."

He turned and disappeared into the bathroom, the door slamming behind him.

Mishella wiped at the tears on her face and pulled her clothes on in silence. Finally she stood, glancing toward the bathroom door. She needed to see him, to feel his arms one more time.

Go, Mishella. She heard the voice in her head and she knew it was him. *Leave... and know that I do love you. No matter what happens.*

A swell of tears spilled over as she hauled open the door and stepped out into the drizzle.

The sky opened up a second time as she drove the highway back to the farmhouse. *Leave, Mishella.* His voice followed her, urging her faster.

"I'll be back," she whispered. "As soon as Stacey is well, I'll be back. I love you."

CHAPTER ELEVEN

Raphael shoved the curtains aside and watched her from the motel window. Only the barest remnant of control kept him from yanking open the door and begging her to stay with him.

He needed her. She pulled him from the darkness into the light.

But she couldn't stay, and he wouldn't let himself go after her. Belial wouldn't have her.

"Damn you," he growled, slamming his fist against the wall. Sheet rock crumbled, and his hand throbbed, but the pain didn't help this time.

A wave of nausea swept through him. His head reeled. He flung his back against the door, sliding down the cracked surface until he slumped onto the floor.

Tilting back his head, he squeezed his eyes shut as unseen hands shook him with a bloodthirsty vengeance.

"This isn't fair," he wailed. "I never wanted this. I never wanted *you,* damn it!"

But I want you, came the voice.

And in the blackness of his mind, a light sparked. Then he heard an anguished cry and saw the small child—an innocent young boy with fearful eyes and sinful black hair.

And the hands reached for him....

"No, Papa," Esteban cried, inching back into the shadows, away from his father's strong fingers.

"Esteban, the time has come." The fingers closed on his sleeve, dragging him forward into the magic circle. The candles blazed all around him, closing in, barring his escape.

Hands clamped over his shoulders, shaking him until his teeth rattled.

"You will do as I say, Esteban," his father commanded.

The flames swam together when his father released him. Esteban swayed, but he didn't fall. His father wouldn't like it if he fell.

Eyes wide, Esteban watched as his father pulled the dagger from its sheath.

"The time has come, my son. You are flesh of my flesh...blood of my blood..." He touched one finger to the blade, mesmerized at the trickle of red that appeared. Then he yanked his shirt open and made a scratch across his chest. Reaching for the jeweled goblet on the altar beside him, he caught the river of blood that flowed down his skin.

"He sent you to me," his father went on. "You are of *his* blood, and you shall serve him just as I have all these years." Placing the goblet on the altar, his father turned and advanced. "Like your grandfather. Then when you pass from this earth, you shall join us."

"No—" Esteban began, but the protest stopped when his father reached for him, ripping his nightshirt from neck to waist.

"Please, Papa!" he cried, tears pouring down his cheeks. "Please don't hurt me. Please—"

"Silence!" The roar filled Esteban's head, making his ears ring.

His father raised the dagger high in the air, eyes closed, voice filling the sanctuary beneath the castle.

"My flesh and blood I give to you . . . another soul to do your bidding. Fill him with your power. Your ways will be his throughout this lifetime . . . throughout eternity."

"Please, no—" Esteban begged as the dagger descended. A burning pain wrenched through his shoulder.

"Stop!" But fire shot through his arm as the blade swept down again. And the pain came yet a third time. Esteban crumpled to his knees.

Then the stone floor started to shake. A rush of frigid air surrounded them.

"Papa," Esteban choked out, staring up into the strangely glowing eyes of his father.

"You are mine now, Esteban," his father said, only the voice wasn't his. The eyes burned brighter. "Mine . . ."

Esteban screamed, but not loud enough to drown out the voice. The voice came from inside him now. Inside.

Raphael forced himself upright and staggered to the bed. The pounding in his skull escalated.

The forbidden memory stirred his bitterness and his hatred for a man who'd forced the darkness upon him centuries ago. He'd been a child, frightened and confused, at the mercy of an evil father greedy for power.

A man void of compassion who had willingly sacrificed his own soul and that of his six-year-old son.

The memory had remained buried for a long time. Only now he needed to remember, to make him all the more hardened against the past and the demon. He had to fight.

Raphael collapsed onto the bed. The drumming in his head neared a maddening tempo.

Eyes closed, he focused his thoughts on Mishella—the silky blackness of her hair, the velvety feel of her skin, the heat within her.

The bitch will die!

"No!" Raphael cried, flinging a lamp across the room. The shaking seized him. With trembling fingers, he wrenched the sapphire ring from his finger and threw it to the floor. Still the shaking didn't subside.

"Run, Mishella," he murmured as he plunged into unconsciousness.

Belial had never lost a battle.

When Mishella returned to the farmhouse, she found Inez sitting on the sofa, tears streaking her ruddy brown cheeks.

"You're back," Inez gasped, her expression startled.

"I—I'm sorry I took so long," Mishella said. Without bothering to take off her jacket, she rushed into her bedroom and yanked a suitcase from the closet. After dumping the contents of several drawers onto the bed, she began stuffing the clothes into the case.

Inez watched from the doorway. "You're taking the child," she said flatly.

Mishella glanced up, her gaze locking with the woman's. "I have to, Inez. There's something you don't understand." She took a deep breath. "Stacey and I didn't come here for a vacation...."

"I know, *mija,*" Inez admitted, her face solemn, betrayed by the anguish in her eyes. "I had prayed it wouldn't come to this. Night after night I prayed." The woman twisted a handkerchief in one hand. "I had hoped you wouldn't be forced to run again. Me and Mingo were here to watch over you. We should've been able to hold him off long enough for you to make the third touch."

A blouse slipped from Mishella's hand. She turned her full attention to Inez. One look into the woman's eyes confirmed Mishella's suspicions. Inez knew.

"It was only a month. We thought we could fight him for you, but my Mingo wasn't strong enough. That left only me.'' Inez shook her head. "But I failed you, like I failed Maricela.''

Mishella noticed the crucifix Inez clutched in her other hand, the one she'd given to Stacey. Maricela's crucifix.

Time sucked her backward. She felt the guards shoving her along, heard the pleading voice begging them to halt. Someone had slipped the crucifix around her neck as she was led to the fire.

"There were so many people,'' Inez went on as if reading Mishella's thoughts.

Correction, Mishella told herself. Inez *could* read her thoughts. She was the guardian. Suddenly pieces of the puzzle fit—the crucifix, her attentiveness to Stacey. *The guardian.*

"But I made sure you had this,'' Inez held out the worn cross, "for those last few moments. Then I picked through the ashes later to find it. I pray it sees you through this time,'' she said. "Take the child and go.''

Stunned, Mishella sank down on the edge of the bed, her fingers tightening around the crucifix. "All this time you knew,'' she murmured.

"I tried to keep him away,'' Inez said, her voice bordering on a sob. "I really tried, but the evil is too strong. I knew today you would uncover the truth when you left.'' She touched a hand to Mishella's cheek. "I didn't want you to see what *he* is.'' She sagged onto the edge of the bed next to Mishella. "I wanted to keep you from him, *mija.* I wanted to protect you.'' She buried her face in her hands. "I should have warned you, but I was afraid. I've always been afraid. So very afraid.''

"You did what you could,'' Mishella whispered, patting the woman's back. Inez lifted bright, pleading eyes to Mishella.

"I wanted to warn you, but I was frightened of him. Some protector I was." She shook her head. "I wish I could've done more for you. I failed you."

"You watched over Stacey for me. For that I'm very grateful."

Inez shook her head. "It wasn't enough. I should have made you leave when you first came here. I shouldn't have let you go into town today. I had a bad, bad feeling this morning. And when I saw you and Thomas drive away, I knew..." Her words trailed off.

Silence descended, disturbed only by the ticking of the clock on the nightstand.

Raphael's image flashed in Mishella's mind. She felt the warmth of his touch. Not that of a demon, but a man. Yet she couldn't deny the evil, and she couldn't let it win. Raphael would be lost to her forever if that happened. And Stacey...

When Mishella finally spoke, determination fueled her words. "But now I know who the evil is. I know and I can fight him—long enough to make the third touch." Even as she said the words, doubt niggled at her. *Please,* she cried silently. *Help me, Raphael. Help me. Be stronger than the demon.*

Inez pulled her hand from Mishella's. "Go, *mija.* He will come soon. I will try and stop him this time, I promise, but I don't know if I can."

Mishella set the cross on the nightstand. After shoving a few more pieces of clothing into her suitcase, she hurried to Stacey's room and began packing her stepsister's clothes.

Minutes later, Mishella leaned over the girl and nudged her shoulder. "Wake up, sleepy," she whispered.

Stacey's eyes fluttered open.

"We have to go, baby," Mishella said.

Alarm registered on Stacey's face. "What's wrong?" She struggled to sit up. Fever glazed her eyes.

"We're taking a little trip. Just sit up long enough for me to put on your sweater."

Mishella made quick work of the buttons. Then, with Inez helping, she managed to move Stacey from the bed to her wheelchair.

"Go far away from here," Inez told her when at last they stood by the car in the steady rain. They had settled Stacey into the passenger seat and stowed the luggage in the trunk.

"I'll be back as soon as the touch is done," Mishella said.

"No!" Inez replied, her voice sharp. "Don't come back here, Mishella. You take Stacey and go far away. Cross the border into Mexico. Make the third touch, beg God to forgive you for using the demon's power and keep going. Don't ever come back. There is nothing but grief here."

There's something more than grief, Mishella thought as she backed the car out of the driveway and waved a final goodbye to Inez. *Raphael.* For him, she would come back.

The rain pounded harder and Mishella flipped the windshield wipers on high.

"Where are we going?" Stacey whispered, leaning her head back against the headrest, her eyes closed, a blanket pulled tight around her.

"I thought seeing some of the countryside might do you good for the next few days. It's been so cold and rainy."

"Thank you, Shell. I hate being cooped up inside all the time." Stacey smiled a weak smile that tugged at Mishella's heart.

She patted her stepsister's hand and murmured, "I know you do." Then, blinking away the tears in her eyes, she struggled to see through the downpour. The headlights did little to penetrate the stormy night.

"What we need is a little music." Mishella turned the radio on, desperate to fill the nerve-racking silence.

They glided along for a good half hour. A soft melody drifted from the radio. Mishella heard Stacey's even breaths. Her own nerves started to relax.

"We'll make it, Raphael," she whispered, seeing the lean lines of his face, feeling his skin beneath her fingertips. "I'll come back—" Her words stopped short when the engine missed and the car jerked.

"Damn," Mishella said under her breath. Her fingers tightened on the steering wheel. The car jerked again.

"What's wrong?" Stacey's eyes snapped open.

"Probably nothing." Still, Mishella could feel the front end tremble. Then the engine died.

She veered to the right and skidded to a stop near the side of the road.

Turning the key, she prayed desperately for the engine to catch. Instead, she heard a dull click. Then a few more clicks as she turned the key again and again.

"Is the car messed up?"

Yes! a voice screamed, only Mishella didn't want to listen. They were stuck on the road, God only knew how far from the nearest human being, in the middle of a rainstorm, and Stacey couldn't walk. And Mishella couldn't leave her.

"The car's messed up." This time Stacey's words were a statement.

"I'm sure it's nothing. Let me try it again." Another click.

Mishella slammed her palm against the steering wheel, then turned the key again. Nothing.

"What are we going to do, Shell?"

"You're going to stay inside, and I'm going to see if I can flag somebody down."

"But there aren't any cars on this road," Stacey said, struggling to sit up.

"Somebody is bound to pass, baby. Just stretch out here, and I'll wake you when somebody stops."

She glanced at the clock—8 p.m. The road was practically deserted. Few cars traveled this stretch during the day, much less at night. And the rain reduced the visibility almost to zero. Mishella doubted anyone would be foolish enough to venture out.

"You can't go outside," Stacey protested. "It's raining."

"A little rain won't hurt me." She kissed her stepsister's cheek. "Now close your eyes and rest. Before you know it, we'll be moving again."

Mishella braced herself and opened the door.

The rain beat down on her and she pulled her jacket tighter. Raising a hand to her eyes, she tried to shield them from the onslaught of water.

Get back in the car. But she couldn't. If a car passed, she wouldn't see it until it was nearly upon her, and she couldn't blow her only chance at help.

She had to get Stacey away from here. She could feel the cold in the air, lashing at her, seeking possession.

Wiping her eyes, she opened them wide. Then she saw the faint yellow glare in the distance.

She threw her arms in the air and waved frantically as the vehicle rumbled toward her. The lights grew brighter.

He's going to pass me, she thought when the driver didn't appear to be slowing. Then the truck swerved toward the shoulder, coming nose to nose with Mishella's car.

She rushed forward, never so happy in all her life to see the familiar form that climbed from behind the wheel.

"Mishella?" Thomas shouted, his voice barely audible above the roar of the storm.

"Thomas, I'm so glad to see you." She flew around the front of the truck to the driver's side. "I need a ride to the nearest town—"

"Wait a second." He held up a hand. "Slow down. What are you doing out here?"

"The car stalled. I have to rent another one."

"Shouldn't you be at home with your sis—" He squinted at the windshield of Mishella's car. "What the hell's going on?"

Mishella searched her brain for a plausible answer. "Stacey wasn't feeling well. The weather's been so bad lately that I thought we'd drive into Mexico and soak up some sunshine."

"Mexico? Tonight? Why, that's the craziest thing I've ever heard. There've been tornadoes spotted in this area, and—"

"Just help me, Thomas," she cut in. "The car is dead and—"

"But Buddy fixed it."

"Apparently he didn't fix everything." Though Mishella had the impression that the car's stalling had nothing to do with Buddy and everything to do with her needing to leave.

"Then I'll take you back to town, and we'll get Buddy to follow us here with his tow truck. He'll have it up and running in no time. When the weather clears, tomorrow or the next day, you and Stacey can head for Mexico."

"I haven't got that much time!" she shrieked.

He gave her an odd look and she knew he thought she was hysterical. When she spoke again, her voice was soft and deadly calm. "I need another car *now*."

Thomas frowned, his stare searching her face. He reached out to push a few strands of hair from her eyes. "Something's wrong. Something besides the car."

She nodded. "I have to get Stacey away from here. Just for the next couple of days. It's very important."

He hesitated, but only for a few seconds. Then he nodded.

"I'll get her in the truck," he said, his fingers lingering near her cheek, his touch cold like the rain.

No, a voice whispered inside her. *Don't let him touch her.* But Mishella couldn't stop to rationalize her reluctance. She had no choice. Time was essential.

She hurried after him, watching him pull Stacey from the car and carry her to the truck.

Go back to the house . . . to Raphael. A battle waged inside her—the love that blazed in her heart rivaling the truth that Raphael was all that he claimed.

He would come for her, but love wouldn't be the driving force. The demon would be. She had to get her stepsister far away before that happened. Once the touch was complete, then she could settle things.

Soon Mishella found herself crammed into the cab of the pickup, her suitcases on the floor beneath her feet, Stacey resting on the seat between her and Thomas.

"Tilden is the closest town. About another hour in this weather."

"Thanks, Thomas. I don't know what I would have done if you hadn't come along. Bless your mother for sending you."

"My mother?"

"She sent you, didn't she? I mean, I know she was worried when I told her I had to leave."

"I haven't seen my mother since this morning," he said, his knuckles white against the steering wheel. "I had to work late, so my father said he'd pick her up. My boss needed me to make a delivery to Tilden. I was on my way back from there. Lucky for you, I guess."

But Mishella felt anything but lucky—uneasy, worried, scared—but certainly not lucky. If only she understood why. She had nothing to be frightened of now, not with Thomas helping her. Still, she couldn't shake the ill feelings.

Wrapping an arm around Stacey, she rested her cheek against her stepsister's forehead. "Soon, baby," she murmured.

She stared out the window at the rivulets of rain trailing down the glass. Her eyes felt heavy. She tried to remember the last time she'd slept.

Her thoughts turned to Raphael. She wondered what he was doing, how he was doing.

I love you, she said silently, her eyes drifting shut. *I always have and I always will.*

Raphael shot straight up, the headboard pounding against the wall.

I love you. The phrase echoed in his head, pulling him from the blackness, tugging at his very soul. And despite the evil that fought for control of him, the words were enough to force him from the bed.

He pulled on a shirt, his jacket and boots, and left the dark motel room, the urgency to see Mishella overriding all else, even the voice that warned him against it.

You can't let Belial have her.

That thought should have turned him around. The demon was a part of him. To go after her would mean risking her life should he lose control. Yet he felt compelled, but not by the evil. Rather, he realized as he sped down the highway toward the farmhouse, by the need to protect her.

I love you. Every time he heard those words, he felt her—her pain, her fear—and sensed danger.

She needed him.

I told you she must die, the voice roared in his ears. *You have disobeyed me. I knew she would weaken you. Still, she won't get away. Try to stop me and you both shall die.*

In that instant, Raphael knew he wasn't the only threat to Mishella. Belial, one of Satan's most powerful demons, had sent someone else. Another one of his minions to fulfill the bargain.

With a vicious curse, Raphael floored the gas pedal. The car went faster. But the faster he went, the farther away she felt. He knew even as he pulled into the driveway that he might already be too late. And the realization ripped his very soul apart.

"Mishella!" he called, tearing through the front door. He stopped, his gaze sweeping the remains of the living room. Chairs had been overturned, curtains ripped, tables broken. It looked as if a hurricane had hit the room. Or something much more powerful.

"Where is she?" he growled, towering over the Mexican woman huddled in the corner.

"He really is a good boy," she mumbled. "My boy." Her eyes were distant, faraway.

"Where is Mishella?"

The woman broke into sobs when he said the name. "I failed her again!" she cried. She wrung her hands, shaking her head from side to side. "I tried, Mingo. Really I did. But I couldn't do it on my own. Why did you leave? I needed your strength."

Raphael leaned down, grabbed her under her arms and hauled her to her feet. "Where is she?" he asked, giving her a shake.

The woman's eyes seemed to focus. "Dead by now," she replied, "or she will be . . . like my Mingo." She closed her eyes, tears trailing down her cheeks. "I can't believe he's gone. It's been over three weeks, but it still doesn't seem real—''

''What are you talking about, woman?'' Raphael noticed the darkening bruise on her cheek.

''Thomas,'' she whispered.

Then she opened her eyes and stared straight at Raphael as if seeing him for the first time. ''He really is a good boy,'' she pleaded. ''He really isn't bad. How could a tiny baby be bad? He was so small when he came to us, just a few months. I wanted a child so bad. Mingo and I never had any of our own. We couldn't. Then I found Thomas abandoned in one of the houses I used to clean. He was so helpless lying there as quiet as a mouse in this cardboard box. I brought him home, thinking he only needed someone to look out for him.''

She shook her head. ''But he was different. He never cried. Ever. And his eyes . . . so pale and frightening. I used to stare at him when he was a baby, just a baby, mind you, and I would feel afraid. He sensed the fear, and he hexed me. Made me love him. But he couldn't fool my Mingo.

''I told Mingo not to see the evil, only the good. Thomas grew up and he turned into all that we feared. I begged Mingo to leave him alone. I begged,'' she wailed, ''but he wouldn't listen.''

''Where is Mishella?'' he growled. ''Tell me, woman!''

''It doesn't matter. He'll find her, anyway. He's strong.'' She clutched a crucifix in her hand. ''Mingo always knew the truth about Thomas even when I didn't want to see it.'' She shook her head.

''We were childless for so long. At first, I thought Thomas was a gift from God.'' She laughed then, the sound brittle, hinting at madness. ''Mingo had the sight much stronger than me. He recognized exactly what evil filled Thomas even when he was a baby. When we took him to St.

Peter's for his christening . . .'' Words failed her as her eyes filled with fear.

She stared past Raphael, watching some unspeakable horror only she could see. ''We knew then,'' she whispered. ''Everyone knew, and no one who was in that church will ever forget. The whole town of Del Rio will never forget.''

Her tears came faster and Raphael loosened his hold. She slumped against the wall, a flash of silver catching the lamplight.

He reached for her hand and pried the crucifix from her fingers. The cross felt warm, comforting, against his palm.

The slight trembling of his hands ceased altogether.

It was hers. Maricela's. Mishella's. He felt it. He would need it if he intended to find her. He *had* to find her.

''Thomas,'' he repeated, his fingers closing around the crucifix so tightly he felt the metal slice into his palm.

Belial had sent Thomas since Raphael had no intention of stealing Mishella's soul come time for the third touch. Thomas was to be the thief. Tonight. When the sun set and darkness caressed the sky.

Time for the third and final touch.

Now Raphael knew.

Mishella felt the cold glass against her cheek and forced her eyes open. The sun peeked over the horizon, bathing the highway in pink brilliance. Not a cloud hung in the sky. The day promised to be crisp, cold and beautiful.

''Where are we?''

''About ten miles from the next town.''

''Which town?''

''Del Rio.''

''Del Rio!'' She stared at Thomas in disbelief. ''What are we doing in Del Rio?''

''You said you needed to get away.''

"I didn't mean for you to drive us, Thomas. You said you would take us as far as Tilden."

"You were sleeping when we drove through there, and that town is smaller than Three Rivers. There wasn't any-place to rent a car. I had a hard time just finding a gas sta-tion that was open. Besides, as exhausted as you looked, you had no business driving."

Heat crept up her neck. "I—I appreciate your concern." She took a deep breath, choosing her words carefully. "But I would rather rent my own car. This is something I have to do myself, Thomas. It's not that I'm not grateful for your help or that I don't like your company—"

"You just don't want it."

"No," she replied, "I simply need time alone with Sta-cey. Please try and understand."

"I do understand, Mishella. More than you think." There was a hardness to his voice that unnerved her.

When she spared him a sideways glance, his tone soft-ened. "I know she's sick and you want to spend as much time as you can with her. She's dying, isn't she?"

"No," Mishella shot back. She wouldn't let Stacey die. "Stacey's trying a new medication. The doctor said it would take a little while to work, that's all. In the meantime, she needs lots of sunshine."

"Then I'm glad I kept driving. We've left the bad weather behind."

"Look, Thomas, I know you're only trying to help—"

"I'll take you as far as Del Rio," he cut in, "then I'll head back to Three Rivers and look after your car." He flashed her a smile. "You can cross over into Mexico, and you and Stacey can have a holiday."

He's only trying to help, she reasoned. *And you need all the help you can get.*

"I didn't mean to sound rude," she said. "I don't know what I would've done had you not rescued us from the rain and—"

"I told you before that I'm a pretty understanding guy. Whatever you want, I'm glad to do. If you need to get away by yourself, that's fine with me."

"Thank you."

"Don't mention it. I know you don't want me along, but I'm glad I didn't wake you last night. You needed some sleep."

Mishella brushed a few strands of hair from her face. "I guess I was tired."

"You look a lot better."

"That doesn't say much for me last night, because right now I look a mess." She attempted a smile.

"No," he said, his voice serious. "You don't look a mess. Well, maybe a beautiful mess."

She murmured another thank you, her cheeks flaming, more from the intense gaze he directed at her than his words.

Glancing away, she turned her attention to the passing scenery. Yet she could still feel his eyes.

"We'll never make it to Del Rio if you don't keep your eyes on the road," she said, trying to keep her tone light.

He said nothing, but when she sneaked a glance, she saw that he had turned his attention back to the road.

Mishella scanned the empty fields. They might well have still been near Three Rivers. The landscape looked the same. But she felt the emptiness, and she knew she was far from the town . . . far from Raphael.

The distance should have eased her mind. Tonight she would make the final touch. As soon as they arrived in Del Rio, she would say goodbye to Thomas and find a hotel. Then she would wait until dusk.

She heard a small sigh and glanced down. Stacey lay on the seat, her head in Mishella's lap.

Instinctively Mishella's hand went to the girl's forehead. Hot. Then again, Stacey would get even hotter. By this afternoon, the fever would be raging . . . and tonight it would end.

". . . is a border town."

"I'm sorry—what did you say?" She glanced at Thomas.

"I said Del Rio is a border town. It's near Laughlin Air Force Base. It's a pretty big town. I'm sure they have someplace you can rent a car."

"Great," she said, watching as the town materialized in the distance.

A good while later, Thomas was weaving in and out of early-morning traffic.

"For a border town, this place is more urbanized than I would have guessed," Mishella commented.

"This place has changed a lot."

"Have you been here before?" she asked.

"I used to live here."

"Really? When?"

"Not for a long, long time." He scanned both sides of the street when they stopped at a red light. "It feels the same, even though it looks different."

"Progress," Mishella murmured, delight surging through her as she spotted a familiar rental-agency insignia. "Over there, Thomas."

He turned into the parking lot. "I think it's too early, Mishella. They're not open."

She stared at the darkened windows. In her haste, she hadn't even considered the time.

"Give them a couple of hours. In the meantime we can get something to eat." He shoved the truck into reverse. "But I need gas first."

They pulled into a nearby service station and Thomas climbed out.

"Stay here and I'll be right back," he said, and she nodded.

Mishella glanced at her watch, then at Thomas who strolled into the station. Her gaze riveted on the phone booth near a soda machine around the far side of the building.

Call him, a voice whispered. *Make sure he's all right.*

For some reason, she had the feeling he wasn't. Maybe it was the trembling in her hands, the prickling of her skin or the emptiness in her heart. Whatever it was, she needed to hear his voice. Just for a second...

Scooting out from underneath Stacey, Mishella settled her sister on the seat and strode toward the phone booth. She fished in her purse for the folded piece of paper with his phone number. Feeding a quarter into the slot, she punched in the numbers.

"Operator, may I help you?"

"I need to make a collect call."

"Your name, caller?"

"Mishella."

"Please hold." The quarter dropped from the phone and Mishella stuffed it back into her pocket.

"I told you to stay in the car." She turned when she heard Thomas.

"I'll accept the charges, operator," came Raphael's familiar voice. "Mishella?"

"Yes—"

Thomas slammed his fist into her temple. The receiver crashed to the ground.

"Stupid bitch," Thomas hissed.

"Mishella!" she heard Raphael's voice from the dangling receiver.

"Stacey," she whispered, then everything went black.

CHAPTER TWELVE

"Mishella?" Raphael gripped the receiver of his car phone. "Talk to me," he begged, his voice urgent.

"Sir, the line's still open, but the caller doesn't seem to be responding," the operator told him.

"No..." He closed his eyes, fear like a cold fist in his stomach. *I told you she would die,* came the voice. "No!" he growled.

"Sir, is everything all right? I could connect you with emergency services—"

"Where was the call coming from?" Raphael demanded.

"One moment and I'll check the area code."

After what seemed like an eternity, the operator came on again. "Del Rio," she said. "Del Rio, Texas."

The receiver slipped from his hand.

The whole town of Del Rio will never forget. Inez's words replayed in his mind.

I told you the bitch would die, came the harsh grumble. The demon's voice, filling the car, roaring in his head.

Raphael gripped the steering wheel, the tremors in his hands starting again. He slammed on the brakes. He'd been driving for hours, searching every town near Three Rivers. When he'd found her car, he'd come close to crying.

He—a man who had never felt sadness, regret or any other emotion, even when his parents had died. He'd been too young to realize how final death was. Too young to feel the emptiness.

Ah, but he felt now. He felt her, smelled her, tasted her, even.

He wheeled the car around and floored the gas pedal, calculating the hours to Del Rio. Damn it, he should've known Thomas would take her there. Inez had said that was where the demon had revealed his hold on Thomas. The place was evil. Thomas would go back there to do Belial's bidding, to sacrifice Mishella and feed the demon's power.

Raphael drove faster. He had to reach her before sundown.

The morning sun glinted off the pavement, momentarily blinding like the blade of a dagger reflecting a flicker of candlelight. The highway turned red as a river of blood spread before him—Mishella's blood. Belial would settle for no less.

And your blood, too, Raphael. You have forsaken me and now you shall pay. You'll see her die like you were always meant to.

"Damn it, no!" He clutched the crucifix. "No sacrifice this time. Not this time." The battle waged in his soul, but his heart had sworn allegiance. Mishella had an ally. If only he could reach her in time—before the demon claimed her, before the demon claimed him.

Mishella forced her eyes open to the blinding sunlight. The hammering in her head increased, keeping steady tempo with the persistent banging coming from somewhere close by. Stretched out flat on her back, she groaned and tried to sit up. Then she realized her hands and feet were bound. The gag knotted around her head cut into the corners of her mouth. She tried to breathe, to move . . .

With a shiver of vivid recollection, she went deadly still. Time pulled her back through the centuries, to the torture chamber, to the days of agony—of waiting to die, of *wanting* to die.

She steeled herself against the thought. Now, she didn't want to die. She wanted to live. She *had* to live.

Turn, a voice whispered, and she managed to move her head an inch. The sun hung directly overhead, casting a glare on everything around her, but still she saw the shadow. She tried her hardest to focus.

Thomas, bare-chested despite the freezing wind, stood a few feet away. He leaned over a large beam, his blond hair flowing loose, his features harsh, intense. She flinched as he slammed the hammer against the wood, over and over.

Thomas. She remembered the strange light in his eyes, heard his voice, felt his fist smash into her temple. He was the evil she'd been waiting for. The evil that had been waiting for her. For the third and final touch when he could kill her and claim her soul.

She relived the past four weeks in a rush of visions. Thomas had been responsible for the shower, her car, the constant cold, and all along, she'd blamed Raphael.

I had a bad, bad feeling this morning when I saw you and Thomas drive away. Inez's voice came back to haunt Mishella. *I wanted to protect you from him, but I was afraid.*

It had been Thomas all this time.

Forgive me, Raphael, Mishella silently begged. Only now it was too late.

With each pound of the hammer, her fear escalated.

Thomas pounded away and Mishella twisted around, taking in the destruction around her. They were in what remained of an old building. Half the roof had been ripped away. Part of the walls had crumbled. Rubble littered the wooden floor. The place looked old, abandoned. A few benches remained. No, not benches. They looked more like pews. Pews?

A glint of light caught the corner of her eye. She stared at the cut edges of what had once been a stained-glass window and saw the cross. A church . . .

Mishella lifted her head and strained to see. Relief filled her the moment she spotted her stepsister's familiar form curled up on a bench across the room. Her eyes were closed and she trembled. The fever was raging hotter.

The sun was well past its zenith. There were still a few hours till it set, however.

Mishella struggled at the ropes, feeling them cut into her flesh, relishing the pain, for it grounded her in reality and kept the blackness from closing in. She jerked harder and the pain grew more intense, but she didn't care. She knew only a desperate urgency to reach her sister. To touch her.

Thomas couldn't win—the evil couldn't win, not when she'd come so far.

"You're awake." It was Thomas's voice, yet it wasn't. It sounded deeper, more guttural. The same voice she'd heard in the telephone booth. The same voice she'd heard each time she'd made the touch. An ageless voice filled with doom, laced with the agony of hell itself.

He towered over her, a silhouette against the burning sun, his face a black shroud. Still, she saw his eyes. They glowed with a demonic light that iced her blood. A fright as black as nothingness swept through her and she tugged at the ropes.

"Struggle, dear Maricela, but you'll never get loose. Don't you know there isn't any escape? You must make restitution for using the power. *He* commands it." Thomas tilted his face toward the sky. "It will be time soon," he declared, "and I still have work to do."

She tried to scream, but the sound died in her throat.

Her strangled cries drew his attention. He glanced back down. "I need quiet to work," he growled. Then his fist came down again. Pain ripped through her skull, numbing her arms and legs, pushing her toward the edge of blackness.

But she couldn't give in. She had to fight, to help Stacey. With a strength that surprised her, she forced her eyes wide until the fog started to subside, enough for her to focus.

Thomas had taken up his spot a few feet away and resumed his hammering.

Mishella breathed in, again and again, until the cold air rushed through her, clearing her head.

I love you, her mind cried as her thoughts went to Raphael. And in that instant, there was no more emptiness where her heart had been. A peace filled her and she saw only him. She *felt* only him.

Stay strong, querida. Strong.

She glanced at Thomas, her sister, then the sky above. Yes, she still had a few hours. Enough time to get free.

She moved her hands again, straining against the ropes until she managed to work about half an inch of space between her wrists. Bending her fingers as far as she could, she began working at the knots.

"What do you mean, you've never heard of it?" Raphael demanded, slamming his fist on the store counter.

The young man behind the counter flinched and stepped back.

"I—I told you, mister. I ain't never heard of St. Peter's. There ain't no church by that name around here. You get on outta here or else I'm gonna call the pol—"

"Call whoever the hell you want. I've been all along this interstate trying to find St. Peter's. This is my last stop and I need some answers. There *is* a church by that name," Raphael insisted, clenching his hands, willing the shaking to stop. "Or there was. Think, man!"

The clerk shook his head, his eyes wide. "I'm telling you, mister, there ain't."

Raphael reached across the counter and grabbed the man by the collar.

"What are you doing?"

"Think," Raphael growled.

"I—I...listen, mister, I don't know any church by the name of St. Peter's. Please don't hurt me. I haven't got much in my register—"

"Bobby, what's going on out there?" a man's voice called from the rear of the store.

"Gramps, we're being robbed—"

"No," Raphael cut in. "All I want is the location of St. Peter's." He unclenched his fingers and released the frightened clerk who inched backward just as an old man appeared, shotgun in hand.

"Whatcha doin' with my grandson, fella?"

Raphael turned on the old man. "Asking a question. Nothing more," he said.

The old man eyed him for a long moment, not missing the trembling in Raphael's hands.

"St. Peter's, you say?" Recognition sparked in the old man's eyes along with fear, and Raphael knew he'd hit the jackpot.

"You've heard of it," he stated.

"Wish I hadn't, young fella. But that church ain't no more. God done come and took care of that mockery. Sent it to hell where it belonged. Ain't nothin' left but a wall or two now. Whatcha want with that old place?"

"I need to find it," Raphael said.

"I can't imagine why. Ain't nobody goes there anymore. They built that church back when I was a young man about your age. Attended a few services myself until that tornado came through. Damnedest thing, that tornado. Stirred up from nothing, but then folks figured it was God's way of tearing down that place. Wasn't nothing but evil there after Father O'Neil died."

The old man shook his head. "It was the evil that killed him. I saw it. One minute he was giving the blessing and the next he was bent down over that baby. A roar filled the whole place. It wasn't human. That little babe wasn't human. When the father touched the babe, or whatever it was that looked like a babe, he went white. A fright filled his eyes, like if he was looking at the Devil hisself. He keeled over then. The babe started to cry—no, more like howl. A demon's howl. The wind picked up, shattered the windows. Things started flying, folks started running..." He paused to pull a handkerchief from his pocket and blow his nose.

"Yep," the man finally went on, "God took care of it. Folks was lucky to get away when that twister come through, but then it wasn't the folks God was mad at. The Devil was in that child, as sure as I'm standing here. Doctors said it was a heart attack that took the Father, but I think he was scared to death. Ain't never seen a look like that in any man's eyes before—except maybe in the parents' eyes. Folks speculated on why that couple took the babe home after Father O'Neil's death like nothing happened. The couple didn't see the child for what it was. The babe bewitched them, some said. I think they just feared for their lives. Rightly so, seeing the mess that little bugger stirred.''

"How do I get to the church?" Raphael asked.

"Hell's bells, boy, you can't mean to go there.''

"Just tell me, sir. I have to find it.''

A long silence stretched between them. Finally the old man muttered, "Take the interstate down to Miller's Road. Hang a right. It's a few miles down—a real isolated spot. Folks say the Devil still walks around there at night. Ain't nobody ever had the guts to go out and tear down the rest of that place. It still sits up there in the middle of all those trees—smack-dab in some of the prettiest country you ever seen.''

Raphael thanked the man, then turned and strode out.

Moments later as he steered the car onto the highway, he scanned for signs marking Miller's Road. Time was running out. The sun was inching lower.

"Hold on," he whispered, but he knew she wasn't listening. He couldn't feel her anymore, and that scared the wits out of him. And the sun dipped a little lower.

"It's time, Mishella," Thomas announced, stalking toward her. "Time to give up your soul. The demon wanted Maricela's soul. She had the power—his power—given to her to heal her husband in return for her soul. Only the bargain was never fulfilled. She never gave up her soul. The time hadn't been right. She and Esteban hadn't mated, and death came too soon for the both of them. Now the power rests with you. The time is at hand. You and Raphael completed the physical union. Now Belial will finally have what was promised him—your soul as final payment for the power you possess.''

Mishella pulled and twisted at the ropes. They gave slightly, but not enough to slip her hands through. Just a few more minutes and she'd have another knot loose. Damn it, she needed more time. More time!

The sun was below the tops of the trees now, a ball of fiery brilliance visible through the branches, hovering close to the horizon. Too close. Panic seized her. She tugged all the more against the blasted ropes.

Thomas loomed over her. His features were hard, like an ivory statue, with not a hint of remorse or any other feeling. More disturbing, however, were his eyes, which gleamed with a cold ruthlessness that sparked nothing short of terror within her.

"Time," he said again, his voice gruff, grating. "*He's* ready for us, Mishella."

As Thomas leaned down, her terror turned to something else. Anger maybe, or determination, or a little of both. For greater than her fear of what Thomas would do to her was her fear of losing Stacey.

When he started to untie her legs, she gave one last furious jerk on the ropes. The flesh scraped from her wrists. One hand slipped free. She grabbed for the hammer hooked in his belt loop.

But Thomas was quicker and much, much stronger.

"Traitor," he growled, catching her wrist in a death grip. Her fingers went limp from the bone-crushing pressure he exerted.

She whimpered, gasping and chewing at the gag that stifled her screams.

"Come on," he ordered, yanking her arm. He half-dragged, half-carried her to the tablelike structure he'd been pounding away at all afternoon.

"You'd think a church would have an altar," he said, shoving her down on the rough surface.

She clawed at the hand locked around her wrist. If she could get loose for even a second . . .

"Stop it!" He backhanded her across the cheek. Her head jerked to the side. Her struggles ceased. The blackness closed in.

No! she screamed silently as he pulled her arms above her head.

He tied her wrists together again, then slipped the knot over a protruding nail. With his hammer, he began forcing the nail deeper into the table.

"Yes, you'd think a church would have an altar. But I'm pretty handy, right, Mishella? I think this will work just fine." He slammed a fist against the tabletop near her head. "Just fine," his voice rose a notch—louder, more grating, more frightening. "*He* ain't particular about his altar. Only the sacrifice. As long as the sacrifice is what he wants." He laughed then. "And you're exactly what he wants." He spared a glance behind him. "Your stepsister—she'll make a nice offering, too."

Mishella shook her head, and his fingers closed about her chin. He leaned down until his face was inches from hers, his breath cold. "The blood," he said, his voice suddenly thick, low. "*He* needs the blood. Your blood."

As he stared at her for endless seconds, she felt the coldness of his hands, his breath. In his eyes, she saw death, and she smelled it—a rank, putrid odor of rotting flesh and cold, musty earth.

Finally he let go of her. Straightening, he closed his eyes. "I need the blood. It makes me stronger. It makes *him* stronger." He swept up the hammer and slammed it down one final time. Mishella jumped. "You have to die . . . to finish the bargain that damned Esteban was too weak to see through.''

He slammed the hammer down once more. ''There,'' he announced.

His features started to blur then.

She blinked and found herself staring up into the smiling face of a priest, his face creased with wrinkles, his hair snowy white. He wore spectacles perched on the end of his round nose. His soft brown eyes were warm, comforting, as he surveyed her for a thoughtful second before inching his finger under the gag and pulling it down.

''Any last words, my child?'' he asked, his voice rich, *human.* Maybe God had indeed heard her prayers. Maybe he'd sent this man to help her.

''Please,'' she croaked. ''Please don't let him hurt my sister. I don't care what happens to me, but he can't hurt her. Not her,'' she begged, her tears spilling and streaming down her cheeks.

His mouth curved upward, his brown eyes firing to a bright red, and Mishella knew it was the demon even before she heard the laughter—the cold, soul-chilling laughter.

''Sorry, but I need her almost as much as I need you. You'll both die. You both *must* die!'' His features transformed—smoothed, hardened—and he was once again Thomas, the demon manifested.

''Burn in hell,'' she whispered.

''I intend to, with you by my side,'' he replied, a freezing smile curling his lips. ''You escaped before, but not this time. You'll burn for an eternity, like you were always meant to. And your stepsister can keep you company.''

''No—'' But his fingers were at the gag, stuffing it back into her mouth.

She clamped down, sinking her teeth into the hard, leathery skin of one of his knuckles.

He grinned as he surveyed the teeth marks and the red dots that appeared. "You have a thirst for blood, too, I see."

He forced the drops to her pursed lips. Mishella's stomach rolled.

"That's good, Mishella. Very good."

She turned her head away and he slapped her again.

"I wonder how much you can stomach," he mused. "How much pain. We'll soon see."

He bent down and rummaged in his knapsack before extracting what looked to be a large bloodred rock. He touched the stone to the floor and rounded the makeshift altar until he had enclosed Mishella in a circle.

When he stood, his face was emotionless, his eyes like gleaming coals. It wasn't until he stepped forward that she saw the dagger in his hand, its handle encrusted with jewels. Her memory replayed a similar scene, only it was Esteban who had held the dagger. Esteban, instead of Thomas. Yet the same demon drove both men. Filled them, ate away at their souls.

Her heart lunged into her throat.

Thomas raised the dagger high, catching the waning sunlight with the blade. The light blinded her for a second.

"Now we'll see exactly how much you can stomach," he said. He tilted his head back, his arms stretched to the horizon. "No more light," he said. "Only darkness. The darkness is the power. The evil."

At that moment, she heard her stepsister's faint cry. Mishella strained to see past him.

Stacey stared at them, her eyes wide, her mouth moving, but no words came out. Only small, frightened whimpers.

"The bargain must be completed. A life for a life."
Thomas seemed oblivious to everything around him. His
arms began to shake as if an invisible hand had seized hold
of him. His fingers clenched around the jeweled handle of
the knife. "She dies for the darkness," he said, leaning over
her.

His eyes snapped open just as Mishella bent her legs and
landed her feet against his chest. He staggered backward.

He growled, his face twisting in a murderous scowl. Then
he advanced.

With a strength that surprised her, she yanked at the ropes
on her hands. The nail ripped from the wood. She rolled to
the side and scrambled to her feet.

"You won't escape," Thomas screamed, lunging over the
altar, the dagger swinging in her direction.

White-hot pain shot through her as the blade sliced into
her arm just below her shoulder. Blood streamed out.

She stumbled backward, closer to one of the walls. He
came at her again. The knife entered her arm an inch lower
this time. More pain streaked through her. More blood
spilled.

Thomas shrieked at the sight. "The blood!" And in his
voice, she heard the torment of centuries. He raised the
knife again.

Mishella ducked to the side, and the blade landed in the
corroded wall.

She darted around him, coming up behind and shoving
him forward. He turned on her. His eyes glowed brighter
and she knew she faced death—her own and Stacey's.

Fight, Mishella. Raphael's words rang in her ears. She
moved back, never taking her eyes off Thomas or the knife.
Fight.

She felt the edge of a pew behind her, blocking her line of escape. She felt her blood dripping on the dusty floor, felt her life slipping away. Her soul would soon follow.

"The third time, Mishella," Thomas chided, stalking her, the knife raised. "The *last* time."

"No!" She heard Raphael's voice. But this time it didn't come from inside her. It came from the doorway, thundered through the ruins of the church and wiped the smile from Thomas's face.

She took the opportunity to skirt the bench and gain some distance from Thomas. Raphael moved toward them, his gaze fixed on Thomas. Bloodlust flared in his eyes when he saw the dagger in the other man's hand.

"You'll die," he promised, his voice low, dangerous.

Thomas smiled. "*You* will be the one to die. You betrayed him. And for that you will pay."

"We'll see," Raphael growled, his eyes as black and as intimidating as midnight. And then he closed the distance between himself and his adversary.

Thomas lunged.

Mishella screamed as the dagger sliced across Raphael's chest. Immediately blood seeped through, turning his white T-shirt red. Raphael didn't even flinch. His eyes turned a shade darker. And he grabbed the other man's wrists.

"Traitor," Thomas accused, struggling against Raphael's grip. The dagger fell from his grasp. "You'll both die," Thomas vowed. "First you, then her. He wants her—"

Raphael smashed his fist into the man's face. Thomas slumped to the ground.

"Mishella," Raphael said, staggering toward her.

Pulling at the gag around her mouth, she rushed to him. "Oh, my God," she croaked, touching the bloodied T-shirt. "You're hurt."

"*Querida,*" he murmured, his eyes filled with concern. He reached for her. "Are you all—" The moment he saw the blood trailing down her arm, he went rigid.

"Raphael." The name stuck in her throat as she watched his eyes flame. And as much as she wanted to believe that he had saved her, that their love had won, she couldn't deny the evil within him any more than he could control the demon that seized hold of him.

"You won't escape," he said, but it wasn't his voice.

"No!" she cried as he swept her into his arms and threw her across the altar.

"You promised me eternity," he said. Then she saw that he had retrieved the dagger. He held it poised above her. "Eternity."

"I'll love you for eternity," she whispered, her eyes locked with his. "Forever." And she would, no matter if he killed her then and there. She would always love him. Always...

His hands started to shake and she saw the turmoil deep inside him. The two sides warred, the good with the evil, the light with the dark, in a battle begun with man's first temptation. A battle that had to end here, at least for the two of them.

"Fight," she whispered. "Please..."

The wind whipped through the church, stirring up the dust. Mishella blinked against the onslaught.

Raphael became a blurry outline. She felt his pain, his indecision, and she pleaded again, "Fight him, Raphael."

The wind blew harder.

He dropped his arms to his sides. "No!" he wailed, the sound reaching inside her, clear to her soul.

She widened her eyes, determined to see him. To help him.

"No," he said again. He raised the dagger, but he didn't aim for her this time. He aimed for himself.

"Fight him!" she screamed, scrambling up and ramming herself against him. "Fight him!"

Her action did little more than sway him, but enough to lodge the dagger from his grasp. It clattered to the floor.

The wind whirled about them with the fury of a thousand demons. But it was only one demon. One very powerful demon.

Raphael pulled Mishella into his arms and held her as if he never intended to let her go.

"Raph—" But her words fell short as a heavy beam crashed into the backs of her knees.

All feeling left her legs and she slumped against him.

In that instant she saw him turn straight into the edge of a pew being sucked into the wind. He stumbled. The pew seemed to swing at him. He fell to the side and she crumpled on top of him.

The wind tangled her hair, lashed at her skin, burned her eyes, and she clamped them shut. The blackness hovered.

"Shell . . ." Mishella heard the voice, small, weak, calling her name.

She forced her eyes open. They watered, but through the blur she saw a shaft of light piercing the dust cloud. She still had time.

"Such a touching scene," Thomas said as he materialized from the haze to loom over her.

And then he changed.

She saw the leathery skin, the claws, the slitted eyes, and she felt the heat, the incredible heat, as hot as hell itself.

"I will have you both," came the harsh grumble.

Beneath her palm, she felt Raphael's heart quicken, his muscles tense. He'd heard.

"You won't..." she heard him breathe.

The demon swooped an arm out just as Raphael shoved Mishella aside and grabbed the dagger. Welts appeared along his jaw, his neck, where the demon's claws grazed him. But Raphael was mindless to the pain. In the space of a heartbeat, he was on his feet, facing the demon before Mishella could stop him.

Seemingly oblivious to the knife in Raphael's hand, the demon lunged, claws ready to rip Raphael open from neck to gut with one fatal swoop.

"No!" Mishella screamed, charging toward the demon. He glanced at her for a second—a fatal second, for Raphael took the opportunity to thrust the dagger into his chest.

"No," the demon screeched, shock contorting his features. "You are the sacrifice. *You!*" The word was garbled as blood spurted from his mouth.

Raphael stepped back.

The demon sank to his knees, the edge of the dagger protruding from his chest. He crashed facedown on the floor. And then the flesh turned human.

Thomas lay in a pool of blood, a lock of his pale hair over his lifeless eyes. The demon had left him once and for all.

Yet Mishella knew it wasn't over. The demon still wanted them.

The wind howled more fiercely. But above the noise, Mishella heard Stacey's familiar voice, and she felt the pull.

Blindly she stumbled in the direction of her stepsister.

"Shell," came the small voice, guiding her way. And finally Mishella saw her.

She saw death.

Stacey's hair whipped about her deathly white face. Fear glazed her eyes, along with the fever. "Shell?"

"I'm here, baby," Mishella cried, falling to her knees beside the girl. Then she reached out.

Skin contacted skin and Mishella felt the heat surge through her. She heard Raphael behind her, calling her, but she couldn't turn away from Stacey.

The twister increased in fury. She heard the wails then— the desperate cries of lost souls condemned to the darkness. They called to her, beckoned her to join them. She closed her eyes.

"...Brighter, brighter, overcome the sin," she recited.

She felt icy fingers close over her shoulders.

"Darkness awaits..." The cold gripped her, but she kept praying, holding fast to Stacey.

"Die!" came the demonic roar. And she realized the hands closing around her throat were real. They were Raphael's.

"...within my hands rests heaven and hell." And at that moment, she felt the power unlike anything she'd ever felt before. The heat filled her, along with the light. They fused into one mighty force, channeling into Stacey, into Raphael.

"Mishella..." It was Raphael's agonized voice. His fingers loosened from her neck. He started to slip away.

The wind pulled him.

The evil called him back to the darkness.

"No!" she cried, reaching for his hand.

With fierce determination, she held tight to both Stacey and Raphael. Just a little while longer...

You'll lose, came the demon's voice. Only she knew she wouldn't. The light was stronger. *She* was stronger.

She said the prayer, over and over.

Wood crashed around her. Then she felt the vibration as what was left of the building crumbled. She held fast, never pausing, never losing her concentration.

The wind reached a deafening pitch, then silence descended.

And then it was done.

She rested her head in Stacey's lap and listened to the beat of her own heart.

"I love you." It was Raphael's voice, clear, distinct. His fingers tightened around hers, and she felt the electricity flow between them, the light cleansing and joining them in that last and final union.

Their souls met, never to part again, and the third touch was complete.

EPILOGUE

"Everything looks the same," Mishella said, trailing her fingers over one hand-carved bedpost. "I still can't get over it."

Raphael rested one broad shoulder against the doorjamb, his eyes riveted on the inviting picture she presented.

Standing across the spacious bedroom near the foot of the bed, she had her back to him, her ivory nightgown hugging her hips to perfection. A single candelabra burned on the nightstand, bathing her bare arms and shoulders in a soft light. The sight stirred a similar memory and he felt a tightening in his groin.

"Inez sent me up here to give you a lecture about not drinking all the tea she made for you."

"She fusses too much," Mishella replied. "Besides, the tea makes me sleep, and I don't feel like sleeping. I'd much rather have you tell me about this castle," she said. "I still can't believe it didn't fall into ruin."

"It should have," Raphael replied after a thoughtful second. "After Esteban's execution, the entire estate went to the local authorities, but not a single person would set foot inside these stone walls. The place was cursed, or so rumor had it. When a distant relative, a woman married to an Englishman, showed up and claimed to be Esteban's sister, the locals gladly granted her full ownership."

"Sister?"

"Yes, a real blood relation. She was an illegitimate child of Raul Malvado. He had refused to acknowledge her because she was female. The demon's power could only live on through a male child."

"And this sister was married to an Englishman? A Dalton, maybe?" She glanced over her shoulder, her brows raised, her lips curved in a knowing smile.

"Very astute." Their gazes locked. They might have stood side by side, for he felt the heat from her body—the soul-saving heat—and he took a deep, calming breath. They had all night. Every night, in fact, for the rest of their lives, and then some.

"Did she live here?" Mishella continued to caress the bedpost, her strokes slow, easy, torturous.

Raphael cleared his suddenly dry throat and tried to force his attention away from her fingers. "No. She and her husband had come only to find her father. When she learned of his death and her brother's fate, she couldn't bring herself to live here. She saw that the castle was cared for, however. It has remained in the Dalton family ever since."

"And now it belongs to you."

"Yes." He paused. "And you, too, Mishella. You became a part of this place a long time ago. You know, people used to say the castle cried at night."

"That's foolish. We've been here for two weeks and I haven't once heard any crying."

"*You* were the one crying, *querida*. Maricela's spirit walked these halls, searching for Esteban. I even heard the crying one time when I was a boy. My mother and I came here for a visit while my father stayed in Barcelona on business. We heard the crying. My mother didn't understand it, but I did. I knew it was Maricela's spirit—your spirit. I felt you even then."

"But I'm not crying anymore," she murmured, her willowy fingers drifting down the carved wood, then up again.

Raphael felt the touch along the length of his spine, soft yet persistent. "I don't want you ever to cry again," he said, his voice taking on a serious note. "Ever."

"I do feel like it sometimes," she admitted. "But only because I can't believe all that's happened—that you finally came back to me and we're together." She glanced toward the window. "Nights here are so beautiful."

Moonlight streamed past the parted draperies, silhouetting her profile. His stomach clenched.

"I still can't get over this place. Not a thing has changed. Not even a piece of furniture is moved out of place. It's as if time stood still and I'm seeing it exactly as I did then."

"Everyone was frightened of this castle. Even thieves kept their distance. The local folk say it's still haunted by the evil Esteban."

"And is it?" One dark brow rose as she cocked her head in his direction and waited for a reply. Amusement danced in the sapphire depths of her eyes.

"Haunted?" He shook his head. "My spirit might be Esteban's, but I'm very much a real man, Mishella. One with an insatiable appetite for his wife."

She faced him then, giving him a luscious view of her breasts spilling over the lace bodice of her nightgown. The shiny silver cross nestled in the deep cleavage. "Insatiable, huh?" The Devil himself was in the smile she gave him. "And what if I'm more insatiable than my husband?"

"Impossible."

"Nothing's impossible," she countered.

"True," he conceded, "but some things are more extraordinary than others. Like the way you make me feel. I don't have normal urges around you, love. They far exceed anything I've ever felt before. I can be quite a handful where you're concerned."

"I can see that," she replied, her gaze sweeping down his bare chest to the waistband of his black silk pajama bottoms. His manhood grew another inch beneath her scrutiny. A reaction that didn't go unnoticed. An inviting blush crept up her neck.

She met his stare again, and when she spoke, the playfulness was gone from her voice. "I'm glad we came here. There was so much pain here before, but there was love, as well. I needed to know how it would feel to stand in this room again, to be near this bed."

"It feels right," he said, thinking that *nothing* had ever felt so right. To him, it seemed only fitting that they should come back to the very place where their destinies had merged.

"It doesn't feel so cold, so empty. It feels like home," she said. "That's what Inez told me, and it wasn't just because she was grateful to us for bringing her along since she no longer has any family. She truly loves this castle. She loves everything about her new life, especially waking up in the mornings and not being afraid."

"There's no reason for her to be frightened anymore," Raphael said. "Thomas is dead."

"I know, but she spent a lifetime raising him, living in fear each and every day. It'll be hard for her to put so many memories behind her. But now at least she's made a start. Three Rivers was too vivid a reminder. Leaving there was the best thing for her."

"She belongs here as much as we do," Raphael replied. "She's a protector—a reincarnated spirit meant to preserve the light and help those lost in the darkness. She was born into the world to protect you this time just as she protected you before."

"I remember the woman with the crucifix," Mishella said. "It was Inez—her spirit."

"The crucifix is part of the reason your soul was pulled into the light rather than the darkness. Inez protected you. Now it's our turn to protect her, to show her some peace."

"It still amazes me that the demon knew all of this. I lived it and I'm still having a hard time accepting the truth."

"Belial is second only to Lucifer. He's all knowing, all powerful. He knew that Inez would one day help you, so he intervened by sending Thomas to her as a baby, hoping to curse her and keep her away from you when the time came. Had Thomas not been so powerful, so fully controlled by the demon spirit born inside him, Inez might have overcome him. But he was too evil, too black. She couldn't fight him and win. That's what Belial anticipated.

"Then," Raphael went on, "when I failed to follow through and condemn you myself, Thomas was there to take my place. He almost succeeded, too."

Silence descended as the memories passed between them. Vivid images of the ruined church, the hellish twister that had ripped through the place, and Thomas.

Mishella shook her head, her mouth curving in a slow smile. "But you saved me. You really were my guardian in the end."

"And you were mine," he replied, knowing he wouldn't be standing there today had it not been for the strength of the woman in front of him. The woman he loved beyond reason. The woman he wanted with a fierce desire that made his hands tremble.

"Belial is gone from our lives. Smothered in the blackness," he said. "We're free of him, love."

Free! The word sang through his head. Free of the evil, the darkness, the torment.

"I only wish we could have saved Domingo," she murmured, her smile turning to a sad crook of her mouth. "Inez still cries for him."

"She probably will for a long time. Hopefully she'll start to remember only the good memories they shared and not the bad. That goes for us, as well. We all have a chance to forget and put the past behind us."

"Stacey loves the castle, too. She told me she couldn't wait for Christmas break."

"I'm sure you can't wait, either."

"It shows that much?"

"You were quiet all the way from the airport."

"I still can't get over how much better she's gotten."

"She's healed, *querida*. You healed her."

"It all seems like a fantastic dream. I still wake up at night thinking I need to check on her, make sure she has her medicine, all the things I did while she was so ill."

"Past is past," Raphael said. "She's better, back at school and doing all the things she loves."

"I know and I'm very glad. I'll miss her, but . . ."

"But?" He folded his arms across his chest, his gaze again riveted on her breasts.

"But I'm sure you'll keep me happy until she returns." She took a deep breath. Her chest quivered and his blood fired.

"I certainly intend to try."

"Why don't you try a little now?"

He glanced at her face and noticed her gaze had darkened to a deep blue. "I think you read my mind." His voice was thick, raw with his need for her, which always seemed to take precedence over everything.

"I'm no mind reader. But you've been staring at my chest with those damnable eyes of yours. How can I not know what you're thinking?" The blush suffused her face and she put her back to him.

"If anything," she went on, her voice somewhat unsteady, "I thought seeing this bed would bring back the hurt."

"But it doesn't?" He closed the distance between them, coming up behind her.

"Not as long as you're in it with me," she replied.

"Fear not, Mishella. You'll never spend a night alone," he promised. "Now that I've moved the headquarters of Dalton Shipping to Barcelona, the farthest I'll be is a half hour away. And should you miss me during the day, you're welcome to come and visit. I'd like to try out that sofa you talked me into buying."

"A sofa is much easier on my bottom than a desk," she replied. "I had bruises for days after you gave me a personal tour of your New York office."

Laughter rumbled from his throat. "But I so loved kissing away the hurt." He eased his hands around her protruding waist, up under her breasts, which were nearly too big now to fit his hands.

When he spoke, the laughter was replaced by a huskiness that betrayed his feelings. "I can't believe you're having my baby. The son I've always dreamed about."

"I hope you won't be disappointed with a daughter." She gasped and arched back against him as his fingers found her puckered nipples.

"Daughter, is it? With you as her mother," he murmured, his lips grazing her ear, "my daughter will be the most beautiful girl in Spain."

"Or your son the handsomest—" Her breath caught.

He circled one extended peak with his fingertip. "I thought you said daughter?"

"I was just reminding you that it might be a daughter. It makes no difference to me. I'll love this child either way...." Her words died as he pulled her flush against him, grinding his hardness into her soft bottom.

"And will you love me?" he asked, his voice rough with emotion.

"I already do." Her words were breathless.

"With your heart, I have no doubt. But I had something a little more earthly in mind for the moment." He lifted her, placed her on the bed and lowered himself over her.

He trailed his finger down the curve of her shoulder, over the three tiny lines that were no longer a reminder of the bitter past they shared, but of the love that bound them together.

A love that had seen them through the long months when Raphael had stood accused of Thomas's death. A love that had rejoiced when the jury had delivered the verdict of self-defense, clearing his name and setting him free. And a love that had called them home to Barcelona to lay the past to rest and begin their life together, free of the evil once and for all.

Capturing her stare with his own, he eased first one silk strap, then the other, down her shoulders, the length of her arms. Then he tugged the lace bodice to her waist.

The air lodged in his chest at the sight of her creamy white breasts, swollen from her milk, the nipples a rich red wine and undoubtedly as tasty.

"So beautiful," he whispered, dipping his head and closing his mouth over one inviting peak. He sucked and nibbled until she cried his name.

Loving her was so easy, so right, and he marveled again at how he'd spent centuries alone in the darkness only to return and find heaven on earth with the one woman he'd blamed for all his misery.

The one woman who had touched his soul when no one and nothing else could.

He freed her of the gown, discarded his pajama bottoms, then slipped inside her. She closed around him, and he knew he had finally come home. Whether they loved an eternity or not, a moment with her was worth more than money, power, revenge. He knew that now, just as Esteban had known then.

"Raphael, I love you," Mishella moaned.

Yes, he'd finally come home. They both had.

* * * * *

SILHOUETTE®

Desire®

He's tough enough to capture your heart,
Tender enough to cradle a newborn baby
And sexy enough to satisfy your wildest fantasies....

He's Silhouette Desire's MAN OF THE MONTH!

From the moment he meets the woman of his
dreams to the time the handsome hunk says *I do*...

Don't miss twelve gorgeous guys take the
wedding plunge!

In January: *WOLFE WEDDING*
by Joan Hohl

In February: *MEGAN'S MARRIAGE*
by Annette Broadrick

In March: *THE BEAUTY, THE BEAST
AND THE BABY*
by Dixie Browning

In April: *SADDLE UP*
by Mary Lynn Baxter

In May: (Desire's 1000th book!)
MAN OF ICE
by Diana Palmer

In June: *THE ACCIDENTAL BODYGUARD*
by Ann Major

And later this year, watch for steamy stories
from Anne McAllister, Barbara Boswell,
Lass Small and Jennifer Greene!

MAN OF THE MONTH...ONLY FROM
SIILHOUETTE DESIRE

MOM96JJ

COMING SOON FROM BESTSELLING AUTHOR

LINDA HOWARD

The follow-up story to DUNCAN'S BRIDE!

Linda Howard is back—and better than ever—
with her December 1994 Silhouette Intimate
Moments title, LOVING EVANGELINE, #607.

No one had ever dared to cross Robert Cannon
until someone began stealing classified
information from his company—a situation
he intended to remedy himself. But when the
trail led to beautiful Evie Shaw, Robert found
both his resolve—and his heart—melting fast.

Don't miss award-winning author Linda Howard
at her very best. She's coming your way in
December, only in...

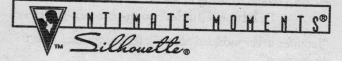

HOW MUCH IS THAT COUPLE IN THE WINDOW?
by Lori Herter

Book 1 of Lori's Million-Dollar Marriages miniseries
Yours Truly™—February

Salesclerk Jennifer Westgate's new job is to live in a department store display window for a week as the bride of a gorgeous groom. Here's what sidewalk shoppers have to say about them:

"Why is the window so steamy tonight? I can't see what they're doing!" —Henrietta, age 82

"That mousey bride is hardly Charles Derring's type. It's me who should be living in the window with him!" —Delphine, Charles's soon-to-be ex-girlfriend

"Jennifer never modeled pink silk teddies for me! This is an outrage!" —Peter, Jennifer's soon-to-be ex-boyfriend

"How much is that couple in the window?" —Timmy, age 9

HOW MUCH IS THAT COUPLE IN THE WINDOW?
by Lori Herter—Book 1 of her Million-Dollar Marriages miniseries—available in February from

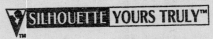

Love—when you least expect it!

For an *EXTRA*-special treat, pick up

TIME AND AGAIN
by
Kathryn Jensen

In January 1996, Intimate Moments proudly features Kathryn Jensen's *Time and Again*, #685, as part of its ongoing Extra program.

Modern-day mom: Kate Fenwick wasn't looking for a soul mate. Her two children more than filled her heart—until she met Jack Ramsey.

Mr. Destiny: He defied time and logic to find her, and only by changing fate could they find true love.

In future months, look for titles with the EXTRA flash for more excitement, more romance—simply *more....*

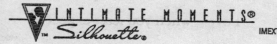

IMEXTRA3

What do women really want to know?

Only the world's largest publisher of romance
fiction could possibly attempt an answer.

HARLEQUIN ULTIMATE GUIDES™

How to Talk to a Naked Man,

Make the Most of Your Love Life, and Live Happily Ever After

The editors of Harlequin and Silhouette are
definitely experts on love, men and relationships.
And now they're ready to share that expertise with
women everywhere.

Jam-packed with vital, indispensable, lighthearted
tips to improve every area of your romantic life—even
how to get one! So don't just sit around and wonder
why, how or where—run to your nearest bookstore
for your copy now!

Available this February, at your favorite retail outlet.

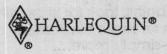

When desires run wild,

Confessions

can be deadly

JoAnn Ross

The shocking murder of a senator's beautiful wife
has shaken the town of Whiskey River. Town sheriff
Trace Callihan gets more than he bargained for when the
victim's estranged sister, Mariah Swann, insists on being
involved with the investigation.

As the black sheep of the family returning from Hollywood,
Mariah has her heart set on more than just solving her
sister's death, and Trace, a former big-city cop, has more
on his mind than law and order.

What will transpire when dark secrets and suppressed
desires are unearthed by this unlikely pair? Because nothing
is as it seems in Whiskey River—and everyone is a suspect.

Look for *Confessions* at your favorite retail outlet this January.